not all memories are the same

BEFORE THE TEA GETS COLD

a novel by

AMELIA VENJOY

For all of us moms
who feel incapable of laying down
the guilt and judgment of ourselves.

May this story serve as a reminder that you
are doing an amazing job, and you are not
alone in your journey of motherhood.

chapter 1

Margo

OH MAN, MARGO. *You've done it again.* Staring up at me is a large, bold 8 drawn with a thick black marker on the crumpled pink paper in my hand. The worn edges are creased from the many other times I must have grabbed it before heading out the door on my daily walk. When I pulled on my cardigan, I instinctively grabbed the paper from the bowl where I keep my house keys. I tucked it into my pocket, slipped on my shoes, and left my house. Grabbing the note is an established habit, and I didn't question myself when I placed it into my pocket.

When I grabbed the note, I hadn't even given it a second thought until halfway through my walk. The cool wind outside had made my nose run, and I reached for a tissue in my cardigan pocket. Instead of a tissue, I pulled out the note and now, standing here at this moment, I couldn't tell you why I have it. I keep glancing down at it, urging something deep within my brain to spark alive, but the 8 remains an eight.

It's not that I don't have any memories. I can tell you many things about who I am and the world around me. I could tell you it is fall, as the tinted leaves stop clinging to their branches and settle around me on the ground. The crisp air blowing at my cardigan is my favorite shade of robin's egg blue. The gray clouds are clinging to the horizon like a delicate blanket, putting the world to sleep for a winter hibernation.

I could point to my house, the blue and white gabled house on 427 Violet Street. It's nestled to the left, exactly where it should be, tucked in between a brown-sided house that still appears new and a duplex with red crumbling plaster on the side. Jake and I bought that house together a lifetime ago. Funny how it feels like only yesterday we pulled up to that "For Sale" sign, but I also know many years have passed in this neighborhood. And that's not just the age creaking in my joints. All those years and memories are forever embedded deep within my soul. Unfortunately, I can't tell you what all those memories are. Not because I don't want to, but because they are out of reach.

Finally, I can tell you that I am Margo. There's nothing that stands out as unique or special about me, but I have a husband and a daughter who are my pride and joy. Simply Margo, a woman who loves snickerdoodles and peppermint tea, wearing matching sweatsuits in various colors, and taking leisurely walks on both familiar and unexplored trails.

That walk brings me to exactly where I am right now, facing what I cannot tell you. This number 8, what does it mean and why am I holding it? The worn edges of the paper tell me I have grabbed this paper more than once. Did I need eight dinner rolls for dinner tonight? No, I do not buy eight dinner rolls every day. Maybe I need to take Alice to piano practice at 8pm tonight? No, that can't be right either.

The more I press my brain to remember what it can not, the larger the blank grows. And unlike the soft grey of the clouds above, this blankness of my brain is not comforting. My breath catches in my chest as I shove the paper back into my pocket. *But what if it's important?*

"It can't be important if I can't remember it," I mutter to myself and turn down the street away from my house. If I have no answers out here, there won't be any waiting for me at home. As much as I want to ignore the puzzle, the faster the questions of *what is it?*, *why do you have it?*, and *why can't you remember?* flood my brain.

"If you fall into the lake, Margie, step one is to not panic." My dad's words ring in my ears from when I was five. "Thrashing at the edge of the ice will only cause it to break off all around you."

Growing up on a farm, the life advice passed down to me is unique compared to the life advice I give my daughter. Don't stop walking when feeding the baby chicks in the barn, wear proper shoes when chopping the firewood, and don't panic if you plunge into the frozen lake out back.

As if one has the choice to simply not panic. Whether bobbing in the frigid waters, walking into that first job interview, or thrashing on the edges of a loose memory thread barely out of reach. I do not make a habit out of anxiety. Life can either happen to you, or you can pivot and roll along with life. That's much easier to do when the various strongholds of your life aren't steadily falling away, one by one.

Fine, Dad. I'll walk around the block again and breathe.

"Good afternoon, Margo!" A woman excitedly greets me as an equally cheerful black lab tugs her along towards me on the sidewalk.

Her face triggers a familiar memory, but her name is coming up empty as I sort through the library of my brain. She is well-dressed, in her 40s, and her heels click along the sidewalk with confidence. Impressive. I would trip like a newborn fawn on those heels, even without a dog dragging me at a brisk pace. Her cheerfulness is comforting, even if I may not remember her name. I watch her long, blonde hair fly out around her with each step, the only part of her that is not under control and in place.

I wave a polite hand. "Hello. It's a beautiful fall day." When in doubt, always talk about the weather.

Her dog is now panting at my feet, expectantly staring up at me to give him (or is it a her?) some love. I bend over to scratch the pup behind its ears. The lady rattles off her sentences, one after another, like falling dominoes. "Are you out checking your mail? Peter went out first thing this morning and they had delivered the fall activity calendars this morning." She pulls her hair to the side and I mirror her, tucking the stray hairs from my chin-length bob behind my ear.

My mailbox! The satisfying click of the last puzzle piece falling into place. Mental note: write "mailbox" under the number 8. How is it I can remember my house, but not my mailbox? My mailbox has not moved or changed in all these years. Or has it?

This is what is most frustrating. How memories and thoughts are left to their own devices to stay or leave on a whim. I can easily forget the simple task of checking a mailbox, but I can remember in specific detail the day I tripped and fell on the playground in front of my class. It was sixth grade if you were curious. I knocked out my front tooth in front of Graham, the red-headed boy with a dimple in his left cheek that half of the girls were in love with. I would trade in that memory for remembering my mailbox number.

"Well, will you be joining us for pottery again?" The woman says and my attention snaps back to the lady in front of me waiting for an answer to a conversation I have missed. She gives me a knowing smile, as if she can tell I wasn't listening, like this has happened before.

Whoever she is, she is pleasant and appears to know me. She might even know me better than myself at this moment, but pottery also sounds like it would be fun. I nod and offer a smile in return. "Maybe. That sounds nice."

She reaches over and gives my arm a gentle squeeze, which I appreciate. If she had offered to hug me, I would have felt more awkward than I do now. "Peter and I will see you later, Margo. Have a great walk." And just like that, her heels clicking off back in the direction I had come from. Her dog bounding on his paws to keep stride as they round the corner out of sight.

Alright, Margo. Another puzzle for another time. Let's go check that mailbox.

Fishing into the other pocket of my cardigan, sure enough, there is a keychain with only two keys on it. The top of each key is marked with a piece of masking tape and a label neatly written on each one. "Mail" on the small, round key. "Home" on the larger key. The mail key slides into slot number 8 and turns open. Some coupons, an activity calendar that the lady mentioned, and a parcel are waiting for me to collect them.

Now, time to go home and see if Alice finished her homework. Maybe next time I should take Alice with me on my walks. That girl has a memory like a high-rise library. Although, that could be because she's got youth on her side. No, Alice would have us on a mission. A walk to the mailbox would be to the mailbox and back home again. Typically, there isn't time in her self-made schedule for smelling the roses or exploring a side trail.

I had tried to take her with me hiking a handful of times, but even when she was only nine years old, she was committed to following the map. Sure, it was the safe option, but there were so many grown-over side trails that were scattered with beautiful wildflowers. I could have spent hours wandering them, but for Alice, the purpose was to reach the top.

I stack the mail under my left arm and grab a rock resting at the base of the mailbox. *This one will do perfectly.* Hugging it in my right hand, I stroke the edges of the rock. Almost all the edges are scuffed and worn down, but one jagged side still remains.

I. Am. Margo. Using my thumb to stroke over the rough edge as I say each word in my head. *Mailbox. Number. 8.*

One step in front of the next, heading back to the comfort of my fenced yard.

I. Am. Margo. Stroke, stroke, stroke. *Mailbox. Number. 8.* Step, step, step. *427. Violet. Street.* Stroke, stroke, stroke. A memory sandwich. It's like the game of two truths and a lie. Except it's two things I know and one thing I forgot. Today I didn't know the number 8, but tomorrow I will. Even if I have to rub my thumb raw.

Opening the front door with a slight push and a creak, the cold in the air seeping in and settling into the hinges. I remove my cardigan and hang it on the hooks behind the door and place my keys in the bowl marked "Keys here". I kick off my shoes to trade them in for my fleece-lined slippers and putter into the living room to my left. It's not a big room, but it is my favorite in the house.

My red leather armchair is tucked off to the side with a quilt draped over the back. The slightly cracked seat is faded from many hours spent in it, but it is the best seat in the house. Across from my chair, along the wall, is a floral-printed couch. The fireplace tucked into the opposite corner isn't a real one. I miss the wood-burning stove from the farm growing up, but I enjoy flicking the switch with ease to make it glow and give heat. No more chopping firewood is required.

I set down the mail on the edge of the couch to sort through later. Squeezing the rock one more time, I will the information I stroked into it to implant firmly in my memory. A quick kiss for good measure. Then, place it gently onto the stack of other rocks, waiting to welcome their new companion in the crystal bowl on the coffee table.

"Alice. Alice, honey!" I call out as I head towards the staircase that heads up to the bedrooms. "I'm home and going to start the kettle if you want some."

My calls are met with silence. 13-year-olds listen about as well as a toddler, I swear.

Rounding around the corner of the stairs, I enter the kitchen. Small, but cozy, and bright yellow. Exactly the way I like it. A round wooden table with four chairs is tucked in the far left corner by the sliding door exiting to the patio. It may not be the most practical for any company, but perfectly intimate for shared morning coffees and family dinners.

The faded pink doors on the kitchen cabinets remind me they need a fresh coat of paint, but what a shame to paint over the colorful flowers that are stencilled along the bottom edges. Each handle is the perfect yellow circle in the center of a flower. What a fun project that had been. The first summer after Jake had left. The first summer that it was only me and Alice, and I needed to keep us busy.

"You mean I can paint the cupboards, Mama?" Little 5-year-old Alice's eyes had been wide as saucers that she was going to be allowed to paint anything in the house. Especially after always being told that "Crayons are for paper. Not walls, tables, or pockets." She reached for a paint bottle and held it up to inspect it. "Can we make them pretty?"

"Let's make them the prettiest cupboards in the neighborhood, Alice. You, me, and all the colors in the world." I had dabbed my paintbrush playfully on her nose, leaving a wet, pink dot behind.

The cupboards turned out beautifully, but they have shown their age over the years. Tea and mugs belong in the cupboard closest to the stove, with the orange and purple daisies. The mug with a chicken for me, the mug with a cat for Alice. A bag of peppermint tea settled into each, waiting for the steaming water to pull out the satisfying aroma and flavor.

That's when I see it. The yellow note stuck to the side of the dented metal kettle. With one hand, I grab the kettle and head to the sink to fill it up. With my other, I peel off the note so it doesn't fall into the sink. In my handwriting, neatly written to take up most of the note, it reads: "Alice is coming to visit at 3pm. Remember." Why would Alice be coming to visit? She lives here.

"Alice?" I call out again with a voice that cracks anxiously. Her name echoes through the empty house that I am now realizing is too quiet. I place the kettle down shakily and head back to the stairs. "Alice, are you upstairs? Answer me, please."

My voice continues to echo through the house. Grabbing the railing, I climb the thick, carpeted steps and will my heart to fall back into rhythm. Alice's room is at the top, on the right. Perhaps she has her head buried in a book.

Except she's not. When I reach the top step, her door is open. No lights on, no book, no Alice.

I cross into her room and see the bare furnishings around the room. Like a thud of bricks, I'm ripped away from thrashing at the edge and I'm pulled under. I remember.

chapter 2

Alice

FORK, FORK, KNIFE, SPOON, AND DONE. Closing the utensil drawer after filling it with the last clean dish, I click the dishwasher closed. I could start filling the dishwasher with the dirty dishes, but I might as well wait until Sadie comes home from school with her lunchbox. I hate doing only part of a task and then having to complete it later. Chewing on the back of my pen (a nasty habit, I know); I scan over my list. Shoot, I forgot to add *empty dishwasher*. I immediately scribble *empty dishwasher* to the list, underneath *wipe down counters*. Then, promptly cross it off with the satisfaction of an accomplished job washing over me.

Empty dishwasher, check. Laundry, check. Shower, check. Prep dinner, check. Unfortunately, that isn't the end of my list. A scattering of items still stare up from the notebook. Call Mom's doctor, buy Sadie new shoes, pick up Mom's groceries, and go to Mom's for tea. Chances are, they won't all get checked off today, no matter how hard I try to end the day with an empty list. It doesn't help that I'm always carrying a notebook and pen with me, collecting all the tasks and to-do items like a magnet as I go about my day. Mom's doctor and groceries are both highlighted in orange, which means I forgot to do it yesterday or I ran out of time. If I don't do it today, I will circle it boldly with a marker, as if making it more obvious on the list will magically make it more achievable tomorrow.

There was a time when I crossed off everything on my list by the end of the day. It was easy to knock everything off back when it was before her diagnosis. Now I am living in the after. Sure, becoming a new mom threw some bumps into my time management abilities, but that was years ago. I promptly found my way back to being the better version of myself. Now, though, managing my house and my mom's house, I'm not even half of the best version of myself. Travis always says this is only a season and to take it easy on myself. But, seasons are short and they cycle through. I'm basically writing my history at this point.

The glowing green numbers of 2:14 on the stove say the rest of my list will have to wait for tomorrow. Sadie's bus will be here in 15 minutes, which means I am out of time. Once she crosses that threshold, it will be a shuffle of hellos and how was school. Then, time to hop in the car because we're going to Granny's. It is a song and dance we are familiar with by now. Not that familiarity makes it any easier, but it helps make the gears run smoother as we do what we need to do. Also, what we want to do. We want to spend time with my mom, but it is a need, nonetheless.

My mom went from being an item floating somewhere on my to-do list to being my entire list. She is no longer something I can push off for another day. My mom's needs now exist as multiple line items with varying levels of urgency, orange highlighting, and bold circles. They consume my time and energy, and they are anchored weights upon my life. But I wouldn't have anyone else take this plate from me.

I worry about my mom living on her own. She used to say that she had her friends, her routine, and our tea visits. "You worry too much. I've got all I need." But that was before she started getting older. Before the doctor's appointments and the medications. It was back when she was the Mom I always knew before the lines between past, present, and other realities all blurred together in her mind.

To make it more challenging, she only has me. She doesn't even have my dad as a rock to lean on. I may not know what it's like to be fully independent as a single mom, but I know how helpful it is to have a husband and a best friend that you can rely on. Travis is my rock and my biggest cheerleader. He may work long and hard hours at the local law firm, but at the end of the day, he's there.

Even with Travis' support, I could do with another person to lean on too, but my dad has only ever been a blip along the pulse of my life. His presence is strong in all the photos in those early years when flipping through old albums, but then gone by the time I entered school. Poof. I remember parts of him; I remember stories of him, but mainly I remember the pain and anger that have grown over the years. What I don't remember is the day he walked out and never came back, but I remember in kindergarten telling my friends that I didn't have a dad.

"Your turn, Alice." Miss Turnbill said as we took turns going around the circle. "Tell us about your family."

"I have a mom, but I don't have a dad." It was true, I had a Jake.

My phone vibrating in my back pocket startles me and I glance at the call display on the screen. *Oh, no! Sadie's school.*

I swipe the screen to answer the call and lift the phone to my ear. "Hello? Is everything okay with Sadie?" My heartbeat rises.

"Everything is fine with Sadie. This is just Mrs. Anderson calling to ask you about the upcoming field trip in a few weeks." The cheerful voice on the other end of the phone allows me to exhale. *You need to learn to relax. Should probably add a bubble bath to the list.*

I flip the page on the calendar beside the fridge to jog my memory. "The trip to the bowling alley?"

"That's the one! Permission slips are due this week. I sent one home with Sadie last week." A slight pause as Mrs. Anderson shuffles through her desk. "I wanted to follow up with you to remind you to send it to school with Sadie tomorrow. Unless you have a question for me?"

Heat floods my cheeks. How did I not remember the permission slip? I am not the mom who forgets things. I'm the mom who's early and overly prepared. I am not the mom who needs a teacher to follow up with her over simple things. MAYBE during the first month of kindergarten, but that was before the teachers knew I was Alice. Top of her game, A-OK, reliable Alice. I used to be president of the P.A.C. before Mom's diagnosis. Stepping back had been hard, but necessary. What I didn't expect is that the first step back was the beginning of a landslide of the image I want to be known for.

"I am so sorry about that!" I apologize while digging through my stacked piles of paper hidden behind my command cupboard.

It had taken an entire weekend to rearrange items in the limited space of our newly renovated kitchen, but it had been worth it. What used to be the cupboards for cookie cutters I never had time to use and the abandoned pots that took too long to scrub clean, were now the shining home of my organizational headquarters. A corkboard was mounted on the inside of one door and a whiteboard was mounted on the other. The idea was out of sight but not out of mind. Any papers that came into the house had a home to be filed into in that cupboard. Except in the last year, the papers came in faster than I had time to file them. Forms for my mom, forms for Sadie, and most likely, an overdue bill or two.

Before I can embarrassingly admit that I can't seem to find it, Mrs. Anderson interjects, "I sent another one home with Sadie this afternoon, in case the other one got lost in the bottom of her backpack." I nod to myself, trying to align with that being a plausible truth. She continues, "We're also in need of another parent volunteer if you're available."

"Of course! Put me down for that. Thanks again for calling." I add a note to the calendar to remind me that I will be volunteering that day.

We say goodbye and hang up. Not sure how volunteering fits into my list, but I need to show I'm still that reliable mom. I don't know who I need to prove it more to, though, them or me. I also can't say no to anyone but myself. Not on purpose, anyway. Lately, the nos were sliding out in response to easy questions. Questions like, *did you buy the groceries?, is my blue tie clean?,* and *did you sign Sadie's permission slip?*

Sigh. Why don't adults ever tell you how complicated it is to grow up? Or maybe the better question is, why don't we believe them? I always loved the team of my mom and I. "Just a couple of girls" my mom used to say. I never thought to look ahead past the shopping trips, tea times, or late night movies. I never thought about how it would be awfully lonely when the rug gets ripped out from under me. My mom needs me to help her, but what if I still need my mom to help me?

"Mommy! I'm home!" Sadie calls out to me, followed by a crash of her backpack hitting the wall by the front door. I have long given up trying to remind her to hang her backpack nicely on the hook by the front door.

"In the kitchen, Ladybug." I smile, waiting for the familiar thud thud of her shoes being kicked off onto the mat. So long as they aren't covered in water, mud, or snow, I am happy if they land on the mat. Even if the mat is a target to reach from 10 feet away. Some battles aren't worth fighting, and with Sadie's spunk, battles were a guarantee to arise again. Usually, when Travis gets home from work, he will hang up Sadie's backpack and line up her shoes before neatly placing his beside hers. Gotta love genetics math. How do two type-A, highlighter-loving parents create a carefree, wild child? At this point, we're all merely along for the ride and fingers-crossed we don't crash in the end.

Climbing up the stairs of our split-level townhouse, I see her red, frazzled hair pop into view first. Then, followed by her freckled nose and tooth-gapped grin. Playtime at recess and lunch is a serious sport with this one. To help prove my points, she's wearing her favorite shirt, *RECESS IS MY FAVORITE SUBJECT*. Rain, snow, or shine, she always comes home a happy mess.

"Where is your sweater?" I ask. Her bare arms make me subconsciously rub my own for warmth. "It's not summer anymore."

Sadie avoids eye contact and slinks into the kitchen. "Umm, I think I left it at school. But I was running and really hot, Mommy!"

I guess if I ran everywhere instead of walking, I would overheat too. Potentially knock off some tasks faster, too. "Remember to bring it home with you tomorrow."

Sadie nods and she scoots herself up onto one of the black leather stools. I grab a banana from the fruit bowl on the white island in the middle of the kitchen. Apples are Sadie's usual go-to snack, but after losing both her front teeth last week, they are too challenging of a snack.

I peel the top and pass it to her. "How was school today? Did you bring home the permission slip from your teacher for me to sign?"

"Good," Sadie answers, pausing to take a big bite of the banana. "In my backpack." Followed by two more quick bites, stuffing them into her cheeks.

"Make sure you're chewing those bites, li'l monkey." I wink and add *sign permission form* to the bottom of my list. Then, highlight it in orange so I will hopefully not forget. I don't want Mrs. Anderson to have to call me again.

Sadie hops off the stool and opens the cabinet under the sink to toss her peel into the compost bin. "Are we going to Granny's now? It's Teatime Tuesday!"

"Yup, let's get a move on." I motion to the stairs as I turn off the lights in the kitchen and down the hall. "Grab another sweater from the hooks by the door and put your shoes on." I walk over to the patio door and check that it's locked before following Sadie down the stairs.

"Wait!" Sadie shouts as she flies past me back up the stairs, shoes on her feet but the laces dragging behind her.

"No shoes in the house!" I shout after her, knowing full well it's going to fall on deaf ears. When there's something on her mind, there's no room for anything else. "What are you doing?" I ask more calmly, but also still annoyed.

CRASH. What sounds like Tupperware lids spilling out onto the tile floor in the kitchen is abruptly followed by, "I need to bring Granny my muffins!"

I lean against the wall, halfway down the stairs, rubbing my temples, and take a deep breath. *Nope, let's make those three deep breaths*. Even though my life is fairly chaotic right now, it doesn't mean I like to leave chaos behind me every time I leave this house. Just once, it would be my dream for Travis to come home to a homemade dinner cooking in the oven and a house that has been tidied. Exactly like how it used to be, back before dinners became a rotation of crockpot and quick fend-for-yourself meals. Not that he's ever complained about it, but I wish I could make that level of caring a reality again.

As much as I am annoyed, the muffins are a good idea. It can help ease my guilt that Mom's grocery drop-off will have to wait until Sadie goes to school tomorrow morning. "Just leave the lids, Sadie. It's time to go!"

Sadie bounds back down the stairs, two at a time. The tupperware of muffins is tucked under her arm and she jumps to the bottom, skipping the last four steps. Her trail of wet footprints on the stairs makes me twitch and use my feet to mop up most of it, instantly regretting my now wet socks.

"Careful, Ladybug." I rummage through my purse for my keys. "I would like to go to Granny's house, not the emergency room."

Not even missing a beat, she beams up at me. "Billy fell down the stairs last year and got to pick a blue cast, Mommy. Do you think when I break a bone, I could get a rainbow cast for everyone to sign?"

"How about you don't break a bone? At least not until Mommy is less busy." I open the door and she's already off running down the driveway. I pull off my wet socks, toss them over the heat vent, and slip my bare feet into my boots. Not ideal, but we're already heading out the door.

I close the door behind me and turn my key in the lock. "Sorry, Trav, for the mess again," I whisper the words and let them hang in the air, hoping he will feel their meaning when he gets home tonight. "I'm trying."

chapter 3

TODAY IS TUESDAY, and Tuesdays are my favorite day. Well, maybe tied with Saturdays because Saturdays I don't have school. Daddy doesn't have to work on Saturdays, so he watches cartoons while Mommy stays in bed to rest. He even lets me eat the forbidden sugar cereal, and sometimes he has a bowl too. Mommy hides it in the pantry for when she needs a break. She thinks she's sneaky, but we all know. But I also think she knows Daddy and I eat it on Saturday mornings. Even though Daddy washes the dishes before Mommy comes out for breakfast.

My favorite is when Daddy pretends like it's a top-secret mission. "Quick! Check to see if Mommy is coming and I'll go grab the cereal," Daddy will whisper to me as I check down the hall to see if Mommy is coming wrapped in her purple housecoat. If Mommy told us she knew our secret, I wouldn't get to be a spy with Daddy.

But today is Tuesday, my second favorite day of the week. Every Tuesday after school I go to Granny's house. Granny calls it Tea Time Tuesday. Mommy and Granny like to drink tea and talk. I'm too young to drink tea, but I don't think I would like it, anyway. It looks like juice mixed with water and it's hot. Who would want to drink hot juice?

Usually, I go play with the dolls upstairs. That's where I am right now. Granny keeps the dolls in my mommy's old bedroom. Sometimes, I try to imagine my mommy when she was my age sleeping in this room. But every time I try, I only see her how she looks now. Except, she's wearing pyjamas that are supposed to fit me, and her arms and legs are mostly bare because she's much too tall. She looks like the clothes went into the dryer for too long. It makes me giggle.

One at a time, I pull a doll out of the toy box and start by brushing her hair with the plastic, pink hairbrush. Then, I change the doll out of a dress into a nightgown. Granny sewed matching nightgowns for all the dolls. Granny loves to sew, and she's really good at it. Anytime I get holes in my pants, which is a lot, Granny will patch them for me. I love to pick out the fabric Granny will use. I want Granny to teach me how to sew one day. Mommy said she tried a few times but didn't like it. Mommy also said that I used to match the doll's nightgowns with the same pink nightgown and a lace collar. When the first doll, Molly, is dressed for bed, I lay her on my mommy's old pillow and grab the next doll. Mommy doesn't remember what names she called her dolls, so I gave them all new names.

Finally, all five dolls are lined up perfectly along the pillow and I can tuck them in under the faded green quilt on the bed. I kiss each doll and turn out the lights as I close the bedroom door quietly. All the best moms have to learn to walk extra quietly. Otherwise, they'll wake up their babies or get caught eating the special sugar cereal in the pantry. I'm not a real mom yet, but I am very good at walking quietly so adults can't hear me.

I sneak to sit at the top of the landing by the stairs and stick my legs through the wooden bars. Granny is sitting in her favorite red chair. She always says, "It's the perfect size for me and a Sadie-bum." And she's right, it is the perfect size. I hope I never am too big to squeeze into the chair with Granny. Mommy is sitting across from her on the couch covered with flowers, with her feet resting on the coffee table. I wonder if Mommy used to sit here when she was a little girl, too. This would be the perfect place to be a spy. If I had a brother or sister, I would love to throw things over the railing for them to catch below. It's hard to do that when I'm the only kid around here. I guess that's how Mommy might have felt growing up here, too.

Mommy and Granny talk about boring adult things, but sometimes I can listen to them planning Christmas or my birthday. It was my birthday in the summer and I heard them planning my surprise birthday cake. It was a bunch of cupcakes in the shape of a unicorn. I loved unicorns last year. Now, I'm too old for them because I know they're not real. Today they're not talking about anything interesting because Christmas isn't close enough yet.

"Are you hungry, Sadie? I think I have a cookie with your name written on it." Granny's voice carries up the stairs to my eavesdropping ears.

I scramble up from my hiding place, hop down the stairs, and land in the living room. Cookies always make my legs move extra fast unless they have raisins in them. But, Granny only ever has the yummy cookies.

"I love cookies!" I smile and poke my tongue through the giant gap where my two front teeth used to be.

Granny has already put out two cookies on one of her fancy plates with those little pink flowers around the edge. She always says Tea Time Tuesdays are the perfect time to "break out the fine China." Whatever that means.

I take a giant bite of the first cookie, and the shortbread melts on my tongue. "These are better than the muffins I made with Mommy!"

"Cookies tend to taste better than muffins." Granny chuckles and winks at me. "What kind of muffins did you and Mommy bake?"

I take a sip of water from my glass. "Banana oatmeal! Brown bananas make them extra yummy, even if they look disgusting." I wrinkle my nose, remembering how they looked slimy sitting on the counter thawing from the freezer. I kept poking one of the bananas and it made the peel split open. Slowly it oozed out onto the counter. It was pretty gross but kinda cool, too. Mommy didn't like that I made a mess after she told me not to touch them.

My mom picks up her tea and takes a sip. "Sadie packed you some, and I put them on the kitchen counter for you to try."

"I can't wait. I bet they're delicious." Granny grins at me and I grin back with a mouth full of cookie. "I sure wish I could be as talented of a baker as you, Sadie."

"You don't bake, Granny?" I ask.

"Oh, I've baked over the years. My stuff turned out okay, but nothing like what my mom used to make. Now, that was some talented baking." Granny turns to the bowl of rocks on the coffee table, thinking.

I instantly perk up and reach for the bowl. "Are you thinking of one of your rock stories, Granny?"

My mom gently nudges me with her foot. "See if you can find the rock in the bowl for a baking story, Ladybug." Granny always tells stories when we are at her house. It's one of my favorite things about coming to her house.

I dig through and settle on a rock that is shaped like a square with a white line running down the middle. "This one looks like an oven! It must be the baking story!"

I hand it to Granny and nibble the rest of my cookie while she closes her eyes and holds the rock. Granny's stories are always the best.

"When I was about seven years old, I really loved butterflies." Granny opens her eyes and they sparkle.

"Hey! I'm seven years old!" I jump up excitedly. Granny gently places a finger to her lips, reminding me to be quiet so she can tell her story.

Granny closes her eyes again and continues. "I begged and begged my mom to make me a beautiful butterfly cake. I made sure to draw her a picture of a butterfly with orange wings and yellow polka-dots."

I close my eyes now too and imagine a beautiful butterfly cake. Mine would be covered with every color in the rainbow because they're all too beautiful to pick only one.

"My mom told me to stay out of the kitchen while she baked, so it would be a surprise. I waited until I heard her making the icing with her handheld mixer and sneaked to peek into the kitchen while her back was turned. And you know what I saw? Two circle cakes stacked on top of each other and covered in white icing. I ran to my room and cried."

"Why were you crying, Granny?" I open my eyes and take another bite of my cookie.

"I wanted a cake shaped like a butterfly, remember? And the cake I saw was a regular, boring round cake." Granny holds up her hands to show a circle.

I nod, feeling sad too. "Why didn't your mom make you the cake you wanted?"

Granny winks at me. "The story doesn't end there, Sadie-bum. The story always continues."

"My mom called me down for dinner and I don't remember what we had. I do remember my mom announcing it was time for a cake, but I wasn't excited. My dad told me to shut my eyes tight. When I opened them, it wasn't only a plain cake. My mom had covered the entire cake with purple butterflies."

"How did she do it, Granny?" Picturing how pretty the cake must have looked like with all the butterflies. For my birthday next year, I for sure want a butterfly cake.

"I'm convinced that woman was magic. And you know what?" Pausing only to take a sip of her tea. "We ate the cake on these same plates. And one day these plates will be your mom's and then yours, Sadie."

I look up at Granny and back to my now empty plate. "I'd rather have your bowl of rocks. I can't play with plates."

Granny chuckles and places the rock she was holding back into the bowl. "These are my special memory stones. One day, you'll have all of your own and won't have room for any of mine."

I shrug. "I could always just buy a bigger bowl." I pick up the rock she was holding and pass it back and forth between my hands.

"What makes a rock a memory rock instead of a regular rock?" I ask. They seem like regular rocks to me.

Granny grabs my empty plate and places it in a stack with hers. "Well, I remembered that story, didn't I?"

Mommy always says she's losing her marbles when she forgets things. Sometimes I shake my head extra hard, trying to make something rattle around in my brain. My braids only whip my face and sting my cheeks, though. Maybe my marbles are locked up and not loose because I'm not old yet.

I wonder why Granny doesn't have marbles like Mommy. Rocks are much cooler than marbles, anyway. My favorite kinds of rocks are the ones with sparkles or cool shapes. Maybe that's why Granny is different from Mommy. She's got cool rocks bouncing around in her head.

Last summer Granny and I were playing outside in the backyard. She wanted to remember something and grabbed a rock from beside her garden. When I asked her why she grabbed a rock, she told me, "Holding my thoughts in my hands helps me remember."

Later, when we went inside, I grabbed the rock out of the bowl to check if I could hear what Granny's thought was. It only felt like a rock to me. When Mommy knocked at the door to pick me up, I was surprised and put it in my pocket. When we got home, I hid it in my drawer to bring back to Granny's house the next week.

"Sadie, why are you scrunching your face up like that?" Mommy pats my head and laughs at me.

I hold the rock in my lap under the table and rub my thumb over it. Maybe if I rub it like a genie's bottle, I will get the memory into my brain. "Can we go to the dollar store after your tea?" I peek over into Mommy's cup. Ugh. She's still got half of it left. Why do adults always sip their drinks so slowly?

Mommy checks the time on her phone. "Not today, Sweetie. Daddy's going to be home from work soon." She fishes out her notebook from her bag and passes me a pencil.

Mommy has notebooks everywhere- in the kitchen, beside her bed, in her purse, and in the car. "Write what you want on my list and maybe I can stop after groceries tomorrow morning, okay?"

With my best printing, I write *a jar for marbles*. Marbles may not be as cool as rocks, but Mommy should do a better job of keeping hers safe. I tuck the notebook back into her bag so she won't forget it.

Mommy's sipping the rest of her tea and Granny's trying to decide if she wants my mommy to buy chicken or pork chops. I hold my breath and sneak the rock I was holding in the pocket of my jeans. The last rock was only like a rock to me, but this rock shows me a world of butterflies when I close my eyes. I definitely want a butterfly cake for my birthday next year. I'm sure Granny would be fine letting me borrow this memory so I don't forget about the cake. But I'm also too scared to ask, and she says no.

"Can I go back and play, Mommy?" I'm scared the longer I sit here, they might notice I have a secret burning a hole in my pocket.

Mommy takes another sip of her tea. "Why don't you play for another five minutes and then clean up the dolls, okay? Maybe we'll even beat Daddy home for a change."

I hug Granny. "Thanks for the cookies!" She pats my back and I try not to push into Granny so she won't feel the rock inside my pocket.

"You're very welcome, Sadie-bum."

Before I can change my mind, I run back upstairs to wake up my dolls before we have to go home.

chapter 4

Margo

What the Heart Wants - Margo in the Past

I FIRST MET MY HUSBAND while on a date with my boyfriend. It was the end of our fourth date, to be exact.

Mark, my boyfriend, held up my coat for me to slip my arms into and then led me out of the restaurant after our dinner date. The glowing letters of *Ricardo's* shone behind us as we walked hand in hand back to the mechanic's shop to pick up Mark's car.

"How was your dinner, Margie?" It still made me twitch when he called me by the same nickname my dad did. But I can't fault the guy, since he's been around me most of my life.

"Delicious, as always. How was yours?"

"The chicken and rice bowl was great, but maybe next time I'll try one of their seafood platters."

I nodded because it sounded delicious, but we both knew he wouldn't. He always would say he wanted a change, but he always stuck with his usuals. The navy blue button-down shirt, black slacks, and Ricardo's chicken and rice bowl. Like clockwork.

It was the start of summer and the hours in the days were getting drawn out and brighter. At dinnertime, the street lights would be on by now, so I was glad for an extra hour before Mark and I would part ways to go back home. Him, to his apartment downtown, and me, back to my parent's house. First, we needed to pick up Mark's car so he could drive me back home.

When we arrived at the shop, the mechanic greeted us. The receptionist, Shelly, had already gone home for the night, and based on the emptiness of the shop, we were the last customers of the day.

"I changed the oil and fixed the headlight." His oval embroidered name tag read Jake. He wiped the grease off his hands on a well-used rag. His hands still were as heavily stained as the rag he held, no cleaner than before he wiped them. "Paul will pull the car around for you."

On instinct, Mark stuck out his hand to shake the mechanic's hand, but then withdrew to avoid the chance of grease. I had secondhand embarrassment, so stuck out my hand instead. The mechanic's eyebrows shot up in surprise and Mark's annoyed glare burned a hole in the side of my head.

Jake gripped my hand in a firm handshake. "Well, enjoy your evening, folks. Bring her back in six months or so from now."

He released my hand and headed to the back.

"Bring back my car or my girl?" Mark muttered under his breath.

I rolled my eyes. A handshake was simply a handshake. There were no butterflies, no thoughts of him nagging at the back of my head. Only a man named Jake who fixed my boyfriend's vehicle. No different from Paul, who pulled it around for us, or Janice, the waitress who had served our dinner.

I placed my hand in Mark's hand, and we walked out to the car. I may not have experienced any butterflies when I first met Jake, but I also had none slipping my hand back into Mark's either. Mark wasn't the right choice, but he was the obvious one. Our families were friends. He had a job my dad approved of, and our paths always crossed and intersected with each other.

Two years after first meeting Jake, and one year and a bit since breaking up with Mark, I headed to the mall for a routine shopping trip. The parking lot was busy for an unsuspecting Thursday afternoon in June. I circled the lot twice before finding a spot to pull into. The black compact car beside me was backing out, so I took the extra few minutes to check my reflection in the rearview mirror.

Thud. I lurched forward and hit my head on the mirror. I turned to the back and, sure enough, a white van had rear-ended me. The woman driving, eyes bulging, appeared as shocked as me.

Opening my door, I stepped out at the same time she did.

"I am so sorry! Oh my goodness, are you okay?" The woman ran her shaking hands through her shoulder-length blonde hair and gripped the roots while staring at the crater her van had put into my back taillight and bumper.

"Luckily, we're only in a parking lot. What happened?" I understood that she had bumped into the back of my car when trying to pull into the too-small parking space with her too-large van. But it still seemed like the sort of question you ask after an accident. Was this even considered an accident?

"Are you ladies okay?" Jake asked as he approached our tangled vehicles. Of course, I didn't know it was Jake at first, and he didn't know who I was either. It's not like it mattered. We weren't some lover ships passing each other in the dark of night.

He handed each of us one of his cards for the mechanic's shop. That was when the dots connected for me. "My information is on the card if you need it for a witness statement for insurance purposes." He eyed up the crunched metal and shattered glass of the taillight. "Looks like the van was lucky with only a couple of scratches, and it shouldn't be too much to fix up your car. Feel free to bring them by the shop. It'll be a quick fix, and I'll have you on your way."

I couldn't help myself from taking the bait. "Is part of your job description patrolling parking lots looking to drum up business?"

The poor woman still looked horrified about the entire incident, but Jake removed his hat, scratched his head, and laughed. "Nope, only a bonus after shopping." He held up a shopping bag with his left hand. "But seriously, ladies. No charge."

"Thanks, Jake," I said and placed his card in my purse. "I'll try to drop by this week."

Jake headed back down the aisle of cars until he spotted his blue truck. A bit of rust on the back and dried mud splashed up the side. Durable, old, but useful. It suited him, was my first thought. I didn't know the guy, so it was an assumption on my part, but it clicked together as a winning match in my brain.

I glanced back at the lady beside me. "No harm, no foul." *Well, no harm to me, anyway.*

Three small faces inside the van pressed up against the window, looking out as wide-eyed as their mother. They were like an entire family of raccoons caught when the porch light turned on. I could only imagine the stories they would tell their father around the dinner table that night. The poor mom exhaled relief. It was as if she had been holding her breath from the moment she felt the crunch until I told her I didn't need her insurance information.

"I am so sorry! My husband recently bought me this beast and I'm still getting used to it. But, with all the kids, I needed something bigger." It was the longest she had spoken yet. She dropped her head, both out of guilt and the embarrassment of the tears threatening to spill over.

I hugged her, and the way she collapsed into me confirmed she was most likely long overdue for one. Little did I know at that moment that I also owed her a thank you.

It was strange pulling into the mechanic's shop later that week. The last time I was at the shop was after my date with Mark. The man my dad had loved and made my mom dream of a fall wedding followed by a summer grandbaby. They weren't the only ones who swooned over Mark, either. I never missed the glances he got whenever we were out together. I know he was aware of them, too. Not that he ever acted on it. That man was 6 feet tall, but the attention he received entirely inflated a foot of that height.

He was nice, polite, handsome, had a good job, opened the doors, paid for dinner, and dropped me off at a respectable hour with a respectable kiss. On our sixth date, he walked me around the pond in the middle of town with the cute gazebo on the far east side.

"I love you, Margo." He looked down into my eyes. "I hope you know how much you mean to me."

This was one of those moments that you're supposed to swoon. You confess your love, you kiss, the sun fades, the butterflies fly, the curtain closes, and you end the scene. But I couldn't say it. "I care about you a lot too, Mark."

I tried to think of something that would show him I cared for him too, because I did. However, if you're not saying "I love you, too" there is no other option that makes it better than saying "I do not."

We only went on two more dates after that. Mark decided there was no point hanging around. He was heading off to college a couple of states away, and if he couldn't take me with him as a wife, then what was the point of waiting for me to be ready? I had more guilt than heartbreak when he left. The day he moved was the day my parents had to accept the fact their daughter let one of the good ones get away.

I guess that's why it was uncomfortable to be back here at the mechanic's shop again. Two years had lapsed, and I was still as unsure about my life now as I was then.

"We got the dent and light fixed and we couldn't find any other damage." Jake had found me in the customer lounge sipping at a coffee in a styrofoam cup. Same overalls, the same name tag, same greasy rag in his hands. But this time I was seeing him.

Jake was tall and had a relaxed posture. He had a short beard that wasn't a mess; he took some care and attention to his appearance. His hair was dark and in need of a haircut as it stuck out the sides of his stained cap, sitting snug on his head. When Mark entered a room, he commanded attention. Jake's presence was more of a subtle slip into the room, but you felt welcomed to be talking with him. His eyes were gentle and content, but a smile didn't tug at his lips without coaxing. So, when he did smile at me, it was like I had earned something special.

"I can't let you fix it for free. How about I treat you to a coffee better than this one?" I lifted the cup that I had been nursing for the last hour, not wanting to chuck it into the garbage can with the half dozen other cups sitting at the bottom in a pool of dark liquid.

"So, first you accuse me of preying on poor ladies in parking lot accidents, and now you're insulting the fine coffee of my establishment?" Jake rubbed the rag over his hands some more. "Which was free, like the labor I did to fix your poor car."

I laughed. "How much of the coffee do you drink?" I offer him the rest of mine.

Jake scoffed and smirked. "Absolutely none. That coffee will put some grit in your blood."

"Oh, is that what you're calling it? How about a proper cup of coffee?" I had never been this bold before.

He looked like he was going to say no. Either he wasn't interested or he was uncomfortable with the boldness of my offer. "I suppose I can't say no." His eyes twinkled a little.

"No, you definitely can't."

Jake snorted and gave the stubble along his chin a scratch. "Alright, we can get coffee. But I'm paying."

Turns out it only takes some extra scrubbing and Jake's hands clean up surprisingly well. So did he, for that matter. Our coffee date that weekend turned into dinner. The dinner turned into a stroll around town, followed by ice cream, a kiss under the gazebo as the sun set, and a walk back to my basement suite. It was cheesy, but everything clicked together without even trying.

His dad was also a mechanic, his mom stayed home to raise him and his five siblings. Neither of his parents were alive anymore. His dad had passed away in a car accident when he was on the cusp of becoming a teenager. Shattering their grieving family even more, their mom joined their dad a couple of years ago after a brief battle with breast cancer.

"What do you want out of your life?" It wasn't a normal question I would ask on a first date. But, out of anyone, Jake grasped the weight of how finite our lives were.

"I want a simple life. No, a happy life." He put his arm around me as we walked back to my place.

I leaned into his denim jacket. "And what is happy?"

"I guess I'd like to have a family of my own. Have it the way it was before my dad died. Family dinners, board games, and too many people piled into a vehicle for a camping trip. Work at the shop and come home to my family."

I closed my eyes and pictured that life, and I was in it with him. I only had a brother who was older than me, and the large family upbringing he had enthralled me. My dad, a farmer, also worked with his hands so I could relate to the simple but challenging life.

My family and friends were still getting used to saying Margo and Jake in conversation when he got down on one knee a month later. A family ring, of course. It all perfectly made sense. Mark made sense on paper, but not in my life. Jake made sense in my life, in my heart, in every breath I took.

When he had first said he loved me, all I had wanted to say was "Yes!". Yes to you, yes to us, yes I do.

"It's you and me always, Mar." He squeezed my hand. "I promise."

"No matter what. I've got you." I squeezed back.

chapter 5

Margo

RED HOUSE, GREEN HOUSE, empty lot, park bench, and a garbage can. I amble down the streets of my neighborhood, the gentle rustling of leaves and the distant hum of traffic, as life moves on around me, lingers in the distance. The sun is high in the sky now, making this late fall day unusually warm. Sitting on the park bench, I rub my left leg. It has a dull ache which is annoying me, and a brown stain on the left knee of my orange sweatsuit sticks to my fingers when I rub it.

My fingers fumble with the zipper of my grey, wool coat. "Too hot, everything is too hot," I mutter to myself. My hands tremble and lose their grasp as I struggle to pull my arms free from my coat. The soft fabric of my orange sweater resists the fibers of the wool coat, causing a tug of war as I try to break free. With one more tug, I break free from its vice grip.

"Stupid thing." I place my coat beside me on the bench in a crumpled heap.

Shielding the sun from my eyes with my right hand, to my left is a purple car, white fence, yellow house, and stop sign. To my right is an empty lot, green house, red house, and crosswalk. *Which direction is my house?*

A young man crosses the street in front of me with long, white wires hanging out of his ears. His hands in the front pockets of his faded jeans, hanging low on his hips and a hole in dire need of a patch over his left knee. However, by the size of it, it might not be worth the effort. He's fresh out of high school but missing a backpack. His shirt is someone's art project, if you could call it that, with a handful of paint thrown at it. The boy's blond hair combed off to the side, his mouth moving but no words coming out.

"Excuse me," I call out. I point a finger shakily in his direction to get his attention, but he continues walking without noticing me. "Excuse me, young man!" This time I raise my voice loud enough so he glances in my direction.

He removes the wire from his left ear and steps towards the bench I'm sitting on. He flips the hair out of his eyes and lets out a huff of air. "Yes?"

"I'm looking for Jake. Do you know where he is?" I ask him and wait expectantly. Surely he will tell me the exact answer I need. *Go up the road and turn left. I saw him just a couple of minutes ago.* Everyone in the neighborhood knows Jake. The people who live here are friendly and always chatting as they go about their day. It also helps that the mechanic's shop Jake works at is the only one in the area.

His face shifts from annoyed to confused. "I'm sorry, I don't know a Jake." He pauses for only a second, studying me.

"Wait, I remember you! You deliver our newspaper, right?" I ask and slap my knee with realization. "I'm trying to find my house. It's the blue one with the fence in the front yard and it's always full of sunflowers."

He shifts his weight on his feet and runs his hand through his hair. "That was probably my dad. He used to deliver the paper around here when he was a teenager."

"Umm, did you like want to come home with me? My mom will be there and maybe she can help you get back home?"

I pull out a tissue that is tucked up the sleeve of my shirt, wipe my nose with it, and shake my head. "No, I want to go back to my house. Not yours."

We stare at each other and I wonder if he has remembered something after all, but he makes that face you make when talking to a small child. I hate that face. "We live in that house down the road with the yellow birdhouse in the tree if you want my mom," he says, putting the wire back into his ear and continuing on his way.

"Why'd people have to go and build so many new houses?" I mutter as the young man walks away. I glance around at all the many strange houses that are blurring together the more roads I walk down.

I tentatively push myself off the bench and turn towards my left. It must be one more road over. I pull the stone from my sweatpants pocket and rub it in my hands. *427 Violet Street.* Stroke, stroke, stroke. Turning the rock over in my hand slowly. *Blue and white house beside an empty lot.* Step, step, step.

The pains in my stomach plague me with thoughts of toast and eggs. The once-warm sun has now gone to hide behind a dark cloud. That's the thing about fall; the weather can change so fast. I hug my arms around my body as I walk. I can't believe I didn't think to bring a jacket. *Foolish.*

My pace has slowed to a shuffle, the ache in my left knee now a painful throb with each sluggish step. Purple car, white fence, yellow house, stop sign. Are all the streets the same around here? The stop sign looms above me and the green street sign reads *Violet Street.*

Jake, I'm home. I squeeze the rock in my hand and turn down the street towards our house. The home Jake and I bought after we got married. When we first toured it, the outside had seen better days. The inside needed some elbow grease and love. But there was nothing about it that was too big to handle. We worked hard together that first year, building up our home while building our life together. Jake let me pick the color for the outside and I went with the perfect deep navy blue. He painted the trim and the fence a pure white and the house stuck out beautifully on our quiet street.

"We'll only have one neighbor," Jake had said when we first toured the house.

I nodded excitedly. "The empty lot beside us will be perfect for all the kids to play in." All the kids we didn't have, yet.

Green house, red car, brown house, blue house, red duplex. I stop and look back behind me at the street sign. It still reads Violet Street, the street of our home.

"No, no, no." I shake my head, trying to clear my vision. "Where's the empty lot?" My blue house and white fence are visible, I think, but where's the empty lot? Our house is not next to a brown house. Where is my house? Where is Jake?

I frantically rub my rock and pace back and forth on the sidewalk. My knee is begging me to sit down, but I can't sit down on the road. I must sit down in *my* chair, in *my* house. I turn back around towards my house again and I nearly crash into a couple walking towards me. *Where on earth did they come from?*

If I had to guess, which I am not excelling at these days, they both appear to be in their early 50s. The woman is of average height and has sleek dark hair that barely skims her chin. She is dressed in a long, winter jacket and balancing on high heels. Heels, heels, I've seen that before. *Right!* That woman with the dog. Holding her hand beside her is a tall man. His hair is deep red with thick curls and he looks like he was due for a shave a week ago. They both are standing awfully close to me and looking at me intently.

"Where is your dog?" I ask.

She chuckles softly. "Oh, he's at home. You remember Duke?" she asks.

"I remember you walking him before, and he isn't with you now."

"Margo," the woman says my name and reaches for my elbow.

I snatch my arm away from her and back up. "Don't touch me." Did she always go around touching strange people? "How do you know my name?"

We all take turns looking back and forth at each other, waiting for someone to say something. They are having a silent conversation between themselves, and me trying to decide how crazy these people must be. When they make eye contact with me, I see that look again. *That* look. And then comes that voice.

"It's Peter and Suzanne, Margo," the man, who must be Peter, says in a slow voice, like he's trying to console a child who is crying. "We're your neighbors in that brown house right over there." He points as if I can't see what is, without a doubt, an imposter of a brown house sitting on what should be an empty lot beside *my* house.

"Are you the ones who moved my house? Does Jake know you moved it?" I accuse them and stare pointedly at them. But, despite my fury, they remain unchanged in their soft expressions and furrowed eyebrows.

"Why don't we walk you home, Margo?" Suzanne reaches for my arm again. "We can find out why your house got moved once we get you settled in."

I eye her suspiciously, but home sounds good. I pull my arm back and respond, "You may walk with me, but I am perfectly capable of walking myself."

Jake will know what to do about the house.

Nestled in my favorite red chair in the living room, my body shivers beneath the quilt Suzanne has wrapped me in. They had insisted on coming into the house when we got here. Suzanne is comfortable on the couch across from me and I figure if they were going to rob me, they would have done it by now.

"Where's Jake?" I ask Suzanne for the fifth time, who is watching me closely. Jake wasn't home when we got here, and neither Peter nor Suzanne would answer any of my questions. "I need him to come back home from work to move our house right away." Where would Alice ride her bike when she got home from school?

Peter steps into the living room, holding a cup of hot tea and hands it to me. The warmth is a comfort for my chilled fingers. He settles beside Suzanne on the couch, draping his arm along the back of the couch behind her. Burglars wouldn't make their victim tea unless maybe they're trying to poison me.

"Wait," I say as a realization hits me and my heart races again. I pat the pockets of my sweatpants and don't feel any keys. "How did you get me into the house?"

Peter leans into Suzanne on the couch as he reaches into the back pocket of his jeans and pulls out his keychain. He lifts a key away from the rest to show me. "We have an extra key, in case you ever need us."

My brows furrow and the tea sloshes in the cup as my shaking hands are barely holding on. "I never gave you a key." I set down my cup of tea, which spills slightly over the side onto the table beside me. "Please, I need to call Jake." I try to push myself to stand, but the pain in my leg and my tired muscles fail me and I fall back into the chair.

Suzanne slides forward on the couch and pats Peter's arm. "Why don't you go into the kitchen and give Alice a call, okay? I'll wait here with Margo." She stands up from the couch to reposition the blanket around me after I knocked it off in my failed attempt to stand.

That's when I know these people are the ones who have completely lost their minds, not me. "Now, why would you call Alice? She's a child." I shoo away Suzanne's fluttering hands as she tries to reposition my blankets. "Please, I need you to leave." If everyone would give me a second. I'm not a child.

Peter opens his mouth to say something, but Suzanne cuts him off. "Peter, please go." Once Peter leaves, she turns back to me and pats my hand.

"You can't do this to me. It's not right." I grab hold of her hand so she will stop and listen to me. "It can't change. Nothing can change."

Peter calls from the kitchen, "Suze, I just got Alice's voicemail. Do you have Travis' number?"

"Try calling Alice again and leave a message. We can wait around for a bit and then try Travis if we need to."

"Travis?" I ask, gripping onto Suzanne tighter.

"He's gonna go call Jake, okay? Jake will be here soon." She kneels in front of me and squeezes my hand.

"I've been asking you to find Jake since we first got home," I complain and shake my head in disbelief. "Was that so hard?" I lean my head back into the headrest of the chair, feeling a heaviness overtake me as I fight to keep my eyes open. It's okay. *Jake is coming.*

chapter 6

Alice

AFTER DROWNING IN MY TO-DO LIST of failures last week, this week is going much more smoothly. I was even able to drop off groceries on our way over to Mom's for tea yesterday. My list is still long, but nothing is urgent. And, more importantly, nothing is overdue. To help matters even more, Mom is also having a positive week.

"She will have good days and she will have bad days," the doctor had said after he handed us the official diagnosis. "Eventually the amount of good days will become fewer and scattered amongst days that prove to be much more challenging."

"So, good days mean her normal self?" I had asked, hopefully.

The doctor had folded his hands on his desk and leaned in. "The definition of a good day will change. Now, a good day means she has a firmer grasp of reality. Down the road, a good day could mean she's not agitated about something. You can still have a great day without the memories."

Good days and bad days. My ever-present notebook had been cracked open in my lap as I diligently took notes while the doctor talked. I had phone numbers for different support groups down the margin and a handful of options for in-home or long-term care.

I never knew my dad's parents. My mom's parents hadn't lived a long life, and I only remembered them in bits and pieces. Grandpa had a heart attack when I was young. Grandma followed him a few years later. Her daily cigarettes took her away from us before I was even in school. But my mom had always been healthy. She had a routine of staying active, eating well, and vowed to never smoke in her life. She was supposed to live long into her 80s and experience her grandbabies grow up and move on with their lives. But life is never a recipe that we can follow perfectly to get the results we desire. A few months ago, Mom passed the 60th milestone, and she is now losing memories faster than I can keep building them with her.

She could still live for many more years, but only those around her could keep any future memories made. We are the ones who will be front row when she retreats within herself as the memories recede from her reality. She could still live to see Sadie grow taller, older, and graduate. But, when Sadie walks across that stage, would Mom even recognize which grandchild was hers?

Since today has been uneventful and it has been a great week, I am giving myself permission to go out tonight. Two Wednesdays every month, some local moms gather at a local restaurant to eat, chat, and remember how to simply be ourselves. It is our chance to forget about school pickup and packing lunches, at least until the next day.

Making and maintaining friendships as an adult are two very different things, both equally challenging. In school, we are all grouped by age and we form friendships within that circle. Once we are adults, though, we all scatter along different life paths. Some of these childhood friendships stay strong and others fade away.

Most of my high school friends moved away to attend college on the quest to start a new life in a bigger city. I stayed behind and went to the community college to become an education assistant. I told myself it was because Mom would be lonely if I moved away, but I also couldn't grasp how my life would look without her being a central part of it anymore. Thankfully, I didn't move away because I never would have run into Travis late at night studying at the library.

When Travis and I had Sadie, I once again lost my main circle of friends. They were still working, and I was changing diapers. They talked about the latest school political drama, and I was binging Netflix while nursing Sadie at 1am. Now, with caring for my mom and raising Sadie, I could feel the chasm growing in my circle of friends again. They were all relishing in their freedom after doing the school drop-off or juggling pickup times and work schedules. None of them were balancing how to help an aging parent and checking their child's math homework.

And it was because of that juggling that I hadn't been able to go to the last couple of mom meetups. Either Mom needed me or I was too tired myself. But tonight is going to be moms' night out. Tonight I can simply be Alice.

I climb out of the shower and wrap my hair in a towel. Wrapping another towel around my body, I sit on the closed toilet lid to scroll through my phone.

2 missed calls. I click on the notification and see I have missed the calls from Mom's neighbor, Peter, while I was in the shower.

Peter and Suzanne had bought the empty lot by our house a couple of years after Jake left. After school, I would eat my snack in the driveway while I watched the house being built. I imagined who would move into the finished house, how many kids they might have, and where they would move from. Turns out the new owners were young and never did have children of their own. Instead, they welcomed all of us neighborhood kids into their hearts and were like an aunt and uncle to me growing up. When Mom got her diagnosis, they were more than happy to help fill the gaps by helping out however I needed.

I only missed the calls by a couple of minutes, so I dial back and urge my heart to settle into a normal rhythm.

"Oh, hey Alice. Suzanne and I are over at your mom's right now," Peter says when he answers the phone.

"Is everything okay? What's going on?"

The background noise fades away as Peter steps into a different room. "Your mom was pacing back and forth across from her house on the sidewalk. Suzanne and I went to talk to her, but she didn't know us or where she was."

"Is she at home now?" I'm already removing the towels from my hair and body while shuffling into the bedroom to grab some clothes from the end of my bed to put on.

Peter's voice remains calm, which helps me to focus on the facts and not the panic rising up inside my throat as it tightens. "Yes, she is settled in here with some tea. She is focused on wanting Jake to come back home."

I squeeze my eyes shut and pinch the top of my nose. Jake's not coming. "Okay, I'm coming over right away. Do you mind sitting with her until I get to her house? Ten minutes, tops."

"Of course, Alice. We're not going anywhere."

I hang up the phone and in record speed pull on some light grey yoga pants and a faded pink t-shirt. My still-wet hair is soaking through the back of my shirt, so I pull it up into a messy pile on the top of my head with a fuzzy black scrunchie. Heading down the hall, I turn left and run down the steps to the front door. I slip on my shoes without socks because I don't want to rummage through the mountain of laundry I still need to tackle. After pulling on my jacket, I flip off the lights and throw my purse over my shoulder.

Grabbing my phone and keys, I shoot Travis a text as I head out the door and lock it. *Mom had a bad day. Headed there now. I'll let you know if you need to be home for Sadie. xx.*

Three typing dots, and then Travis responds. Let me know if you need anything. *I'll wrap up here and finish the rest of these documents at home. Breathe.*

The good week has ended. My plans shattered into a million glimmering fragments, like my mom's memory. The weight of it all settles in my chest as I try to take Travis' advice and breathe.

I open the oven door and put in a casserole from the freezer for an early dinner for Mom. She's been upstairs and resting in bed since I got here a couple of hours ago. My phone is on the kitchen counter playing the traditional waiting room music while I wait on hold for Mom's doctor. With nothing else for me to do, I stand and watch the timer on the stove tick down. One slow minute at a time.

At home, I always have a basket of laundry to fold, a dishwasher to unload and load again, sticky crumbs to mop up, and lists to make. Here, the stillness is so foreign it is almost suffocating. I have already washed and dried the lonely teacup and plate that sat inside the sink. The dishwasher is rarely used because it would take a week to fill it with the dishes of only one person. I may be drowning in my busyness, but I don't know who I am without it.

By the time I got here, exhaustion was setting in for Mom. She was alternating between sleep and agitation, mumbling about Jake and her house. She recognized me right when I walked through the door and reached out for me to hold on to. I thanked Peter and Suzanne for bringing my mom home and walked them to the door so they could return to their normal lives. It never fails to amaze me how two distinct realities in her brain can blend and still be true to her. A world where I am a young child and Jake is still my dad can be as true to her as me stepping through the front door as a grown adult who she knows by name.

At some point on her walk, she must have tripped and fell, but she didn't remember when I asked. The dried blood on her left knee had soaked through into her sweatpants. Upon further inspection, I found nothing major, only bruising and slightly swollen. I cleaned it up, no different from her cleaning my wounds or me cleaning Sadie's. I changed her into one of her nightgowns and tucked her into bed. She had only mentioned Jake twice since I had arrived, and who knows what reality she would awake into.

I had noticed her wool coat was missing from the coat rack, so I made a note to check for it outside. Peter beat me to it, though. After leaving, he and Suzanne wandered back through the neighborhood. They found it one street over, lying on a bench. Still tucked inside one pocket was her set of house keys. Suzanne dropped it off on her way back to their house and offered to make us dinner. I had thanked her but assured her we had been enough of a burden on them for one day.

"Thank you for waiting. This is Dr. Ramirez." The voice abruptly cut through the classical instrumental.

I grab my phone and switch it off speaker mode before bringing it to my ear. "Thanks for fitting me in between patients. It's Alice Hughes calling on behalf of my mother, Margo Reynolds."

"How is Margo doing? I didn't have you guys on my calendar for our usual appointment until next week," he says. Dr. Ramirez is clicking on his computer, ready to take some notes.

"Well, she's had a great week, but today Mom was really confused and agitated. The neighbors found her wandering on the street, unable to find her way home. She also didn't remember who they were," I answer. The words come pouring out like a full-pressure faucet. The faster I can relay the information to him, the faster he can bandage it all back together for me.

"You know we've touched on this before, Alice." Dr. Ramirez types some more notes and then pauses. "I think it's time that you look into other options for your mom's care."

"But we still have so many good days," I interject, not ready to talk about options that mean my mom is getting worse. "She has a routine that she follows regularly. She walks, she makes herself food, and she's very independent."

"And those are all positive things that she can still do, but she needs someone to be around her more. At some point, someone won't be around to help her back home. At some point," he has finished typing now, "she might get really hurt."

I let his words sink in. "I'm not ready," I admit. The words barely make it past my tight throat.

"I'm sorry, Alice, but you need to get ready. Whether it's you, an aide, or a long-term care center, something needs to change. If you need numbers or forms for anything, please call Dorothy at the front desk, okay?" Dr. Ramirez asks.

Okay, to what? Okay, to the fact I heard you? Okay, that I will do it? Okay, that I am okay? None of this is okay. I take a breath and say the only thing that I am supposed to say, "Okay. Thanks, Dr. Rameriz."

"I'll keep you on the calendar for next week still, and we can touch base more then."

I'm grateful he took the time between patients to call, but this isn't what I wanted him to say. I also can't monopolize any more of his time to discuss this further. "Talk to you next week. Bye," I say and end the call.

I lay the phone back down on the counter. The stove timer only has ten minutes more to go. Travis is home with Sadie, possibly ordering some dinner for the two of them shortly. I'm not sure if I should wake Mom up or let her sleep. Waking up can be startling for most people, especially so when Mom's mind is already agitated. I won't rest easy tonight if I slip out while she's asleep. So it looks like my moms' night out might be an impromptu sleepover at my mom's house instead.

I shoot out a quick text to the moms' thread. *Something came up with my mom. Catch you ladies next time.*

I'm stuck between the roles of mom, wife, and daughter. It's a life that is so busy and exhausting, but fulfilling and challenging. Yet, here I am on a Wednesday night, straddling the chasm of two worlds being constantly pulled further apart. I pull out a single plate from the cupboard because I'll most likely eat alone.

chapter 7

Margo

THE EARLY MORNING LIGHT streams into my bedroom through the curtains I forgot to close last night. My body craves another hour of sleep, but when the sun says it's time to seize the day, I listen. With winter approaching sooner every day, I will welcome every ounce of sunshine, even if it wakes me from sleep. I roll to my side and throw back the quilted bedspread so I can swing my legs off the edge of the bed. My feet find the warmth of my fuzzy pink slippers as I slide the rest of my body off into standing.

I fold the covers on the bed back up under the pillow. The quilt on the other side of the bed lays crisp, as the still-made side of the bed, beside my still-warm side. After all these years, I still sleep on only the one side of the bed. The other side always has and always will belong to Jake.

Walking into the adjoining bathroom, my mirror has three notes placed in a row. Each card has its own title: *Important, Morning,* and *Night.* I don't remember when I first made the morning and night cards, but they are helpful in the moments I forget if I have already brushed my teeth or washed my face. In the grand scheme of things, I still have most of my originally-issued teeth, so I'm sure it is fine to forget to brush them now and then.

The notes were my way of channeling some of Alice's order and rhythm. I am doing fine all on my own. Well, that's my well-rehearsed line to Alice's ongoing worries, anyway. But, I will secretly admit that there is a comfort in simply following the instructions on the cards and not having to think about it.

During the past couple of weeks, Alice had added multiple cards of her own throughout the house. Each of her cards is marked *Important* and in a bright pink color while mine are on sunny yellows and peaceful blues. I told her it was foolish, but she was still very worked up from what she keeps referring to as "the incident" from earlier this week. I am happy with my notes scattered minimally around the house, but all the additions from Alice everywhere are just as annoying as they are sometimes helpful. Nothing like constantly being reminded that I need help to function.

"Mom, you need to work with me and stop fighting with me," Alice had chastised me over breakfast when I woke up after "the incident" and found her sleeping in her old room. I don't remember the last time she spent the night here, but she claims she's done it a handful of times when I've had one of my bad days.

"Last I checked, you were my daughter, and this was my house." The waffles were a pleasant change from my usual morning oatmeal, though. And every mom loves to have her little chicks around, especially when they are too big for the nest.

I had humoured Alice, though, and let her place notes throughout my house. Knowing I had fallen on a walk that I don't remember taking bothers me. It eats at my brain and the facts of what happened are out of reach from what I can grasp. I'm frustrated Alice feels like she needs to micromanage my life, and I'm angry at the fact I need her to. I wonder if there will be a time in the future when we can simply download these notes as programming into our brains. Then, as memories slip away, we can reboot them with a new update. I'm not a real fan of technology, but that's an invention I could get behind. Wouldn't that be something?

The pink important note from Alice stuck to my mirror is a new addition. Alice must have placed it there yesterday. It reads: *No showers without Alice at the house.* I glance at the tub in my bathroom and smirk to myself. She never said no baths. I turn to leave the bathroom, chuckling to myself as I hear Jake's ever-present voice in my head, "You're nothing but trouble, Mar."

With breakfast dishes done, I fold the dish towel and hang it on the stove's handle. Another one of Alice's notes taped to the stove fan catches my eye: Important: Turn off the stove. I roll my eyes, but still double check I turned off the burner from making my pot of oatmeal. *Dangit, Alice. Now I'm questioning if I am capable of anything.*

Normally, I would go for a walk around the neighborhood after eating breakfast, but I had promised Alice I wouldn't go for walks by myself anymore. What am I supposed to do with myself when my routine of two decades is now deemed "too dangerous" for me? Ridiculous, I tell you. These are supposed to be my golden years, not my bubble-wrapped years.

I grab a glass from the cupboard closest to the sink and fill it with tap water. I guess I will sit on the patio this morning. That's when I notice another of Alice's notes taped to the sliding glass door. *Important: Take the phone with you outside.* I pluck the note off the door and crumple it in my hand. Enough! I toss it onto the kitchen table and it bounces off the side and lands on the floor.

To my right, I grab the cordless phone off its charging stand and tuck it into my sweater pocket. "Rules are rules," I grumble to myself as I slide open the door and step outside.

I settle into a worn, wicker rocking chair and spread out the blanket that was draped over the armrest. I rarely find myself out here, there's no need. My well-worn path across the faded brown carpet from the bedroom to the kitchen to the living room is my daily routine. The upstairs has bedrooms collecting dust, some have been collecting it longer than others. Alice's bedroom is full of her childhood memories and another room is full of broken dreams and wishes for a house full of children. The garage is full of storage and memories of what feels like a lifetime ago. The backyard and patio were a place of planning for our future family. It was also Sadie's first push on a swing, empires built in the sand, and learning to balance on a bike.

The delicate gold watch on my wrist ticks its way past 9am. I pull the phone from my sweater pocket and wait for the ringing that will soon fill the quiet- like clockwork. Staring out at the neighbor's rose bushes, withered for the season, the familiar ringing breaks the silence. I click the talk button and bring the phone to my ear.

"Good morning, Mar." The familiar warmth of his voice fills my entire being.

"Morning, Jake. How are you?" I ask.

A thud in the background causes me to jump. "Oh, just the usual. Trying to tackle some projects around the house this week. What's new with you?"

"Is breaking your house one of your projects?" I tease and chuckle at the rhythmic banging of what must be a hammer.

"Alright, I'm done. I'll put down the hammer." He grunts and then claps his hands together. "Okay, you're off speaker now. I was hanging up another new piece of art I got at a garage sale. It was a beautiful bouquet of sunflowers and made me think of you. Remember when you first started the tradition of growing them all in a line along the front fence of the house?"

I close my eyes and pull the memory into focus. "That must've been, what? Our first summer in this house?"

"Our second. You were pregnant with Alice and I had to water them for you," Jake says.

I cut him off, "Because I was too busy puking. That pregnancy was a doozy." I chuckle at the memory. The dirt was not ideal for planting and was full of so many rocks. I stained the knees of multiple pairs of pants, digging out all of the rocks. The more I dug, the more I found. It didn't take long before I had a growing pile of rocks by the driveway and a trench along the fence. The shoveling of new, rich gardening soil was much easier than digging out the rocks.

"These sunflowers better grow after all of this work," I had muttered to Jake. After they sprouted, I was in the throes of morning sickness and had to pass the torch to Jake to keep them alive. When they finally opened, they were beautiful and so worth the effort.

We both stay quiet as the memory hangs between both of us. I imagine his house with the different paintings he has told me about over the many years. Then, I think about all the photos that hang down my hallways. How ironic that my house is full of photographs of the memories I built and created, while he strives to fill his house with art, reminding him of the few memories he can cling to. All the memories I lived through, crumbling into fragments and dust. All the memories he missed haunting him as he continues to live alone.

Jake breaks the silence. "You didn't answer my question of how you are."

I sigh. "You know me, not much new here. Well, except Alice no longer allows me to go on walks."

"What happened?" he asks.

"Why should something have happened, Jake?" I ask. I'm frustrated that the fact our daughter has now banished me to a life inside doesn't surprise him. I'm angry at him too. If he were here, there would have been no incident. No one would have deemed me crazy for searching for my husband.

"Well?" Jake prompts again. The concern in his voice is palpable.

I soften my voice before confessing. "I just got a little turned around and fell on my way home." What I don't tell him is that I had been looking for him.

"Damn it, Mar." He's not mad at me, but he's frustrated. Heck, I'm angry too.

"It's okay, Jake. Really. I'll be okay." I extend my words across the line to him, hoping they reach him like a squeeze to his hand. It's not okay, nothing about this is okay. But we will be okay. Alice, me, and the uninvited third wheel of my ailing brain. Even Jake and I, in our strange reality, were okay, too.

When Alice and I had gotten the news from the doctor, I told Alice it would be okay. I told her we would get through it and not allow me, her old mom, to be a burden on her life. She was a young wife and mom now, too. I held her while she cried as if I had walked into that appointment as her mom in the present and walked out as only a memory from her past.

It had been a Monday, and I sat on the information waiting for Friday. I had stewed, cried my tears, and longed for that Friday to come. Friday mornings were for Jake, when he would call and for only a moment, our lives crossed and intertwined.

"You need to promise me something, though, Jake." I had put off this when I first told him my diagnosis, but after this week I knew I couldn't anymore. "You need to talk to Alice."

"I know," Jake sighed heavily, his voice catching. The weight of decades of disappointment and abandonment lying squarely at his feet was dragging him down.

"You have to take care of her, even if she doesn't want you. It's on you now," I remind him. Eventually, a day may come when I won't remember who he is when I pick up the phone. The doctor had warned me it may come to a point where I wouldn't recognize Alice anymore. Deep down, I feared most for not knowing Jake anymore. If I didn't know him, it would be impossible for me to be that bridge between the lives of Alice and her dad.

"You may have been the one to make the decisions that led up to you leaving, Jake; but the decisions we made after that we made together." I fill the silence, waiting for him to answer. "One day, there won't be a me anymore. Alice needs to understand that there's still a you, though."

A shaky breath and the words come through, "I've got you, I promise."

Oh, how those words have echoed through time to mean so many different things.

IT'S MID-MORNING ON SUNDAY and I am relaxed on the couch, nestled into Travis. He has his agenda opened in his lap looking at the week ahead. I have my notebook beside me ready to plan out the meals and my tasks for the week. I shift slightly on the couch and Travis repositions his right arm around me, his fingers lazily drawing circles on my arm.

If you saw Travis on a weekend, you would never guess he was a lawyer. At least, he never looks like what I always imagined a lawyer to resemble. During the week, he always dresses to impress with a freshly cleaned suit, perfect posture, and confidence that exudes from him. He means business, and he gets the job done.

On weekends, he prefers a casual shirt and dark joggers. He doesn't bother shaving on the weekends and I like the scruff that teases along his square jawline. Travis also doesn't bother taming his curls into place. He still exudes that same confidence, though, but his dark green eyes are more playful and less business for these two days of the week.

"I'm doing the right thing, right Trav?" I break the silence.

"Mmm?" Travis turns his concentration to me.

I shift my head to get a better view of his face. "Hiring the in-home nurse for Mom. Is my mom going to hate her?"

Travis tucks some of my hair behind my ear and thinks for a second. "Your mom could never hate you. I also don't think there's one right solution. I think the nurse is the first step for us to try."

I nod. It didn't feel right to move my mom out of her house into a care facility, and I think moving her into the townhouse with us would suffocate the freedom she still has. That house is everything to her, and hopefully with the nurse, she can maintain some independence. It will also give me peace of mind. Those hours away from her house can fly by for me while I bounce from the store to her house to my house to take care of Sadie. But they're long hours for Mom, and anything can happen without me even knowing.

"I'll tell Mom we will try it out for a couple of weeks and go from there," I say.

Dr. Ramirez had recommended Jennifer to me when I called back to get referrals from his secretary. Jennifer and I met on Friday to talk about my mom and what kind of help I was looking for. She was in her mid-40s and had a soothing demeanor. Unmarried and without children, Jennifer had a heart to serve and care for those around her. She preferred working for families directly so she could fully immerse herself with only a couple of patients instead of bouncing around multiple people in a care facility.

We agreed she would start on Monday, and I would be at Mom's house for the first day to help bridge a connection between them. Since Mom could still cook and reheat simple meals for herself, Jennifer would come by after breakfast and walk with her around the neighborhood. Then she would be around to keep my mom company and offer support as needed. Mom often had a lie-down early afternoon, so Jennifer would head out for the afternoon and come back in the evening before Mom went to bed.

I was hesitant at first about how much Jennifer would be around my mom because I felt like my mom didn't need to be put to bed for naps and bedtime. However, I needed to make sure she wasn't wandering off around the neighborhood and getting lost again. Jennifer assured me it would be beneficial for her and Mom to form a connection before my mom's mind continued to decline. At that point, Mom would rely on Jennifer and me more and more.

I pat Travis' chest with my hand and begrudgingly uncurl myself from the cozy spot on the couch. "I should check on Mom and let her know about Jennifer. I'll be back after lunch if that works?"

"I'm sure Sadie and I can find some ice cream in the freezer for lunch." He smirks at me and winks.

I can tell he's joking to lift my spirits. Well, at least I think he is. Just in case, I call back to him as I head to the stairs, "Only if you save me a scoop."

"A nurse?! I'm not sick." Mom is slamming cupboards in the kitchen while making us each a cup of tea. She hasn't rearranged her kitchen in over 15 years, but she's making a scene out of looking for the mugs and tea bags. I don't want her to be agitated about this, but her tantrum reminds me of Sadie and I smirk.

I stop leaning against the counter and cross the kitchen to grab our usual mugs from the cupboard by the stove and set them on the counter. "Mom, she's only coming to help keep you safe. I worry about you here all by yourself. Wouldn't it be nice to have some company?"

Mom grabs her usual chicken mug and places it back in the cupboard with the other mugs. Instead, she grabs a mug painted like a cactus and places it on the counter. She turns to look at me with a scowl. "I have you and Sadie to keep me company. Or are you going to outsource my family, too?"

"We can't be here all the time, Mom. You know that." I reach out and squeeze her arm to help show this isn't an attack against her.

Mom drops her shoulders only a bit, conceding the battle but not willing to lose the war. "Fine, but I won't like her."

I chuckle to myself. That's the fighter I know my mom is. "Jennifer is going to have her work cut out with you."

Mom stops pouring the hot water into the cups and sets the kettle back down on the stove. She clicks off the burner and touches the notecard without looking at me. She's touching it to show me she's listening, which makes me happy.

She turns and passes my mug to me as we make our way into the living room. "Jennifer, you say? I knew a Jennifer a long time ago. We must have gone to school together, maybe grade 1 or 2?"

"Oh yeah? What kind of trouble did you get into?" I ask and wink at her. Mom always said she couldn't figure out where I got my goodie-two-shoes personality from. As a kid, Mom had always kept everyone on their toes with a healthy dose of joy and excitement in their lives. And if my dad was any good, he would still be here.

"I don't think Jennifer had much growing up. I never went to her house from what I can remember, but she would often come home with me after school. She wanted to learn to ride a bike, but her parents couldn't afford to buy one." Mom sips at her tea while gradually recounting the details, pulling piece by piece together like a jigsaw puzzle.

I think back to what I have heard about my mom's childhood. She didn't grow up with a lot of money herself. My grandma stayed home to raise Mom and my uncle. My grandpa worked long hours in the fields, farming a variety of grains and crops. They both firmly instilled in my mom the meaning of hard work and believing in yourself. Mom taught herself how to find the glimmer of adventure that's been fueling her life ever since.

"Did she ever learn how to ride a bike?" Leaning over, I place my cup down on the table to let it cool off some more. I prefer my drinks warm and not hot. I'll never understand how Mom never burns her mouth. She never fails to empty her cup before the steam has stopped.

Mom smiles as if she's back on that dirt road wrapping around the barn and farmhouse. "Yes, she did. Mom, your grandma, came out one day after school and showed Jennifer how to ride on my new red bike. She was biking laps around the yard by the time she had to head home for dinner. I still can picture that smile on her face and the tassels on the bike handles blowing in the wind."

I can't help but smile at the thought, too. "That was very sweet of Grandma. I wish I had more memories of her."

"My mom was the best. I am merely a shadow of the woman she was," Mom states as if it were pure fact.

I pick up my tea again and blow some of the steam away. "I don't know about that, Mom. You're pretty amazing yourself," I say and smile fondly at her. "Did you and Jennifer spend a lot of time biking after that?"

Mom scrunches her eyebrows together and thinks. "You know, I'm not too sure. I think she might have moved away the next year. I should pull out the old photo albums. I remember a picture of that bike in it somewhere."

Later that afternoon, when I got home, I went straight downstairs into the basement to rummage through some boxes.

"What are you doing down there?" Travis calls down the stairs to me. He knows how much I hate coming down here, so this is usually his domain to fetch and return things for me.

"I was looking for Mom's old photo albums. Remember when I said I wanted to scan them onto the computer to back them up for safekeeping?" I call back to him as I wiggle another box free from a stack. A picture frame I didn't notice balancing on top crashes to the ground.

Travis climbs down the stairs to investigate what the commotion is all about. "Are you sure you're not trying to destroy everything?" he teases.

I glare at him as he comes into view at the bottom of the stairs. "Ha, ha. You're so funny." I lift the lid to the box and brush the dust off an album labeled *Margo Childhood*. "Ah ha! Found it!"

I turn the first page and spot a couple of photos of my mom as a baby. They have yellowed over the years and the plastic protector sheet over the page crinkles under my hand.

"Doesn't Sadie remind you of Mom?" I turn the album so Travis can see the photo I am pointing to. My mom is wearing a frilly dress and a bonnet on her head. Everything is muted colors, yellowed and faded, but I can pick out the resemblance in those chubby cheeks and nose crinkle.

Travis shrugs and picks up the picture frame that had fallen to the ground. "You know I'm horrible with that sort of stuff. Were you wanting me to pull out the scanner?"

I shake my head and flip the page. "No, I only wanted to look. Mom was telling me a story about a friend she had as a kid. My grandma taught her how to ride a bike. Something about the story sounded familiar to me like I could picture that red bike in my head as if I was there. She said there was maybe a picture in her old scrapbooks."

Travis comes alongside me to look at the pictures with me. He points to a balding man on a tractor. "Is that your grandpa?" he asks.

"Yes, and that's my grandma," I say and point to a different picture of my grandma lighting candles on a white square cake from the local bakery.

I turn to the next page and all the photos are of my mom as a young teenager. Frowning, I turn back to the previous page. "I don't see the bike or my mom's friend at all."

"They didn't have digital cameras back then, Alice. There's a high chance they never even took a picture of your mom, her friend, or the bike." He places his hand on my lower back and peers over my shoulder to study the pictures more closely.

"I guess," I trail off, disappointed. "But I was sure I must've seen a photo of that bike before. Mom even mentioned there was a picture here somewhere."

I place the album back into the box and close the lid. "It's sad to think how many stories of my mom will disappear with her as her memories fade. I have so many questions, and I don't know if she could even answer them."

"You're always writing lists. Maybe you should write down her stories, too. That way, you will have something to look back on," Travis says and places the box back onto the stack and grabs my hand to lead me back towards the stairs.

"You know what, Trav? That's not a bad idea." My wheels turning in my head.

"It's why you married me," he says. His back is to me, but I know he's grinning.

"I'm sure I have an extra journal in the hall closet upstairs." To be honest, I have multiple to choose from. I turn off the lights as we head back upstairs. "I'll start by writing out the story of my mom's birthday cake and the red bicycle. Actually, I'll start with a list of stories and questions. Yes, a list is a good place to start."

Travis squeezes my hand. "I'll grab you that scoop of ice cream."

chapter 9

sadie

I BUCKLE MYSELF INTO MY SEAT and then stare out the window, playing with the unicorn clip hanging from the zipper on my backpack. Mommy picked me up from school today. That means no school bus and more time to spend at Granny's house.

Mommy passes a container back to me in the backseat. "I know Granny always has cookies, but I put an orange in here for you to eat first."

I frown. "Why not a banana?"

"We don't have any left. *Someone* ate them all." Mommy laughs. "I already peeled the orange for you."

I pop a slice into my mouth and stare out at the mountains in the distance. "Look at the snow on the mountains, Mommy. Soon we will have snow, too!"

"Hopefully not for a few more weeks." Mommy looks back at me and smiles while we wait in a line of minivans and school buses waiting to turn out of the school parking lot. "Remember, you're going to meet Miss Jennifer today."

I push the slice of orange into my cheek. My throat feels too tight to swallow it. "Is Miss Jennifer always going to be at Granny's house?" I ask as a school bus turns onto the road and I wonder if I'll need to share some of my cookies with Granny's nurse.

"She will be at Granny's every day, but not all day," Mommy says and creeps forward in the lineup. "Granny needs someone to be at the house to help her out with things. That's Miss Jennifer's job. She's a helper."

I swallow the orange slice in my mouth but put the rest of the orange into the discarded container beside me. "Couldn't we help her, Mommy?" I ask and blow out some hot air onto my window and trace a heart into the foggy cloud, watching it fade away.

"We do help Granny out, but we can't always be with her." It's now our turn to pull out onto the road. "You'll like her. She's nice."

I'm not shy like some kids when meeting new people, but I don't like the idea of someone else being at the house when I am there with Granny. I wonder if Granny likes her. Maybe she's really old and smells like old clothes and peppermints. Granny doesn't smell like she's old, and I like that.

I frown and touch my nose to the cold window. "Mommy? Why does Granny sometimes call me Alice?" I ask.

Mommy glances into the rearview mirror at me and gives me that sad, but smiling face. It's the one she likes to use when she's about to tell me we can't go to the park anymore. "Remember when Daddy and I talked to you about how, when we get older, our bodies don't work as well anymore?" Mommy asks.

I nod. "Like how Daddy's back needs ice after he hangs up all the Christmas lights?"

We all love Christmas the most. Every year, Daddy decorates the front of the house with a million lights. Well, not actually a million, but probably close. It takes him all day and Mommy lets me watch in the front yard. After everything is hung up, Daddy climbs down the ladder, stretches his back, and says, "I think we should do less lights next year." But, we never do less, which makes me happy.

Mommy laughs. "Yes, like that. Well, Granny's brain isn't working as well as it used to. Sometimes she will forget things or get things mixed up."

I nod because I think it makes sense. "I guess you must have been a pretty cute kid, too."

"Oh, why do you say that?" Mommy asks.

"Because I'm the cutest. And if Granny thinks I'm Alice, you must have been pretty cute, too." *Obviously*.

I grab the rest of my orange to eat while we drive the rest of the way in silence. Mommy hums along to a song on the radio and I think about Granny's changing brain. Sarah, a girl in my class, had to meet her daddy's new girlfriend last month. Her parents got divorced last year, and she was very sad about it. Sarah doesn't want to have a new mommy, and I wouldn't want to have a new parent either. But, it turns out we become new people when we're older. I don't like that very much, either. I like my old Granny that I had, and I don't want a new one.

My stomach grumbles, but I don't want to go downstairs yet. I'm in my mommy's old bedroom playing with the dolls again. They lay on the bed and stare up at me. I have already changed them in and out of their pajamas twice and my stomach knows I have cookies waiting for me downstairs. I wish Mommy had packed me more than a small orange to eat on the way here so my stomach would shush up.

"I'm not hiding," I whisper at the only red-haired doll, glaring at her laying there in a pink dress. "I just don't *want* to go downstairs yet."

I grab the hairbrush to comb the blonde hair on the smallest doll. Miss Jennifer was nice when I met her. She didn't smell weird, have a scary mole on her face, or talk funny. She asked me about school and told me Granny had told her lots of stories about me. So, I guess she's not a stranger anymore, but she's still not my friend.

I hear a door close downstairs and I hop off the bed to look out the window. I pull back the lace curtains, but all I can see is the backyard.

"Sadie," Granny's voice floats up the stairs. I hold my breath and pretend I can't hear her. "Sadie, the coast is clear!"

What does she mean? I lay the doll I am holding onto the bed with the others and creep towards the stairs. Granny is at the bottom of the staircase, grinning up at me.

"Miss Jennifer left to go home. Do you want to come eat your cookies?" Granny asks. She holds out her hand, motioning me to come down the stairs.

"I wasn't hiding from Miss Jennifer. I just wasn't hungry," I say. My stomach growls loud enough to tell everyone I am lying. Only a little lie, though, because I was not hiding. "Okay, a little bit of hiding." I scowl and Granny laughs.

Once I hop down from the last step, Granny leans in to whisper in my ear. "It's okay. Sometimes I hide from Miss Jennifer, too."

My eyes go wide and I grin at Granny. I have a hard time imagining an adult hiding from anyone, especially Granny.

"What are you two whispering about over there?" Mommy calls to us from the living room. Granny holds a finger to her lips and winks at me. I giggle.

I hold on to Granny's hand and we walk into the living room, where I see two chocolate chip cookies waiting for me on a plate. Yum!

Granny settles back into her armchair and covers her legs with a blanket. "What are you going to do when you get home, Sadie? Ride your bike?" she asks.

"It's too cold, Granny! I can't ride my bike now," I say and Granny glances outside.

"It's November, Mom. There's no snow yet, but the wind outside is too cold." Mommy smiles at Granny and sips her tea. Then she looks over at me. "We packed your bike away for the winter already, didn't we, Sadie? Soon, you will sled at the park!"

Granny looks back outside and then at Mommy. "Oh, I see."

"Did you ride a bike when you were a kid, Granny?" I ask, taking a bite of a cookie and snatch a rock out of the bowl on the table. No new rocks have been added since I was here last week.

Granny pats my head. "No, I didn't learn how to ride a bike until I was much older. There wasn't a lot of time to play on the farm."

"But, Mom, you had a red bike, remember?" Mommy asks and seems confused. She scrunches her eyebrows together so they are almost touching. I try to scrunch my eyebrows like hers but go cross-eyed. "You said Grandma taught your friend Jennifer how to ride on it."

Granny shakes her head and laughs. "And you think my memory is bad? I only know two Jennifers," she says and holds up two fingers, pointing to each one while talking. "Jennifer, who you have babysitting me, and Jennifer, the little girl who lives down the road. She has the cutest little pig tails and comes over for lemonade sometimes."

Now, Mommy's eyebrows are high on her forehead, and it makes me giggle. Granny pokes my nose and grins at me. "I know you believe me."

"You're the smartest, Granny." I grin my biggest chocolate smile at her. When Granny looks away, I slip the rock in my hand into my pocket and hope Granny adds some new rocks to the bowl before my visit to her house next week.

I never did bring the other rock back to Granny's. If I'm being honest, I've snuck a couple more since then, too. I like to hold them when I have a hard time sleeping at night. The rocks remind me of the old Granny. So, I figure if she didn't notice the last rocks, she won't notice this one either. But if she doesn't start adding more rocks to the pile, she might start to notice.

I'm supposed to be working on my math homework in my room, but I hate math. Usually, I do my math at the kitchen counter while Mommy does the dishes. I read out the problems and she helps me solve them. Sometimes we use the spice jars in the cabinet or the forks and spoons from the dishwasher. She's been really quiet since we got home from Granny's house and asked me to start my homework in my room. She only sends me to my room to do my homework when she wants *adult time* with Daddy.

There's no secret place to sit and listen to the adults talking like at Granny's house. But now that Mommy turned off the kitchen tap, I can hear their voices easier from my room down the hall.

"But, Trav, she told me a few days ago she had a bike." The dishes clink together as Mommy stacks them into the cupboard.

"And today she said she didn't have a bike until she was older? Is it possible she wasn't remembering how old she was? Do you remember how old you were when you had a bike or barbies?" Daddy asks. I can remember when I got almost everything in my room, but I also only have seven birthdays and Christmases to remember. Well, I don't remember when I was a baby, but I probably only had rattles and blocks.

"It wasn't only the bike, though," Mommy's voice continues. "She said she had a friend named Jennifer, but today she said Jennifer is a little girl down the road who comes for lemonade."

"Maybe there is no Jennifer at all," Daddy says and the cabinet doors close with a small thud. "It might be a mixture of different memories coming together. You said the nurse you hired is Jennifer, too, right?"

"If I'm going to write her stories, how am I supposed to know what memories are true or not?" I think Mommy is crying now. Her voice sounds squeaky, like the time I drew all over our new couch. I wanted it to be colorful, like Granny's couch, instead of the boring color of sand.

Mommy didn't like that idea. She cried a little and yelled a lot. Then she cried some more when she snuggled me in bed, telling me how sorry she was for yelling. But I made sure I only drew on paper after that.

"What am I supposed to do with them all?" Mommy asks.

"Maybe you can sit with her and remember things how she wants them to be," Daddy says.

I close my bedroom door and walk over to the table by my bed. I open the bottom drawer and pull out the four rocks from Granny's memory bowl. Mommy once told me they are only rocks Granny likes to collect. But Granny says they are her special memory rocks. And I know Granny is magic.

Is Granny losing her memories because I took them? I line up the rocks and carefully flip each one over. Or are the rocks losing their magic? Mommy always says I should say sorry when I do something wrong. Then, I need to do something to make it better. But, if Granny doesn't even remember they are missing, do I need to say sorry?

I place the rocks back into my drawer gently. Then, I go back to working on my homework.

I'll keep them safe, Granny. I promise.

chapter 10

Alice

THE VIBRATION OF THE GROCERY cart on the surface of the bumpy parking lot joins with my already shivering body. Dark gray clouds above me hang low like a blanket, but don't offer any comfort or warmth. The Midwest mountain skyline is now fully covered in snow. I pull my coat closer around me and wonder if we will get snow here in the valley this weekend. If not this weekend, then definitely soon. The ominous feeling of maybe even a snowstorm hangs in the air.

I pull the grocery cart alongside my dark green SUV and open the back. Bags of groceries for Mom on the left, bags of groceries for us on the right. Tea for Mom, cereal for us. Two bags on the left, 9 bags on the right. Do we really eat so much more compared to a single person living on their own?

As I push the cart back to the cart return, my familiar ever-too-popular ringtone announces another incoming call from deep inside my purse. I consider ignoring it and letting it go to voicemail. As often as it is spam, it is just as frequently something to do with my mom. I sigh in defeat and fish it out of my purse, but don't recognize the number on the screen.

"Hello?" I answer as I push my cart into the line of the other abandoned carts with my free hand. I hook the chains together and pull out my coin to tuck into my pocket for next time.

"Hello, Alice," a man's voice responds. He's both certain but uncertain at the same time. "This is Alice's number, right?"

I sling my purse back onto my shoulder and hurry back to my vehicle so I can get it warmed up. "Yes, it is. How can I help you?" I ask.

Silence, and then a shuffle of papers. "I'm sorry. I'm not even sure where to begin," he trails off.

I pull the phone away from my ear to look at my screen again to see his phone number again. It's a local area code, but still no recollection. I reach my vehicle and unlock it to climb in. "If you're trying to sell me something, I'm not interested. Otherwise, I have places to be, so just get to it." I don't mean to be short, but my list is full of items begging for my attention. And if he's calling looking for a donation, he really needs to work on his sales pitch and tighten it up.

"Yes, of course, I'm sorry. I didn't want to be calling you. No, I have wanted to. I didn't know when I would. And so long as I didn't, it wouldn't crack everything right open. I figured I had at least another 15 years, even 20, before I had to make this call. But maybe I wouldn't have even needed to by then either. Maybe I would've been gone. Like really gone this time..." The voice on the other end putters to a stop, like an old car running out of fuel. Silence again.

Was this a prank call? Or one of those scams where someone from internationally calls your phone to run up your minutes or hack into something. I don't know how any of that works, but I remember Travis watched a documentary about it a month ago. What I should do is hang up and drive to my next errand, but I have to admit I am also slightly curious. "I don't have time for this. Who are you?" I ask.

A deep breath fills the line. "Hi, Alice. It's your dad. I needed to call you about your mom-".

End call. My brain races, trying to catch up to the action that my finger seems to have taken all on its own. The black screen on my phone stares up at me. *My dad?* I don't have a dad. Well, deep down, I know I had a dad. Emphasis on *had.* He stopped being my dad over 20 years ago. Why call me now? What about when I sat by the window waiting for him after school, hoping he would come back to us? I spent hours drawing pictures for when he would come back home, but he never saw them. They were long taken away by a recycling vehicle, and my love for him was long ago placed in the trash.

I needed to call you about your mom. What about her? You don't know her. She was your wife; I was your daughter. You chose to be elsewhere. In all honesty, I have been curious over the years to know where he went, why he left, and if he regretted any of it. But I never allowed myself to linger on those questions for too long. It hurt too much, and I had moved on. Early in our marriage, Travis would ask if I wanted to look him up and get some answers.

"Maybe when Sadie is older," I would say and push it down to the very bottom of my to-do list.

He didn't have time for our family back then, and my life was too busy to waste any of my time on him now.

I don't know if I ever would have reached out, but one thing I felt sure of was if we reconnected, it would be on my time, my plan, and my rules. Him calling me out of the blue? No, that wasn't allowed in my world.

My phone screen lights up again with another incoming call, the same number from before. His number. I don't need to answer; I don't owe him anything. But the unknown tugs at my brain and I know it will eat at me for days.

I click *answer*, but I say nothing. I wait. My silence and the silence on his end bounces off each other.

He folds first. "I know you don't want to hear from me. I get it," he says.

"No, you don't. But let's just get to the reason you called so I can end this call." *End all of this*, I stop myself short of saying. I focus my brain on the call at hand and leave all the hurt and unsaid words bolted up tight where I buried and abandoned them decades ago.

"I know what's happening with Margo- your mom," he continues.

He knows? He knows?! How would he know?

I don't respond because this is his call. If he wants something, he's going to have to be the one to say it.

"Listen, Alice. I don't want anything or need anything. But, as things progress with your mom, you're likely going to find some things out, so I wanted to let you know now. Will you be closing down her bank account, or is Travis putting together an updated will for her?" he asks.

"Money? So this is about money?" I ask, incredulously.

The fact that he knew Travis' name is throwing me and the entire conversation is making my blood boil. "I don't know what hole you crawled out of, Jake, but my mom's estate is none of your concern."

"I don't want any money, Alice, but the estate is my concern." Jake let out a long breath. "Margo and I are still married. If anything happens, I don't want you finding out from a will. There will be a lot of things left to me, but I don't want to keep them from you."

This time, my brain was in charge of ending the call. Well, maybe half in charge because my anger is fighting to take the lead. He has to be lying. *I would know if they were still married, right?* I toss my phone onto the leather seat beside me. Why would they still be married?

I take a shaky breath and tentatively pull out of the parking lot and weave through the rows of parked cars, trying to decide if I turn left to my mom's house, or turn right to Travis' office. Will any answers be waiting for me if I ask my mom? Will Travis be able to dig up the facts and put everything back into the boxes where they belong? Secrets and questions to the left, action and facts to the right.

Sitting in the beige leather chair, I swivel to look out through the impressive wall of windows at everyone bustling back and forth. Amanda, Travis' receptionist, had settled me into his office while I waited. I rarely find myself here in the last few years except for holiday functions.

In the early years of just us, I was here often. I would take Travis out for lunch or drop in to simply say hello. Then, work became more than just a job and I became more than just a wife. Travis was working hard to climb each one of those rungs on the proverbial corporate ladder. I was busy dragging myself out of the postpartum trenches.

"It's only a few more weeks of these long hours, Alice. We're close to wrapping up this case," Travis would say when he came home yet again after I had rocked Sadie to sleep hours ago. I had long given up checking anxiously out the window for his arrival home and learned to embrace the quiet. There's quiet, and then there's that lonely solitude that slowly sucks you dry. Those evenings toed the fine line between those two.

Travis was right, though. That case did wrap up on schedule. The case closed, but another immediately opened. The glimmer of hope at the end of each case became dimmer as each fresh case took urgency. Instead, I stopped wishing for those pauses and forced myself to ride the wave of long days and an empty bed at night. Familiarity offered a form of comfort. It was more exhausting to fight reality and long for change.

Depending on how you look at things, Travis' hard work paid off. Everyone knew they could count on him and could pull him in on their case. He was smart. I knew that the day I met him. He was also hardworking, and they needed him. We also needed Travis at home. But they could give him a plaque on his desk stating *Junior Partner*, I could only give him love.

His hard-earned salary gave us flexibility with my mom's care. His new job title gave him the freedom to pass off work to those under him. He could be home more for our daughter, Sadie. We can't get time back, but at least he stayed while time kept ticking.

"Well, this is a surprise!" Travis' voice shakes me from my thoughts.

I smile up at him as he leans down to give me a kiss. He walks around his mahogany desk and sits in his leather chair, placing the file in his hand into a stack on his desk. Travis looks sharp in his dark navy suit and his red striped tie I got him for Christmas last year. He shuffles through some other loose papers and places them into different folders. Then, he touches each one of the files, all of them lined up perfectly in the middle of his desk. One, two, three.

Once everything in his world is in order, he looks up and really sees me for the first time. "Oh, babe." He reaches over and places his hands palm-side up on his desk, inviting me to put my hands in his. "What's wrong?" he asks.

"Jake called," I barely make my voice more than a whisper. I lock eyes with him and feel the tears at the edge of spilling.

Travis' eyebrows scrunch together, taking him a second to place this name that has never been a part of our lives. "Your dad, Jake?" he asks.

I nod. "He knows about Mom. He says they're still married. He was talking about her bank account, the estate, and, and..." The words are flowing as freely as the tears now.

Travis releases one of my hands and picks up his phone. He starts talking in his I've-got-this voice. It's reassuring and I wonder if this is how clients feel. I know he can fix anything, but I'm not so confident that he can fix this. I'm not even sure what *this* is, yet. "Amanda, cancel my afternoon meeting. Also, I need you to pull out the files I have for Margo Reynolds. See if you can also find a copy of her marriage certificate and any divorce certificate, too."

"Wait, you think it's true?" I ask the moment Travis places the phone back down. I may have been thrown completely off orbit by my dad's revelation, but I hadn't believed that it was true.

When someone walks out the door on their spouse, they don't stay married for another 20 years. They don't keep that a secret from their heartbroken daughter, either. But, if he was telling the truth, why would my mom keep it from me?

Travis is in lawyer mode still and I can tell he's trying to choose his words thoughtfully. "I don't know if it's true. We will look at the facts when we get them and find our answers from there."

"But-" I start to say, but Travis interrupts my protests by walking around the desk and grabbing my hand. I don't want the facts, unless they back up what I know to be true. What I desperately need to remain true.

Travis tugs my hand, so I'm standing beside him. "Let's go home, babe," he says.

Where I want to go is back to yesterday, 5 years ago, and my mom's house for answers. But home will do.

chapter

11

Margo

☕ **All That Glitters Isn't Gold** - Margo in the Past

THE FIRST TIME IT HAPPENED was almost six months into our marriage. Late nights at work stacking on top of each other, one after another. Cold dinners reheated in a microwave and the quiet shuffling down the hall to the bedroom to sneak into bed. Him, thinking I was still asleep, or maybe hoping. Me, awake wondering if this was all a terrible mistake.

"Why do you need to go and get married so soon?" my mom had asked me.

I had giggled and twirled in her hand-me-down lace wedding dress in the kitchen. The tiers of fabric created a voluminous cloud around me as I floated on air. "Are you forgetting your engagement? Or Aunt Cindy's? Or Grandma's?" I had asked in return. Sure, I was from a different generation and we weren't getting married as young as our parents. But, surely, our love was no different from theirs. So, why should I wait just because most of my peers were dating for months more than I did?

Grandma scolded me to hold still so she could pin up the hem of the dress. "When you know, you know, dear," Grandma said, on my side. Her eyes twinkled as she looked up at me. She knew. She had been happily married for over 50 years after a chance meeting, followed by a hasty engagement.

Well, what did I know? *Clearly nothing.*

Work at the mechanic's shop might not be a typical 9-to-5 office job, but surely once the streetlights came on, replacing brake pads could wait until the shop opened the next day. I didn't dare voice my frustrations out loud, not because I feared Jake. I didn't. But voicing them out loud made them tangible and something real we would need to address. My friends would ask if I thought he was seeing someone else. They would ask if he was having regrets. I may not have known why Jake wasn't coming home to revel in newlywed bliss, but I knew without a doubt he wasn't cheating on me. Instead, he was cheating on us and breaking my heart. Is that any better?

As soon as I was getting used to our midnight shuffle and morning walks on eggshells, he came home at 4pm one day. It was a typical Thursday, nothing special. I was flipping through the latest housewife magazine my mom was always subscribing to. I wasn't sure if she passed them on to me because I was part of the married club now, or if she was nudging me to do better to keep my house, my man, and my marriage. Regardless, I only scanned the contents, merely waiting for the minutes to pass before I would start making a dinner that I would likely eat on my own, yet again. Jake had startled me from an article about the best tips for waxing a kitchen floor. I looked up to see him standing by the couch with flowers in his hand and leaning down for a kiss.

"Let's go out for dinner tonight, Mar." He grinned down at me in that same way he had not so long before. It awoke the butterflies in my stomach from their slumber and they happily spread their wings.

I put on a shiny dress; he washed up his grease-stained hands. I was first date level nervous to be going out with my husband. We ate, we danced, and we laughed.

"You and me, Mar," he whispered in my ear as we walked along the boardwalk hand-in-hand.

"Welcome back." I squeezed my hand in response.

Those lonely weeks before that night were just a slight bump on the long road of our marriage ahead of us. I just knew it. Or, I thought I did.

I lost track of how many more times I lost him after that. That's the thing with time. We remember the start and the end. But the middle can be a blur unless it's anchored down by something. I remember a variety of times he came back to me, but how long he was gone each time was a mystery to my memory.

Late nights merged into an empty bed come morning light. If he made it home, he might as well have been gone.

"Jake, did you hear me?" I would ask multiple times as my stories or questions hung in the air in silence.

"Mmm? Whatever you think is best, Mar," he would respond without even looking up at me. If he looked my way, it was always followed by a smile that never reached his eyes.

The silence while he was gone was to be expected. *What am I going to do, talk to myself?* But the silence was heavier while he was around. Together, under one roof, but only one of us was present. You can't be in a marriage on your own.

"Talk to me, Jake," I would plead. "Is it me? Is something wrong?"

"It's fine," he would say and fade away. Never upset, never complaining, never anything.

I wished I could be as numb to it all as him. It would make everything easier, but I felt every bit of it. The torture of it all. Was it over? Would he please just yell, fight, or something? The indifference was choking me.

If he had hit me, I could take refuge in his absence. If he was drinking his life away, I could step away. If he was cheating on me, I could hate him. Letting himself fade into darkness? It felt pathetic. I was pathetic if I chose to leave him.

I could hear it now.

"I'm so sorry to hear about you and Jake," friends and family would say, wanting to know what the turning point was. Because there always had to be something that changed the direction of a ship. And a separation isn't a slight veering off course. It was a giant turn to avoid the iceberg, or maybe it was the collision of the unseen below the surface. The collateral damage pulled down to the ocean floor.

"Oh, you know. He was silent and worked a lot. Kind of just disappeared for seasons of time." I could see how they would look at me. A grumbling housewife, who was upset that my husband wouldn't talk to me after a hard day at work. Pathetic.

Welcoming Alice into the world was during a season when Jake was by my side as a strong, supporting force. It was one of those anchors of time in my life. Our marriage still felt like it was so fresh, but we needed to be a firm foundation for this new life resting peacefully in our arms.

"Everything will be okay," Jake assured me. His eyes reached mine and urgently searched to banish my fears away. "I've got you and Alice. I have to be okay. I will be okay."

I didn't believe everything would now be fine. But it was Jake, and I believed in him. That had never changed. "I've got you, Jake. We've got you." *Please. We need you.*

There's only so long you can hold someone above water, though. Especially when you are a sleep-deprived mother, and the baby needs you for all of their survival. At some point, you gotta assess the wreckage and let go of what's dragging you down.

"Now or never, Jake. It's sink or swim," I said to him when I was on the edge of my collapse under the weight of motherhood. The dark circles under my eyes were a permanent feature. Weren't toddlers supposed to have figured out how to sleep by now?

"I'm trying," Jake had cried into my shoulder as we held each other until morning came. Broken apart, but broken together. At least this time, he was honest with me. And maybe, for the first time, he was honest with himself.

He tried for quite a while. Those seasons had stretches of time, just long enough, that all seemed right in the world. I would even miss all the warning signs as he slipped back down, deep, out of reach. Sometimes it was disappearing into work at the shop. Sometimes it was going out late with friends and not bothering to sneak back home. Then, there were the months he found solace amongst Jack Daniel's, Bacardi, and Martell. I told myself it was better than seeking the love of a Betty, Jane, or Mary Sue.

"Daddy home?" Those little eyes would look up at me, still believing Jake hung the moon only for her.

"Not tonight, sweetie." I would snuggle in beside her to read a story for bed.

"I miss Daddy." Alice would snuggle in close to hear the story about little miss bunny for the tenth time this week.

Me too.

It wasn't all misery and heartache. I'm not a glutton for punishment. For all the disappointment and emptiness, there were also equal moments of beauty, joy, and love. Penny for a penny, pound for a pound.

Seeing him light up the first time that Alice uttered the word, "dada". His world shifted right off its axis like it all made sense for him. Every time I would think of those pudgy toddler cheeks and tiny hands, I saw them wrapped around his forehead as she perched on top of his shoulders.

"Careful, Jake! Make sure she's holding on to you," I would remind him as he took off around the kitchen island while she filled the house with sweet giggles.

We were making our own family, carrying on his family name. Jake had always been a family person, deep in his soul. He needed those connections. But when his dad died, it ripped up the roots of their family tree from the ground. As he and his siblings grew up, they fell like autumn leaves and scattered in the winds. Everyone branched off to find their place of belonging and how best to get through their time in this life.

Maybe if he had reached out, he could've grafted their trees back together again. It wasn't my place to air our secrets to a family that felt like strangers to me. I wondered what they were like, though. If they struggled as much as Jake, or if maybe they could hold a key. But, alas, we stayed as a family of three. Even on our happiest days, he still wouldn't let anyone in besides us. *His girls.*

Neither Alice nor I required much from him. He worked hard to provide for us and I was happy with our life, so long as he was present with us. But he was so hard on himself. Jake was constantly striving to rebuild the childhood he remembered having before it all went sideways. He was trying to live up to the pedestal he had placed his father on and bring healing to his own wounds by completing his legacy. Unfortunately, he was burying himself alive in the pressure, guilt, and expectations. I don't think he ever stopped to realize that he was the only one holding a shovel.

The last time it happened was when Alice turned four. Four-year-olds know it's their birthday. They know what they want for a cake and presents. And, most importantly, they know that Mommy and Daddy are present for the special day.

"You've reached J&J Mechanics. Please leave a message after the beep," said the voice recording from the answering machine. I angrily hung up the phone.

"Is Daddy done working?" Alice asked. She was wearing her tiara and twirling in her pretty pink dress for her princess-themed birthday party.

How unfair that I was always the face of her disappointment when he was the one doing the disappointing. "I think we'll need to start without Daddy and he will be a little late." *He promised he would be here.*

"I only need to put in the order for some parts. I will be there and back in less than an hour." He had grabbed his keys, but he looked guilty. Because he knew he was. "I promise, okay? You don't want me buzzing around while you both get all prettied up, anyway."

I had believed him. Well, I had to believe him, otherwise what was the point of doing this dance?

That niggling voice of hope was always in the back of my head. *Maybe he didn't answer because he was already on his way home.* But that voice was fading faster and faster each year. The voice of reason was much louder these days. And it was urging me to make a move. As Alice got older each year, it was a ticking clock I could no longer ignore. Each birthday was another year. Another year, where we settled into a family rhythm and inevitably ripped away.

"Oh, what a shame," friends had said. "Jake works too much. He's a hard worker, that guy."

On queue, I nodded and refilled drinks. "Things will settle down, eventually. Everything always does."

I sat on the stairs outside, waiting for him to come home. The streamers and balloons in the front window taunted me. I left them up after the party because I wanted him to have that visible reminder of what he opted out of. I waited for hours after tucking Alice into bed and wondered if I would fall asleep on the front porch for Alice to find me in the morning.

Jake trudged around the corner with his head cast down. Defeated and sinking. He looked at me and stopped. I stared right back and all our years together stretched out between us. He was used to shuffling in and out, without too much of a fight from me. He wasn't used to me being in his way, letting him know that I saw, and refusing to sweep his guilt under a rug.

"Mar-"

"Stop, Jake." I raised my hand and stood as he approached earnestly. "I can't hold the raft anymore. I don't know what you need, what we aren't filling for you, but you need to go."

Jake sobbed. I held him. I had no tears left to cry. The guilt I felt was so thick around me. For better, or for worse, right? I had been wavering over this decision for years, but his hollow presence was making this decision for me.

"But, Alice?" I knew he loved her, loved me. I never doubted his love. But I refused to be dragged down by whatever was holding him under.

"She will always know who you are, Jake."

He grabbed my face as if I was his last lifeline. For so many years, I wanted to be that lifeline for him, urging him to hang on. But he never grabbed the rope long enough to save himself. To save us. "I'll change. I'll get help. I'll be better. I'll… I don't know."

"You don't know, Jake. That's the problem. I want you to find your why. But don't come back." I paused to make sure he could hear the most important thing I could muster. "Don't come back into Alice's life unless you are going to stay."

He turned and left, and I couldn't breathe. I collapsed to the ground. What was I supposed to do with my life now?

And Alice, oh Alice. We had failed. I had failed. Maybe the difference was I wanted to swim, I wanted to be above the water.

Sink or swim, Jake. Please swim.

But Jake sank. And I was left to clean up the wreckage.

chapter 12

Alice

I STEP INTO THE ELEVATOR and press for the seventh floor. The law firm uses the sixth and seventh floor of the downtown building, but Travis got promoted to a shiny office on the top floor when he became a junior partner. There's no difference between the two floors, except more ego lives on the top floor and more late-night grit and takeout on the lower floor. Thankfully, when Travis traded in his moonlit hours for the promotion, he didn't gain a bloated sense of self-worth in return.

The elevator dings, announcing my arrival, and the shiny doors slide open. Windows and glass offices line both sides of the floor. A desk is stationed outside every office where busy, smiling assistants are shuffling papers and answering phones. Amanda files away a folder and spots me walking towards Travis' office.

"Good morning, Alice. How are you doing today?" Amanda's voice is perky, but not obnoxiously. She's one of those women who is blessed with a desire to ooze sunshine on everyone, and it's contagious.

I can understand how she has kept her job for so long. When Travis first was on the hunt for an assistant, the journey was quite bumpy, to say the least. Some of Travis' colleagues desire an assistant that is equally beautiful as they are competent. But, if they had to choose between the two, they would choose the eye candy. Travis wanted equal competence and a friendly attitude. Someone willing to roll up their sleeves, put his clients at ease, and bring a healthy dose of vitamin cheer to the day.

"I'm doing good, thanks," I answer. I'm not, but you can't immediately unload your problems whenever someone asks you that question. Although Amanda would pull up a chair and strive to ease any burden. "Travis asked me to stop by the office for some things."

Amanda motions to Travis' office door behind her. "Of course. He told me to let you in as soon as you arrived. He doesn't have to be in court for another three hours."

"Thank you, Amanda." I smile and step around her desk to enter the office. Travis is sitting at his desk and smiles as I walk through the door.

"Twice in a week. I should get you an office next to mine." Travis winks at me and goes over to his bookshelf to grab a box of files.

"Only if I get Amanda as my assistant," I tease. I appreciate Travis trying to brighten my heavy mood.

Travis shakes his head. "No way. It took me three assistants and two years before finally finding her." He rests the box on the desk and removes the lid.

"I guess you're stuck with your wife waiting at home for you." I reach into the box and grab a folder to see what it has in it. "Speaking of marriage, what did you find out about Mom?"

Travis sighs. "Well, Jake was telling the truth." He reaches over to grab the folder I'm holding and then grabs my hand. "Your mom and Jake never finalized a divorce."

I move to sit down on the small leather couch tucked off to the side of his desk. "But, I don't get it. Surely, if they've been estranged for all these years, there are laws or something that would help prove he is absent from her life."

Travis sits down beside me and runs one of his hands through his hair. "I brought in a couple of people from downstairs to go over documents. It's been on my list for quite a while, to go over her estate planning, but I haven't gotten to it until now."

"I know. It wasn't ever a priority. Had I known that secrets were going to be lurking…" I trail off and wish I had known before. *Before Jake was the one to tell me.*

"Obviously, his name is on the house and it's not ideal. It's unusual that he still has his name on the house, but there's not much we can do about that."

"But what about Mom's will? I'll still get the house, right?" I ask. That house lives and breathes my mom, and my childhood, and I can't bear the thought that Jake might have any claim over it.

Travis sighs. "Your mom's will was last updated over 10 years ago and it's a joint will with your dad." He pauses, studying the shock on my face. I breathe out, counting to ten in my head, and nod for him to continue. I need the facts first and then I can break down after. "As a married couple, they left everything to each other in the event of a death.

They named you as a beneficiary for several things from both of them. It is also written that if your mom passed away first, the house is to be held in trust by Jake and then offered to you if you are interested. If you aren't interested, the house is to be sold and the money split between you and another trust that is set up for any children you have."

I drop my head into my hands, trying to make sense of everything Travis is saying. "But they're not married."

Travis rubs my back and I want to melt into his touch, but I'm too knotted up. "They are married. They own the house together, they updated this will together 12 years ago. Heck, Jake even makes regular payments into a joint bank account he has with your mom."

I regret wanting more information because with every discovery comes a dozen more questions. "Like child support payments? Wait, you said he still makes payments? I'm an adult now."

"Maybe they started as child support, but I don't have all the answers. It is something they had worked out together, between themselves. No contract or court order outlines any of the payment requirements. He was paying for the mortgage, and various household expenses, and there also seems to be some kind of savings account that they were both paying into until two years ago." Travis pauses and then continues. "They put a lot of effort into their will to consider a variety of scenarios. Not getting divorced wasn't an oversight or something they forgot. They were planning for your future, ensuring you got the house, and even considered future grandchildren."

"How does this affect things with my mom's care? How did she not say anything when we were setting me up to have Power of Attorney?" I ask.

Travis grabs a different folder and opens it to show me. "You still have decision power over her care. She also stated in her will that you would have the final say in all decisions. It could become complicated, though, if Jake wanted to fight you over something since he is her legal husband."

"I guess now I know why she never wanted you to go over anything when we asked a few years ago." But why the need for secrecy? "Can we get her to divorce Jake and update the will?"

"Estate planning is not my specialty. Barry takes on all of this stuff, and I had a conversation with him this morning. It is likely that your mom is no longer considered to have the legal capacity to make changes to her will. She would need a letter from her doctor to prove her mental abilities." He leaned forward to toss the folder back onto his desk. "And none of that matters, since your mom has stayed married to him all these years. She had her reasons for that and likely wouldn't change it now."

My phone rings and I rummage through my purse to find it. I can't see anything through the tears clouding my vision. "Damn it, where is it?" I turn my purse upside down and hastily shake out the contents.

Travis reaches for my phone first and swipes the screen to answer it. "Hello, this is Alice's husband." He places his other hand on my back again. "Yes… I see… Okay, one second. I will ask her."

He holds the phone to his chest. "It's Mrs. Anderson, Sadie's teacher. The class just got to the bowling alley, and she's wondering if you are still coming to volunteer."

My hand swiftly finds my mouth as my jaw drops open. I grab the phone from Travis and press it to my ear. "Hi, it's Alice. Yes, I'm on my way right now."

Dropping to my knees, I shove everything back into my purse. "I'll be there in 10 minutes. I'm so sorry!"

I hang up and Travis holds up my car keys for me. "Take a breath. Everything will be okay."

I snatch the keys and wave over my shoulder as I hurry out of his office. Amanda startles as I rush past her desk and almost collide with someone's poor, unsuspecting assistant. *Breathe, Alice.*

Four hours later, I'm sitting on my mom's couch and waiting for the tea Jennifer insisted on making on my behalf. I had requested herbal tea because my body can't handle the caffeine right now. I'm wound so tight that any liquid energy would be my complete undoing.

"Everything okay?" Jennifer had asked when she greeted me and Sadie at the door.

"Just a day," I answered and forced a smile while removing my shoes.

Sadie beside me had been bouncing, still buzzing from her ice cream sundae. "I went bowling today! We got ice cream, too. Best field trip ever!" She pumped her arms up in the air to drive her point home.

Mrs. Anderson had been wrangling all the excited kids when I had finally arrived. She and another mom were assisting the kids, trying to get them into their rented bowling shoes. To add to the chaos, a set of twins got bored waiting in line and snuck over to lane four, where they were trying to bowl each other towards the pins. Mrs. Anderson had been too relieved to see another set of helping hands to question why I was late. I immediately put on my extra-patient mom cape to go above and beyond. I was drowning in guilt over forgetting (again!) and desperately needed something to go right.

"What has you so worked up, Alice? Surely your day couldn't have been that bad." My mom broke the silence in the air. Sadie was upstairs playing with dolls and I was trying to sort out how to bring up my questions, bouncing around like tennis balls in my brain.

I shake my head. "Oh, it was fine. I just have some things on my mind that I am sorting through."

"Well, spill it out, dear. Nothing is ever as bad once we say it out loud," Mom coaxes from her armchair across from me.

That may have been true when it was a nightmare or fear of a monster under my bed as a kid. My mom was one of those people who always seemed to take everything in stride. I don't have any memories of her getting worked up about something. Only with the aging of her mind does she get frustrated over things. Mom should have been a stereotypical hippie in another life- love, peace, and dance it out. I, on the other hand, am the poster child for overthinking, catastrophizing, and forgetting my natural ability to breathe.

She's staring at me waiting, patiently. "Mom, how is it possible that you are still married to Jake?" I ask cautiously but also impulsively before I lose the nerve.

Mom laughs and smoothes out the blanket on her lap. "What a silly question. Why wouldn't I be married to my husband?"

I stare at her, baffled. "But he left you." Does she not remember the past? "Jake left us," I continue.

Mom shakes her head. "Why do you keep calling him Jake? What has gotten into you, child?" Mom grabs at the edges of the quilt on her lap, holding tight fistfuls of the fabric.

"Don't you remember, Mom? Think." I urge her to pull together the pieces of our history, those lonely nights, solo dinners, and me staying home from father-daughter dances. "It was only you and me. He left us and never came back. Then, out of nowhere, he calls me and tells me he's still married to you. I just want to know why." *And why you never told me?*

"Left us, when? You're not making any sense, Alice." I knew this was a bad idea to ask, but how could I not try to get answers? Mom calls out in a raised voice, laced with a hint of panic. "Jennifer, is that tea ready yet?"

Jennifer comes in from the kitchen empty-handed. "The tea is almost ready, Margo." She walks across the room to pat my mom's hand reassuringly. Her white knuckles relax their grip on the quilt only enough for the blood to flow again. Jennifer turns to look at me. "I wasn't trying to eavesdrop, but I could hear you from the kitchen. I think it's maybe best you leave this conversation alone, Alice."

I am at a loss for words. "I was just trying to understand something," I explain. Then, add a bit more brashly than I intend. "This is a family matter."

Jennifer doesn't back down but acknowledges that she heard my words with a nod. "I'm going to get Margo settled for a nap. Why don't you go upstairs and get Sadie and we will see you tomorrow?"

I blink, not sure if I should obey or dig in my heels. *Who is she to step in and direct everyone to do things on her plan?* Jennifer and my mom are staring at me, the two of them against me. Since when was my mom on Team Jennifer? A duo. And me, her daughter, just standing on the outside looking in?

SHIFTING TO MY SIDE, I hunker down in my armchair and stare out the window. The snowflakes are falling from the dark clouds and quickly piling up on the driveway. Some neighbors have braved the icy winds to shovel a path around their vehicles. The woman across the street leans over her shoulder to help push through the weight of the heavy snow. She's been working in her driveway for the last hour. The paths she had already cleared are now covered in white again. The snow in my driveway is ankle-deep already and growing.

That first snowfall has a special kind of magic. *Well, I think it's the first snowfall of the year.*

"I'm not sure if she's up for a call today." Jennifer's voice drifts into the room.

"Are you talking to me, Jennifer?" I ask and shift in my chair to stand up just as Jennifer walks in from the kitchen. She's holding the phone to her chest and motioning for me to sit back down.

"Jake is on the phone. Would you like to talk to him?" Jennifer asks. She's hesitant, as if I am sitting here busy doing something more important.

I laugh and hold my hand out for the phone. "Of course I will talk to him," I say.

I shift the phone to my ear. "Hello. How's your day going?"

"It's a usual day here. How are you, Mar?" Jake asks.

I notice none of the usual clanging or banging in the background. "It sounds quiet over there. Are you not working today?"

"Not today. Today, I wanted to chat and let you know something," he says.

"Oh?" I urge him, as he seems hesitant to continue.

Jake sighs deeply and I can imagine him running his hand through his hair like he does when he's nervous. I always joke he will give himself a bald spot with all the tugging that poor scalp endures. "I called Alice."

"That's a good idea, babe. The snow is picking up outside and I was worried about her walking home from school." I look up and see Jennifer hovering in the living room's entrance. I shoo her away. She's a sweet woman, but for a housekeeper, she dotes and mothers me comically.

"Jake, are you still there?" I ask.

"Yes, of course, Mar. I will pick her up from school."

"Okay, it's settled then. I will make hot chocolate and cookies and the two of you can sled before dinner." I'm not sure if enough snow has fallen yet for them to sled, but surely they could scrape together more than enough to build a snowman and create some memories. "You work too much, you know? This will be good for you. For us."

The winter season is magical, but also comes with an invisible burden. It's the pressure heaped onto parents to make Christmas a cherished memory in our young children's minds. There are mazes of traditions to navigate and things to prepare for, all fueled by the look of wonder and excitement in their little round faces. Oh, but it's a blessing to get to relive our years of whimsical Christmas memories implanted deep in our hearts. It's being able to recapture those feelings and pass them on that spurs us on.

As a child, I loved skating on the pond and making gingersnap cookies with Mom in the kitchen. I have used the same recipe with Alice over the years. The smell never fails to bring me right back to my parent's farmhouse. My brother, Henry, and I would sneak cookies when Mom wasn't looking. We would stuff a few of them up each of our sleeves and scamper off to eat them in our rooms. We were always extra careful to not leave too many crumbs behind as evidence.

Over the years, I have taken on so many of the traditions and festivities. Baking cookies with Alice, setting up the Christmas tree, and helping her write letters to Santa. Christmas, like any holiday, could cause Jake to relive his memories that were cherished but still a raw ache in his soul. So, I always made sure to gently encourage him to find his own ways of making memories with Alice each Christmas. Sledding was always enjoyable for both of them, and I hoped this year he would be fully present for the holidays.

Jake interrupts my wandering thoughts. "It sounds perfect. Listen, I should get back to work."

I smile and glance at the clock. "Hurry home, Jake. I miss you."

By afternoon, the snow had stopped falling and lay like a soft blanket on the front yard and driveway. Jennifer had shoveled a path on the driveway while I napped after lunch. The rhythmic scraping of the shovel on the pavement had lulled me into a deep winter's sleep. The dark clouds blocked out the sun and made my bedroom darker than usual when I woke up. I don't like napping with the curtains closed because it can feel like the middle of the night when I wake up.

As I come down the stairs from my bedroom, Alice is opening the front door.

"Hurry in, dear. You must be freezing." I motion her to move more snappily to come inside to the warmth. The wind blows in some of the loose snow onto the entry carpet.

"Hello, Mom. Did you just wake up?" Alice asks and unzips her boots, placing them on my boot mat.

I rake my fingers through my hair to breathe some life back into the bedhead. "Yes, it was lovely. You should try napping more often," I suggest.

"I'll add it to my list." Alice smirks at me. Too busy, that girl. Scurrying around like a chipmunk collecting nuts for winter, but time always beats the same whether you walk or run.

Jennifer comes around the corner and nods a greeting to Alice. "The tea is already in the living room for you ladies." She squeezes my arm as she passes by me on her way to the front door. "If you don't need me, I'm going to step out now to have some dinner and run a couple of errands," Jennifer says.

Alice steps out of her way and moves towards the living room. "Of course. I am staying for dinner tonight."

"Oh, Jake will be so happy to hear that." I beam at Alice. I turn back to Jennifer before following Alice into the living room. "Can you grab me an extra roast from the store, Jennifer?" I ask.

"Of course, Margo." She passes a look to Alice and then smiles back at me. "I'll see you later."

As Jennifer heads out the front door, Alice and I settle into our usual spots to sip our hot teas.

"How are you doing today, Mom?" Alice asks. She rearranges the throw pillows to create a nest in her spot on the couch across from my chair.

"Oh, you know. A little bit of this and a little bit of that," I say. Nothing special comes to mind, but that's expected when I'm holed up in this house hibernating as winter roars outside.

Alice blows on her tea while watching me. She spends more time coaxing her drink to the perfect temperature than she does enjoying the taste of it. "Sadie's class went ice skating today. Now we have another thing that she now wants to throw herself into full-time."

I can't help but grin. Sadie's a firecracker and Alice could use that spice in her life. "I used to love skating on the pond at the farm. My mom would teach us on Sunday afternoons when all the chores were done," I reminisce.

"I have a hard time picturing you and Uncle Henry playing together," Alice admits while tentatively testing out the temperature of her tea.

I shake my head. "Uncle Henry would skate with his friends." I understand how it would be hard to imagine. Henry and I never got along, and the divide between us only became larger as we grew up and moved in different directions with our lives.

"Your Auntie Jennifer and I would skate out on the pond for hours if your grandma would let us," I say.

"Mom, you don't have a sister." Alice gives me a concerned look and places her tea down. *What a shame.* It's my favorite blend of mango and peach.

"Of course, I have a sister. She just went out to get me a roast from the grocery store. I didn't know you were coming for dinner, and I don't have enough to feed all of us." I finish the last of my tea and rest it back down on the table.

"Mom, Jennifer works here to help you. I don't know why you keep creating these Jennifers in your memory," she says and lets out a breath of frustration.

What on earth is she going on about now? "You're not making any sense, Alice. It's a shame that Travis and Sadie can't join us for dinner, too. Your dad would have been excited to see all of you when he gets home."

"Jake isn't coming, Mom. It's only you and me for dinner tonight." Alice stands up and grabs my empty teacup.

I ball my hands into tight fists and slam one of them down on the end table beside me. "Stop it! Stop it right now, Alice. I can't stand you going on anymore about your father like that."

Alice jumps and sits back down on the couch, setting my empty tea cup beside her still full cup. "It's okay, Mom. Next time I'll bring Travis and Sadie." Her face looks stunned, but not remorseful.

"And drink your tea," I say, pointing to it on the coffee table. "It's probably cold by now."

Dinner had been quiet and tense. Alice was right. It was just the two of us for dinner. I can't figure out if I'm more upset that she was right, or that Jake never arrived to eat.

"Did you check the answering machine for a message from Jake?" I ask Jennifer. Alice had already gone home for the night.

"No new messages, Margo," Jennifer says as she counts out some of my pills into my organizer on the counter.

I peek out the window at the snow. "I sure hope he didn't get caught up on any bad roads."

Jennifer glances up at me after placing the pills into Monday and Tuesday's compartments. "I'm sure he is fine. How are you feeling after today?" she asks.

"Tired. You should have heard Alice after you left. She was going on and on, calling her dad Jake and insisting he wasn't going to be coming." I dry the plates resting on the dish rack and place them back on the shelf where they belong. "I don't understand this battle between the two of them. If something bad had happened, I would remember it, wouldn't I?"

Jennifer closes the lid on the organizer and places it up in the cupboard with my tea mugs. "That sounds very frustrating, Margo. I'm sure it's nothing you need to worry about. I know Alice just wants to make sure you're happy."

I yawn, feeling my body's internal clock calling me to bed. "I am happy. I only wish she would stop fighting with me."

"Alice loves you so much. You have an amazing daughter in that girl." Jennifer clicks the light off by the stove. "But I think it's time for you to go to bed."

I grin. "She really is the best, isn't she? I hope Jake won't miss it."

chapter 14

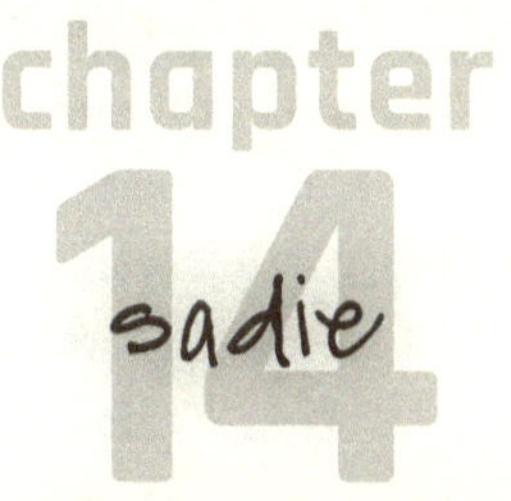

SATURDAYS ARE NO LONGER TIED with Tuesdays for my favorite day of the week. And today is Saturday, the new best day of the week. I still like Tuesdays, but Granny's house is not as fun as it used to be. Mommy says that Granny is still Granny. Obviously, I don't have a new Granny, but she's different from who she used to be. Mommy never talks about it with me, but I know she thinks about it. I hear her talk about it with Daddy sometimes when I'm in my room playing. Most days it ends with Mommy crying, which makes me sad. Mommy never used to cry this much. Now, she cries a lot.

Why won't she talk about how Granny is different with me? If we're all thinking about it, and they're all talking about it, why can't I?

I still love Granny, but I wish her brain wasn't breaking down. Sometimes she calls me Alice, but I'm *nothing* like Mommy. She's all grown up and I'm just little. Mommy has brown, straight hair and mine is red and curly. Everything in her life needs to be perfect, and I like to jump in muddy puddles. Granny and I have done lots of fun things together. Sometimes, we would do things and not tell Mommy about it. Like she would sneak me a cookie before dinner or let me lick the icing in the bowl. The best times were getting to stay up past my bedtime reading stories with Granny when she would babysit me. Does she not remember those things, either?

"Sometimes Granny just gets confused and remembers when I was a little girl like you," Mommy told me on the drive home after tea last week.

I crossed my arms and slid back into my seat. "That's silly. She should remember me, too."

"She still loves you the same, Ladybug." Mommy had smiled back at me from the rearview mirror.

I avoided her gaze. "Not if she thinks I'm you."

Now it's Saturday, and Mommy is back at Granny's house again. She's been going to her house every day this week. Sometimes even twice a day. I thought Mommy and Daddy had Jennifer helping Granny, so she didn't have to help so much. But, ever since Jennifer started helping, it feels like Mommy is helping even more than before. I miss how life used to be.

Sometimes Mommy comes home from Granny's sad or angry. On those days, she and Daddy talk in their bedroom because they think I can't hear them. I don't know why she keeps going back if it only makes her sad when she comes home. I only do the things I don't like when a grownup tells me to. Like when Daddy tells me to eat all of my peas or when Mrs. Anderson makes me do math homework. I thought that was supposed to be the best part of being an adult. You get to do whatever you want to do. When I'm a grownup, I'm going to do whatever I want like Granny does. Except, I want my brain to always work.

Right now, Daddy is in the living room doing important lawyer work. He doesn't normally work on weekends, but Mommy has been gone a lot during the week. When Mommy is at Granny's house, Daddy has to be home with me. It's fun to have Daddy all to myself, but he isn't as good at cooking dinners. Don't tell my mommy I said that, though. Last week, Daddy made scrambled eggs and toast for dinner. It didn't taste bad, but it didn't taste like Mommy's. We also ate it *three* times for dinner that week.

This morning Daddy promised he would only work for an hour and then we could go play outside in the snow. He set the big timer Mommy keeps on top of the fridge to remind us when work time is over. It finally started snowing last week, and I want to make a big snowman. I'm good at rolling the balls of snow, but I'm not strong enough to lift them on top of each other.

"You're not strong enough, *yet*," Daddy always reminds me. He doesn't like it when Mommy or I say bad things about ourselves.

He also doesn't know all of Mommy's rules. So, he let me bring the paints into my bedroom while he works. If Mommy was home, she would make me paint at the kitchen table with the special crafting tablecloth laid out. I would also have to wear a crinkly apron to protect my clothes. But, I can't work on this project where people will see what I am doing. Mommy would ask too many questions, and she might tell me it won't work.

But I know it will work. *It has to.*

I'm not a total rule breaker, so I also grabbed a flattened cereal box from the recycling bin to put on the carpet in my room. If I spill paint in here, Mommy will know my secret and I'll be in big trouble. Daddy would probably get in trouble, too.

I pull out five of Granny's memory stones from the end table beside my bed. Carefully, I line them up on the cardboard box and pull out a few paintbrushes. I figure if I paint Granny's memories on the stones and put them back in her bowl, it will help her remember again.

The first stone I paint is the square one with a line down the middle. It looks like a stove and it was Granny's memory of her special butterfly birthday cake. The rock is too small to paint an entire cake on it, but I can do a butterfly. I squeeze out some of the paint colors onto a paper plate and place it beside the flattened cereal box, being careful not to spill it. I dip my thick paintbrush into the purple and start painting the wings. Then, I use a thin paintbrush to paint the body and antennas brown. I wish Mommy didn't hate glitter, because then I could have found some in the cupboard to sprinkle on the butterfly. Instead, I add a few dots of yellow to the wings. *Perfect!*

For the next stone, I squeeze out some red paint to make a bicycle. I remember Mommy telling Daddy about Granny riding a red bike with tassels when she was little. Granny said it wasn't true though, but maybe she was forgetting. So painting the stone might help her remember it. I know if I had a red bicycle, I would want to remember that too.

I decide to paint a chocolate chip cookie on the third stone. Before Granny had problems with her brain, Mommy would drop me off to play while she went shopping. One of my favorite memories of Granny was one time I went to Granny's house for dinner. I think it was when I was four or five years old because I still had all my baby teeth in my mouth. Mommy and Daddy were going on a special date and I got to stay up late at Granny's house.

"What are we having for dinner, Granny?" I had asked while watching her pull out mixing bowls from the cupboard. I always wondered what Granny ate for dinner. Mommy and Daddy loved to eat lots of vegetables, rice, and chicken. But Granny lived by herself so she got to eat whatever she wanted. That's what I would do when I am a granny. I wouldn't need to eat my vegetables anymore because I was already all grown up. I also wouldn't need to hide the sugary cereal in the pantry like Mommy does.

Granny held a finger to her lips before whispering. "Can you keep a secret?"

I nodded quickly and tried to stand on my tiptoes to see what Granny might be hiding in the bowl.

"Let's bake cookies," she said as she pulled out a big bag of chocolate chips from the pantry. "And then we can eat them while we wait for the pizza to cook."

I couldn't believe my ears. "Do we get dessert *before* our dinner? I knew being a granny was the best!"

Granny leaned down and kissed the top of my head. "It really is the best."

I loved baking with Granny, and the cookies were delicious. When Mommy and Daddy came to pick me up, they brought a brownie for me from the restaurant. So I made sure to keep my lips sealed really tight. I didn't want Mommy to know I had cookies, pizza, *and* a brownie that night. Granny had winked at me when I put on my coat and I knew it was our special little secret. I wonder if Granny still remembers? And, more importantly, if she remembers that it's a secret?

On the fourth stone, I paint a snowflake with white paint. I carefully paint each straight line criss-crossing into a star shape. Then I made small branches off each of the larger lines. Mommy always said one of her favorite memories with Granny was building a snowman on the first snowfall of each year. I have a hard time picturing it because Mommy doesn't play outside in the snow anymore. But, I figure if that was Mommy's favorite memory with Granny, it must be something special for Granny, too.

"That's a thing for Daddy and you, Ladybug," Mommy always says when I beg her to come outside for just a little bit. She would rather clean or cook. Being a mommy must be boring and lonely.

"Please, Mommy! I want you to!" I would even fold my hands together and give her my best puppy dog eyes.

"How about I finish up my list and then I'll come out for a few minutes, okay? You go ahead and get a head start on having fun for both of us," Mommy would say, and I would head outside with Daddy. Either Mommy's lists were never done or she forgot. But every year I would have fun with Daddy and come back inside in time for Mommy to pour out some hot chocolate for us.

I know that Mommy used to go sledding when she was little, though. Granny and I used to look through old photo books sometimes. There were a couple of photos of Mommy when she was younger than me, sledding with her dad. I never met Grandpa and Mommy never talks about him. I wonder if he is more like Mommy. Maybe if he was still here, we could all go sledding.

I look down at the last stone. Granny tells so many stories. *How am I supposed to choose only one more?* I stare at the different colors of paint, trying to think. I could paint a bright egg for all of Granny's Easter egg hunts. Or I could do a sunflower for when I would help her plant them along the fence in the front yard every spring. There was also the time we built sandcastles on the beach. Or Granny having sleepovers at our house on Christmas Eve. Sometimes she even shared a bed with me because I kept sneaking out to see if the presents had arrived under the tree yet.

I look down at the red paint and decide to draw a big heart on the last rock. After painting the heart, I smile. Lifting it slowly to not smudge the paint, I blow on it to help it dry faster. I squeeze out a little bit of the black paint and look for my smallest paintbrush. I paint the letters *L-U-V-E* boldly over the heart.

Love. I want to make sure Granny always remembers we love her.

I gently push the cardboard holding the rocks under my bed to let them dry. Then, I crack open my bedroom door and peek out to make sure Mommy isn't home yet. The coast is clear! Taking my time, so I do not drip any paint, I gather up my supplies and head to the sink to wash the brushes and put everything back where it belongs.

Mommy will be so happy when Granny starts re-membering things again. Then, everything can go back to normal.

Motherhood Ain't for the Weak - Margo in the Past

EVERYONE WANTS YOU TO HAVE BABIES. Okay, well maybe not everyone, but friends with babies want to walk through motherhood with someone else. They need someone on their team. Once we got married, we were getting called off the benches. Calling us into play are the beaming parents, star-struck with the visions of being doting grandparents. Finally, there are the well-meaning people who know we have checked off the adult step of getting married. They are looking for us to hit the next milestone on the path of life that is rushing under our feet at lightning speed.

"So, babies?" I had asked Jake over a stack of waffles for breakfast one morning. A good day had rolled into a pleasant week and then multiple wonderful months. I had written off that blip of Jake retreating as newlywed nerves. Some people had the honeymoon period, so I figured others likely got newlywed nerves. It's not like Jake left and stayed away. We had a rhythm again, and I was ready to build our future.

Chewing his waffle thoughtfully, he nodded casually. "Still want four, right?" he asked.

Jake, having four siblings, loved the idea of a big family. He only wished his parents were still alive to share in the joy of being grandparents. Starting a family with me would be his chance to continue the legacy of the Reynold's family name. A couple of his siblings had a handful of children already, but both were his sisters. All of his siblings had scattered across the map, living very different lives. Anyone could choose to pick up the phone and stay in contact, but no one did.

Having only a brother, I liked the idea of creating my own large family. "Yeah, four seems pretty perfect," I agreed.

My brother and I were close at times, and at war the rest. He seemed to have a temper that grew with him. My mom used to say that he had enough anger for the two of us, seeing as how I had a very laid-back personality. Unfortunately, as an adult, it grew into an anger streak a Texas mile long. Given both of our histories of sibling relationships, I was hopeful our own future nest of chicks would have better odds than we did.

"Then, I guess we better get on it." Jake winked while grabbing my empty plate to start the dishes.

And that was that. A couple of months later, I was staring down at two pink lines while sitting on the checkered floor of our bathroom. I checked the instructions twice, just to be sure. I had no clue what I was doing other than checking off the next milestone on my list. My pregnancy took it easy on me and was completely uneventful, but that didn't stop Jake from worrying about me and our baby-to-be. He doted on me, worked hard to stash up more money, and shared late-night cravings of fries with chocolate ice cream while we spent hours bouncing names off each other.

"What about Nancy or Ed, after your parents?" I had asked.

"I think I would have a hard time calling my child by the name of one of my parents," Jake had responded after some thought. "Also, my oldest sister already had a little girl named Nancy."

I scratched them off my list. "We still have plenty of time to pick a name. I've never met a baby who didn't get named at some point." We laughed and pushed the list aside, yet again.

Holding her in my arms for the first time was nothing like I expected, but everything that I didn't know I needed. Every chance I got, I inhaled her scent right into the depths of my soul. Welcome to the world, little Alice.

We had finally settled on a family name. An aunt of Jake's, his mom's sister, who actively tried to keep their family glued together after Jake's dad died. Jake's mom never managed to work through the first hurdles of grief. She watched languidly from the sidelines as her children grew up and moved away to start new chapters of their own lives. Aunt Alice stayed connected with each of them and worked to make sure everyone got together for milestones and holidays. In the end, the passing of their mom was too much for the weak links between the siblings to endure.

"Aunt Alice fought for what she wanted," Jake had told me a week before my labor began. "But she also didn't lose herself in the process. After my mom died, her strength and love for all of us kids gave me the strength that I could get through losing another parent, too."

And what a welcome baby Alice, the little 6-pound bundle of wrinkles, greeted us with. She screamed, she clung, and she flailed. Those red cheeks, eyes squinted shut, wavering baby cry, and fists pounding the air. She seemed to fight the idea of her very existence. Alice didn't know how to baby, and I didn't know how to mom. Everything was so new and complicated for both of us. I was just floating out on an island, desperately fighting the ever-encroaching tide around us.

Everyone wants you to have babies, but once that baby arrives, you're on your own. We all long for the village of moms from decades prior, but we're all too darn exhausted to build one from scratch.

Those mornings in the first year all blur together. The mornings when waking up at 5am became celebrated because it was better than the uncalled-for 4am. Maybe Alice's tooth had finally popped through, or that development leap was over, or the new fuzzy pajamas brought extra sleepy dust. It's all a guessing game, isn't it? Whatever the reason for her to still be sleeping, my body would be awake out of habit. The blanket of sleep ripped away, and I would eventually give up trying to chase it.

So coffee it was. It was the only actual answer when the sun hadn't even crawled out of its bed yet. I remember one morning I stumbled into the kitchen to start the domino effect of the day. I glanced at the stove and stopped dead in my tracks.

"Nooooo." Last night's dinner sat exactly where I had left it. The dinner I had made one-handed with a baby crying on my hip. The dinner I didn't even get to finish because I needed to transfer the laundry over, so I didn't have to restart it for the third time the next morning. Then, by the time that was finished, Alice was crying to be fed and my plate of food was completely forgotten about.

The shuffling of slippers behind me stopped as Jake followed me into the kitchen, hunting for his own liquid energy. Following my line of vision to the stove, he placed a hand on my lower back.

"Oh, Mar. Don't fret about it. You were tired last night," he had said and kissed the top of my head. Then continued on his quest to get a mug from the cupboard.

My gut clenched at his words. Completely unaware, Jake lifted the pot and poured the steaming coffee into his mug.

"Want me to pour you one?" he had casually asked without even turning around.

"Mmm, please." I bit my lip to fight back the tears and told myself to pull it together.

Objectively, he had said nothing wrong. He could've chastised me for wasting ingredients. He could have thrown salt on my wounds that he worked hard to provide for us on a single income. What he did was try to console my guilt and patch it up. What I needed was for him to come alongside me. Even if I was grieving for something trivial, like room-temperature stew sitting in a pot on top of my splattered stove.

It was simply one more thing that made me feel replaceable in the mundane world that my life was in that season. I could easily make a new meal that night.

Heck, I could have even ordered takeout, and I wouldn't even be needed for that. I probably did order in, since he was most likely working another inevitable late night. He would be completely unaware of all the effort and things I was doing at home. Anyone could mop the floor, fold the laundry, and change the baby's diaper. *But you're the MOM, they could never replace you.* The nursing, the rocking to sleep at night, the snuggles, and the kisses. *Maybe.*

It was a full-time job parenting in the trenches, and they would remember none of these early years once they were older. They'd have me imprinted on their life if we all survived this war. But they could still get through those battles without me even around.

During those first few years as a single parent, everything haunted me. The adjustment was surprisingly harder than I expected, because I was doing so much on my own before Jake was gone. But here I was. Sending off Alice by myself for all of her childhood milestones.

If a village was barely supporting a new mom in those early postpartum years, then it was completely non-existent by the time the school years arrived. Parents had this figured out. They had work, routines, and friends from mommy-and-me groups. I had myself, Alice, and a husband somewhere out in the world, living a different life from us.

There were months of yelling into the empty house, crying over the broken pieces, and urging me to set life into motion for the sake of our only child. But, most of all, I grieved the life that I had planned. When I said "I do" it was for a life with a partner by my side, to a house full of children, and growing together into our dreams. It's not that I was grieving what I once had, it was grieving for something that never even existed.

Poor Alice went from patiently waiting for his return to then writing him out of her life story. It wasn't an obvious external anger, but a fire that brewed under the surface. The older she got, the less she wanted any of the memories. She took down the photos of him from her bedroom. She stopped curling up beside me to look at photo albums, and she started telling people around her she didn't have a dad. It became my responsibility to nurture the memories on her behalf. She might want them one day, and besides, I still needed them.

The closest people in my life were in the same lane as Alice. Moving ahead and leaving behind the wreckage that was Jake in the rearview mirror. I was the one with the truck so I could pull the trailer of hopes behind me in the high-occupancy lane. The shame and ghosts of the past were riding shotgun. Our time together wasn't all roses, but unless you're in it, then you haven't lived it. I had lived it, and it was complicated.

Jake had offered me a divorce multiple times, but I never wanted to move on.

"You know I will keep paying for the house and anything else I can," Jake reminded me more than once.

"I know." Each time, I would answer the same thing. "I'm not ready." I was Jake or bust. I'm not sure what my limit was, but I hadn't hit it yet. I was fine on my own with Alice, but there was still always that hope for matching rocking chairs on the front porch.

"Do *you* want a divorce? Am I holding you back?" I would ask when he brought it up. Maybe he was ready to move on and try again without us. I had always held hope he would find his way to happiness but never imagined that happiness could exist without us in the picture.

"You've never held me back, ever. I'll stay married as long as you want, Mar." And that's all the hope and reassurance I needed to keep the fuel in my tank.

People in my life called it a waste. "Think of Alice, and yourself. You need to let Jake go and move on with someone else. What are you going to do once Alice graduates? Live alone?"

Eventually, it was easier to let those closest to me believe that Jake and I were over. I had cut the cord. But the only cord I had severed was bringing up his name to anyone in my life aside from Alice.

It was Alice's first month in grade three that I stepped into a counselor's office for the first time. Jake had asked me if I would join him. I almost didn't go. He lived over two hours away. By the time I dropped Alice off at school and arrived for an appointment, I would make it back home just in time to pick her up. A whole day would disappear, and a lot of gas.

It wasn't marriage counseling. It wasn't a session to work on us. This was Jake's person and his journey. I was merely being invited along for the ride.

There never was just one cause or one struggle in his life that lit the fuse. It was a mess of webs and shrapnel that he battled, depending on the season. Without being able to pinpoint the one thing, it made it easier to have hope for changing one thing at a time, but trickier to cut ties and leave.

There were seasons while I had been packing school lunches and he was emptying bottles. First, to drown his demons. Then, down the drain to face them head-on.

There were seasons of overworking, overthinking, and being pulled down into self-isolation.

Everyone saw him as the deadbeat who abandoned us. I saw him as the one who gave me Alice. I was pulling myself up to be Mom and Dad for Alice. Jake was trying to heal, so maybe he could be Dad. No one saw that but me. And, no, I'm not an optimist or delusional. It was just, well, complicated.

Jake's therapist saw it all, though. Even things I didn't see, and never will. He made no promises and minced no words. Life was work, marriage was work, and healing was work. And Jake had work to do.

The only thing I knew for sure, I was the only thing that Alice had right now. And I was determined I would always be that village for her. If she became a mom, and she was in those trenches, I would climb down into them with her. So many things about parenting are hard and unknown. I'm sure half of my decisions would be looked back on with judgment, either from myself or from Alice. But being present for your child, that was the easy part of parenting. That was the part I got right.

chapter 16

Alice

FOR THE THIRD TIME in the last ten minutes, I putter back to the kitchen counter and rearrange the two brown coffee mugs. I lift the lid to the kettle, still full of the same hot water from five minutes ago. My hand hovers on the burner dial, considering turning it back on again for a couple more minutes just to make sure it stays hot. I realize how foolish I'm being and drop my hand back to my side.

This is my house, dang it. I peer out the window in the living room. *My house, my life.* I have no reason to be nervous.

And then I see her walking up to my front door. Urging myself to toe the line between prickly confidence and the aching hurt bubbling up inside, I head to the front door to greet her.

"Good morning, Jennifer," I say, smiling tightly.

I open the door wide enough so she can slip inside to escape the icy winter wind from outside.

"Hello, Alice. Good to see you again." Her smile is genuine in a maternal sort of way. The kind of smile that shows she is happy to see me, but also there are some things we need to deal with as well.

She's not about to be blindsided by this meeting, which puts me slightly on edge. It's not that I desired to blindside her, but if she was expecting this conversation, then she likely came prepared. And I'm already feeling like I'm on the losing side, so her not expecting this would be nice. This isn't some deposition at Travis' law firm. *Relax.*

I lead her up the stairs into the kitchen where the kettle sits patiently waiting for me to finally pour out the hot water.

"Want a cup of tea?" I ask and pour water into the mug closest to me.

Jennifer removes her scarf and folds it onto the counter. "No, thank you. Your mom will probably want me to have a cup with her once I head over there."

"Right, of course." I pour the rest of the water in the kettle into the sink and watch it leisurely swirl down, abandoned. I motion to the table and say, "Let's sit."

Jennifer sits in the chair across from me and folds her hands in front of her on the table. "I think it's good for us to get together and talk about these things away from your mom. As things progress, more of these situations will arise, and it's good for us to be on the same page."

I lift my mug to place a coaster under it and try to catch up to the words she's saying. *Isn't it presumptuous that she takes the lead on this conversation?* Last I checked, Margo was my mom. Correction, Margo *is* my mom.

I regain control of the conversation. "I called you because I didn't like what happened last weekend. It was inappropriate for you to interject yourself into a personal family matter."

A startled look flashed across her face only briefly, followed by her usual maternal smile. *Maybe she wasn't so prepared for this meeting after all.* "I can understand that it was a jarring experience for you. I apologize for stepping in like I did, but it is my job to assist your mom for moments exactly like that."

"Exactly like what? A daughter having a private conversation with her mom?" I can feel the heat creeping up my neck.

I hate confrontation and will go out of my way to avoid it. But, I can't people please my way around this one unless I want to give up my place in Mom's life. Travis had offered to be here for this conversation. He likely figured that I was going to get worked up, and he's used to holding the peace in conference rooms even if he's the one bearing his teeth in the courtroom. Mom was my job, though.

Jennifer unfolds her hands and places them in her lap. "Moments of conflict and being probed with questions can get your mom very worked up. I know you already know that. I've seen you gently handle those scenarios firsthand. But in that moment, I could see you desperately wanted answers, but your mom had none to give you. I was only diffusing a situation before it pushed her over the edge."

I brush swiftly at imaginary crumbs on the table. "Pushed over the edge by me, you mean?" I ask. "Her daughter, who recently found out her dad is still married to her mom. The dad who walked out on us when I was so little." I look down at my cup to urge the tears welling up in my eyes to be bottled back up again. "And she doesn't even remember the pain we went through, let alone being able to answer any of my questions."

Jennifer nods sympathetically, as if this isn't the first time she's been on the receiving end of an emotional outburst from a patient's family member. I wonder how many secrets she carries around with her from her previous patients.

"Alice," she treads slowly across the minefield of cracking ice around this conversation. "I'm not telling you what to do, but from time to time I will offer strong suggestions. Margo is your mom, but she is also my patient. She may not remember all her past losses and sufferings, but I'm only trying to ensure that she doesn't spend her last years surrounded by new hurts."

What was I supposed to say to that? As a daughter, the last thing I want to do is purposefully hurt my mom. I'm not a teenager anymore, rebelling and stretching my wings. Any daughter with a normal mom could demand answers to these questions to put the missing puzzle pieces together. Any other person could try to get closure and healing.

I thought I had lived through the same pain and abandonment as my mom. Now, I am the only one left to carry this pain while she lives in another reality. A chasm is growing between both of us. Bringing her back to me will only open her to wounds I can't bear to deliver. But, crossing over to her will cause an entire part of my history and lived experiences to die in the process.

The silence stretches between us and my forgotten tea no longer is tempting me with its fragrance.

"I should head over to your mom's." Jennifer gets up and pushes her chair under the table.

I bring my tea back into the kitchen and place it in the kitchen sink. I grab Jennifer's scarf and pass it to her.

"Drive safe. I'll swing by after I run some errands," I say.

Jennifer squeezes my arm as she passes by on her way to the stairs. "You're doing a good job, Alice. You're being her daughter, and that's all you need to be."

Later that day, I pull into my mom's driveway and park behind Jennifer's dark green car. The smell of warm cinnamon rolls escapes from the two boxes beside me. One box for teatime, and the other box to bring home after. They're the cinnamon bun insurance policy. That way, if the visit falls apart at the seams, at least I have cinnamon buns to binge on tonight. And I can share with Sadie and Travis if I end up home too late again.

I hug one of the boxes to my chest as I climb out and lock my door. In the driveway next to Mom's, I spot Peter shoveling in his driveway. I wave with my free hand.

"Hello, Peter!" I shout.

Peter glances up and leans against his shovel. "Alice! Good to see you! How is your mom doing?" he pauses and then continues, "We keep thinking of stopping by to say hello, but after that last time we saw her… anyway, we don't want to upset her more."

That feels like such a lifetime ago. Isn't time funny like that? "She stays pretty close to home these days. A few more months and the snow will all be gone and make walking safer again and you can say hello." Because I'm pretending that's the only reason she's not walking these days.

Peter knows the same as I do why Mom's not walking around the block anymore. "Have a good visit," he says. "I'll sprinkle some salt on her driveway after I finish shoveling mine."

I wave thanks, head to the front door, and knock. I grabbed the wrong set of keys when I left home and don't have the keys to unlock the door. I'm about to knock a second time when Jennifer pulls the door open. It's still a jolt to my senses. I'm not used to seeing someone else who isn't my mom welcome me into my childhood home.

"Oh goodness, I'm so sorry. Margo has been hearing knocks on the door all day. I was wiping up in the kitchen, but then I heard it this time." She steps aside and waves me to come inside. "Come in and I'll hang up your coat."

"See, what did I tell you? I was right!" I hear my mom call out from the living room and clap her hands together. "Ha! I told you, Jennifer!"

I can't help but smile. Mom always loves to tease, and she also loves to be right. I turn to Jennifer as I shrug out of my coat. "So, aside from the knocking, a good day today?"

Jennifer grabs my coat and smiles. "Aside from the invisible house guests, a good day today."

"Hello, Mom. I brought cinnamon buns for you," I announce, and hold up the box as I enter the living room.

"Jennifer, would you be a dear and bring in some plates? Unless those are invisible, too," Mom teases and winks at her as she walks past us to retrieve some plates from the kitchen.

"Oh, Margo. My job would sure be boring without you, wouldn't it?" Jennifer chuckles.

Mom smooths out the blanket on her lap and calls out. "You wouldn't have a job without me. I am the job."

I guess Mom has come around to fully embrace Jennifer, then. I'm immediately reminded of how unsure I feel about this budding friendship between them. But, who am I to deny the fact Mom is having a good day? And my job as a daughter should be to ensure we keep rolling with the good days as they are dealt out.

"Here you go, ladies." Jennifer interrupts my borderline pity party and places some plates on the table. "I'm going to go upstairs and change over the bedsheets and lay things out for bedtime tonight."

I reach down and hold out the box to Jennifer. "Please grab a cinnamon bun for yourself, too." A peace offering from our conversation earlier, or maybe a promise that I will not disrupt today's good day with my visit. Either way, she grabs one from the box.

"Thank you. They look delicious." Jennifer heads to the kitchen to enjoy it while we visit.

"No Sadie today?" Mom asks me while she dives into her cinnamon roll with a big bite.

"Today's Thursday, Mom." I find the edge of my cinnamon roll, unroll it methodically, and rip off a piece to eat. "Sadie comes on Tuesdays."

Mom frowns slightly and my breath catches in my throat, along with the last bite of my cinnamon roll. *Should I not have said it was Thursday?* Is every conversation going to be dodging trapdoors to prevent an episode?

She shrugs. "Huh. Almost the weekend." *Phew.* "Sadie didn't come this week?" Mom asks.

"No, she didn't. She wasn't feeling well, so stayed home from school," I answer. It wasn't anything serious, but enough that she was better off sleeping on the couch instead of dragging herself through school. Also, it was for the best to not have her coughing and sneezing on Mom and make her sick.

Mom licks a bit of the icing off the top before taking another bite. "Is she still sick?"

"A mild runny nose, but she's trying to milk it for all it's worth to stay home an extra week."

"I remember when Sadie was sick a few years ago, and I watched her for the day." Mom stares at her lap, trying to knit the pieces together in her brain to continue. "You must have had an appointment or something. Boy, that little thing was sick. She puked, she cried, she snuggled, and right when I thought I couldn't watch another episode of that singing cartoon, she slept."

I pull off another piece from my cinnamon roll spiral. "I don't remember that at all. She must have been quite young. And it must have been important for me to not cancel."

"It was like my do-over. Every mom is good at something," Mom says. "Give me emergency rooms, broken bones, and stitches any day of the week over the stomach bugs and head colds."

I laugh. "Really? Hospitals and doctor's offices make my skin crawl. And don't even get me started on blood."

"It's scary, it's fast, and then it's over," Mom explains. "Sicknesses drag on and on. Are they better, or are they worse? Is this the last bucket to empty?" Mom pops the last bite into her mouth and licks off her fingers. "I was not the mom with a doting bedside manner, unfortunately."

"I don't remember it like that at all, Mom. I don't remember being sick much either, though."

I try to think back to being sick as a kid and a few fuzzy memories come to me. I remember lying on the couch in the living room watching cartoons and snuggling under a big quilt. Mom had made the quilt before I was born and had messed up the stitching and spilled her coffee on it. So, it sat in a trunk to be used as the throwaway blanket for times when it might need to be thrown away. As a kid, though, it felt like a special blanket. Going outside for a picnic with my dolls? Grab the quilt. Being bundled up in the car for a winding, carsick-inducing road trip? Absolutely grab the quilt. And on days when I couldn't keep anything down as a kid and was sick with a fever? I would always smile at the sight of that quilt.

"Do you still have that quilt, Mom?" I ask.

"See! Exactly what I was saying. That grungy blanket I used to help protect the couch when you were sick? Not very thoughtful, was it?" Mom points to the chest tucked in the corner beside me. "It is stained and scratchy, and almost made me quit quilting when I made it. But, yes, it's at the bottom of that chest beside you."

Funny, I don't remember it being scratchy at all.

"BUT, MOMMY, everyone is going to Rachel's house to play!" I complain and throw my backpack against the wall. Kicking off my shoes with an extra thump, I stomp up the stairs. I spent the entire car ride home trying to convince Mommy to let me go, but she's still not budging.

"Sadie, please be more careful," my mommy calls after me as I reach the top step. "I think it *feels* like everyone is going to Rachel's house today."

I know it's only Becky and Sarah going, but I don't care. "It's not fair! Why can't I go, too?" I ask and head into the kitchen to wait for a snack. I may be angry, but I still want to eat.

Mommy grabs a cheese stick from the fridge and puts it on the kitchen island for me to eat while she digs in the back of the fridge for some grapes. "I know you want to go, but on Tuesdays we go to Granny's house. You know that."

I open the cheese stick and start peeling it like it's a banana. "I don't want to see Granny today. She won't even care if I'm not there," I mumble and avoid looking at Mommy.

"Of course she will care, Ladybug." Mommy plucks off some grapes and places them in a colander to wash them. "Granny is always excited to see you, and she will miss you if you're not there."

I sigh loudly. I'm not so sure Mommy is right. "Pleeeeease, Mommy," I beg, trying my best to give her my best puppy dog eyes that Daddy says will be the end of him yet. Whatever that means. "It's just one time." There's like what, a hundred Tuesdays in a year, I hardly ever miss a Tuesday. Also, it's going to be Christmas break from school in a couple of weeks and I won't get to see my friends. I could go extra days during Christmas break to see Granny like we usually do. We decorate for Christmas, bake cookies, and play outside in her backyard.

Mommy is at the sink rinsing off the grapes and she's not saying anything or looking back at me. *Please, please, please mean that she's going to say yes.*

I love going to Rachel's house. She has a sister, a brother, and a golden lab. Sometimes, Rachel's mom lets us bake in the kitchen with her or we will bounce on their trampoline in the backyard. One day I'll be brave like her brother, Tim, and do a backflip. Our house doesn't have a backyard. Mommy says that's because we live in a town-house. Rachel lives in a *house* house. Since Becky and Sarah are going over today, they probably will play a board game together or hide-and-seek. Even though Rachel's sister,

Amy, is five years older than us, she sometimes will play, too. If I had a sibling, Mommy could take them to see Granny while I get to go to Rachel's house.

"You're so lucky to live close to your granny! I bet you get spoiled all the time," Rachel sometimes tells me. Most of my friends don't live close to their grandparents. They see them during the holidays and sometimes talk on the phone. That's why I don't understand why Mommy won't let me miss some of the Tuesday tea visits. Granny can't be that lonely now that Jennifer is there all the time. And Mommy could still go and visit her. Mommy is there all the time.

Mommy lays out a towel on the island and dumps out the grapes to dry them off. "After we eat the grapes, we are going to go to Granny's house because she is expecting us."

Nooo! I cross my arms on the counter and bury my head in them. "This sucks!"

"But," Mommy says and strokes the back of my head. "I can call Rachel's mom tonight and set up a playdate for the weekend."

That perks me up a little bit. "Can you see if I can go to her house? And Becky and Sarah, too?"

Mommy smiles. "I will call and see, okay?"

I pop a grape into my mouth. I suppose something is better than nothing. "Okay," I agree.

"Alright, now finish up your snack and then we can go to Granny's."

Usually, I run up the steps to Granny's house, but today I follow a few steps behind Mommy. I was also pretty quiet on the drive over here, too.

"Are you still sad about not going to Rachel's house?" Mommy had asked to break the silence as we drove slowly through traffic.

"A little," I had said and laid my head against the window.

It wasn't a full lie, but a little one. I am still bummed to not go to Rachel's house, but I am excited to go on the weekend. Fingers crossed. Maybe we will even sled in her backyard. Rachel has a little slope going down the side of her house. And, since it would be a weekend, Rachel's dad wouldn't be working and he could build us a jump! I was mostly quiet on the drive because I didn't want to be going to Granny's today. Mommy is sad a lot when she comes home from Granny's house. And Jennifer is always there. It just isn't the same kind of fun anymore.

"Your mom is excited to show you what she did today," Jennifer tells my mommy when she opens the door. I hurry in behind her to take off my shoes because I'm curious to see.

I follow Mommy into the living room and Granny yells, "Tada!" She's standing in the corner and with her arms stretched out beside her like she's revealing a magic trick. "Jennifer helped haul it out of the crawlspace for me."

But this isn't a magic trick. This is a mean trick Jennifer is playing on me and I can't believe Granny is a part of it.

"You did it without me!" Hot tears are running down my cheeks as I look at the Christmas tree.

Not only is the Christmas tree setup, but it is already covered in shiny decorations. It even has the wood decorations that I painted with Granny a couple of years ago. Every year I help Granny decorate the tree. Most years,

Mommy drops me off while she does Christmas shopping and I get to decorate the tree with Granny. She always puts the star on top because I can't reach it, but every year I secretly hope that I would be able to. And now it's ruined because the tree is already decorated. It really is true, Granny doesn't remember anything.

Jennifer steps around me to get into the living room to help Granny settle back into her chair. Granny's hands shake a little as she sinks in her chair. "I wanted to surprise you, Alice. Don't you like the Christmas tree?"

I want to scream, *I'm not Alice!*" but I swallow the words instead. Turning to Jennifer, I fire all my arrows at her. "I hate you! This is your fault. I wish you were never here!"

"Sadie!" Mommy sternly yells at me, but it's too late. I run to the stairs so I can go hide in Mommy's old room until we have to leave. And once we leave, I'm never *ever* coming back. Granny doesn't even care.

I didn't feel like playing with the dolls, so I ran straight for the closet when I got to Mommy's old bedroom. There's not much in here except for a couple of cardboard boxes. I lean against the wall and kick at the bottom box out of boredom. The box shifts on the plush carpet and I notice a piece of paper sticking out from under the bottom box.

I gently pull it out, trying to not rip it. I turn it over in my hands and see it's a picture. Hey! That's the red bike! I remember Mommy was looking for this picture in the photo books in our basement but couldn't find it. In the middle of the picture, Granny is sitting on the red bike with streamers hanging from the handlebars. She's wearing a winter coat and there is snow in the background, which seems like a pretty funny time to be riding a bike. Beside her is a woman wearing a long winter coat. That must be Granny's mom. It always feels strange to think about an adult being a little kid like me, but it's even stranger to see a picture of it.

Knock, knock.

I quickly slip the picture behind the box against the wall to hide it. *I think I want to save it for a Christmas present for Mommy.*

I close the closet doors and sink deeper into the dark corner of the closet to hide. I know I'm in trouble for yelling, but I don't want to hear that I am in trouble yet. Picking at the edge of one of the cardboard boxes, I wait for them to stop knocking and go back downstairs.

"Sadie, I know you're in there. I'm going to come in and talk to you," Mommy whispers. Her head peeks through the door and looks around the room for me. I can see her through the crack in between the closet doors. Maybe if she can't see me, she'll go away. But, I also don't want her to leave and go home without me. I don't want to stay at Granny's by myself.

I crack open the closet only enough that I can see all of Mommy instead of just part of her. "I'm in here," I mumble.

Mommy sits on the bed and strokes her fingers along the stitching of the quilt. "I remember hiding in that closet when I was a young girl, too."

Mommy waits for me to say something, but I don't, so she continues, "I know decorating the tree was your special thing with Granny. She wasn't trying to hurt you. She just didn't remember."

"How could she forget?" I ask. *Maybe I should have painted a Christmas tree rock.*

"Granny can't control what she remembers and what she forgets. It's partly my fault too, Ladybug. December only started this week, and I was so worried about everything else that I forgot to set up a time to do the Christmas tree with Granny." Mommy runs her hands through her hair while she stares out the window. She looks tired.

I had forgotten about the Christmas tree, too. I don't get excited to come to Granny's house as much, so I wasn't even remembering doing something fun like decorating. I didn't even know Granny could still be fun. "Jennifer should have decorated her own tree at home."

Mommy nods. "It's weird for me, too, having Jennifer here with Granny. But, she's helping her out, and I think Granny likes having a friend around. You don't need to be Jennifer's friend, but you can't yell at her like that." Mommy slowly pulls the closet door open a little more and sits down on the floor in front of me. She pulls me into a hug and I wrap my arms tight around her.

"Is Granny mad at me?" The tears in my eyes are threatening to spill over. I'm not sure I ever remember a time when Granny was mad at me.

"Oh no, Ladybug. Granny always loves you." Mommy kisses the top of my head.

"Even if she thinks I'm not Sadie?" I ask.

"Even if she can't remember your name." Mommy pulls me into her lap and turns me so she can brush the hair out of my face. "You can't forget love."

I nod and bury my face in her warm sweater. I wish we could just stay here forever.

"Do you want to go back down and look at the Christmas tree with me?" Mommy lifts me out of her lap and holds out her hand for me to join her.

"I think Granny forgot to put the star on top. Do you think I could put it on if you picked me up?" I ask.

"Yes, I think that can be arranged." Mommy walks with me towards the door and I clap my hands excitedly.

Maybe Granny forgetting was a good thing, after all. Now, I can always remember that this was the first time I got to put the star on top.

chapter 18

Margo

"LET'S ADD NAIL POLISH TO THE LIST," I say to Jennifer. We are sitting in our usual spots in the living room making a shopping list for Christmas. I still feel so bad about the Christmas tree ordeal earlier this week. I know Jennifer feels guilty about it, too. But how was she supposed to know? She only knows what I or Alice tell her. *And, clearly, I told her it was a great idea.*

"Do you have a certain color in mind?" Jennifer looks up from her list. She knows better than to ask me what Sadie's favorite color is.

"Anything bright and colorful. Make it three different colors." I smile, thinking about how Sadie will probably find a way to wear all the colors at the same time. It's also safer than picking one color and it not being her favorite.

"Maybe she could even paint your nails to match hers," Jennifer says.

I am determined to get gifts placed under the tree this year on my own. Well, on my own, with Jennifer's help. Together, we're working on a list and Jennifer will pick them up when she does her own Christmas shopping. I could go with her, but Jennifer suggested I might find the hustle and bustle overwhelming. She's most likely right.

The more time I spend inside my house with the cold weather raging outside, the more I feel safe and snug surrounded by these four familiar walls. The older version of me, the one who had a working brain and her own life, would have balked at the idea of being cooped up inside her house every day. This type of confinement would have felt like a death sentence of suffering, but not anymore. Now it is my cocoon, a welcomed blanket of security. There would be no metamorphosis or emerging into something grander, though.

"Christmas was always my favorite holiday growing up," Jennifer says absently as she scribbles things on her shopping list.

I smile, mentally checking Christmas against all the other holidays I can think of. "Mine too," I agree.

After my brother and I did our farm chores, we would gather in the living room to open presents. We typically only got one gift each, but I didn't care. It was one of the few times when we were all gathered together with nothing to do but spend time with one another. Farm work never stopped because it was a holiday, but once the urgent things were done, we decided to stop and push the rest aside. We were all always so happy and excited to see what everyone got.

It wasn't until I was a mom that I realized how much more exciting it was to be the one holding the jar of Christmas magic. A pinch of it here and a sprinkle of it there. My favorite part was buying the perfect gifts for Jake and Sadie and wrapping them up under the tree.

"Can you also find a watercolor paint set, too? If it's not too much trouble."

Jennifer flips back to my page in her book and writes it on her list. "For Sadie or Alice?"

"For Jake. He's always wanted to get back into art again. Maybe it will help him settle out his thoughts." I glance at the empty mantle over the fireplace. "He still owes me a painting to hang there."

When we moved in, I had told Jake that the vacant spot was begging for something to be displayed.

"Maybe we could hang our family picture there each year. We could start with our wedding picture," I had told him while mentally measuring the spot to buy a frame.

"I don't want to be one of those families that hangs giant portraits of themselves. We can hang them in the hall upstairs by the bedrooms." He walked over to the mantle and turned back to me. "But maybe I could paint a picture. I've always wanted to play around with something."

"You paint it, I'll hang it," I had said, finalizing the agreement.

Now and then I would nudge him to go buy a canvas to start his painting, but he always came home empty-handed. I even bought him a canvas one year as a surprise, but he promptly buried it in storage.

"It's not going to be a hobby if you're pressuring me, Mar," he had complained after I revealed the empty canvas.

I shook my head and dropped my hands in defeat. "I was just wanting to encourage you to get started. Even if you mess it up, you can just paint over it and start again. Paint over it a hundred times if you want. I don't care."

"When I know what I want to paint, I'll paint it. And I'll do it right the first time. No shortcuts, no do-overs."

Jennifer smiles gently at me, bringing me back to the present. "Alright, I think we got our lists figured out. I can grab some wrapping paper while I'm shopping, too. Then we can wrap them on the weekend."

☕

Jennifer sent me off to take my afternoon nap while she went to the store to shop. I lay in bed tossing and turning, but I can't settle. Climbing down the stairs into the kitchen, I stifle a yawn and flip on a light. *Even my body knows I should be napping.*

I open the fridge to see what I can find to eat. It looks fairly empty. I should maybe get some groceries. There isn't enough in here to make dinner for tonight. I move the milk carton to the side and see an abandoned green apple, shriveled and unappealing. Checking the freezer next, I spot a container of chicken noodle soup. I don't remember when it was placed here but looks good to me. Laying it on its side in the sink, I turn on the tap to hot water so it will break free from the sides of the container.

My stomach rumbles loudly at the thought of a hot bowl of soup. The perfect thing to relax me before nap. I open the drawer under the oven, pull out a small pot, and place it on the burner. Carefully, I empty the contents of the soup into the pot and the ice chunk makes a loud thud when it hits the pan. I turn the burner on medium to melt it. *Nothing like a bowl of soup on a wintry day.*

Chicken noodle soup wasn't my favorite soup as a kid. My brother, Henry, used to tease me, saying we were eating one of the family's roosters in the soup. I knew we were eating a chicken from somewhere, but I didn't want to be eating the chickens we named and chased around outside. Mom always assured me it wasn't Billy Bob or Pied Piper, but I still would always run to the window and check outside before taking a bite.

"You shouldn't let him get to you so easily, Margo," my parents would always remind me. "He only likes to get a rise out of you."

And yet, every time I fell for it.

Sometime after he left for college, a parcel arrived in the mail for me. Inside was a small stuffed rooster toy. We never really talked anymore unless he came home to visit. To be fair, we didn't talk a ton while he was at home either. But, even if we were talking about farm chores or occasionally about a book, it was still nice to have a civil companion. Even though it had been a while since he visited, it was nice to know that he still thought of me as his sister. After that, we mailed the rooster back and forth for each other's birthdays.

"I wonder where I put that thing," I mutter to myself while checking its usual home in the cupboard above the fridge. *If it's getting close to Christmas, it means I need to get that thing into the mail.*

I head back up the stairs and check inside the empty room across from Alice's old bedroom. It is full of storage boxes, cobwebs, and dust. A whole other lifetime ago. I weave my way through the boxes and sit down on the bed along the back wall.

Grabbing the box closest to me, I open it up and find a few baby gowns, a bunny-shaped rattle, and some swaddle blankets. *I should pass this box on to Alice.* I stroke the yellow baby gown on top of the pile. It had an embroidered giraffe in the middle with the words "wee one" underneath. It is crazy to think just how little they all start.

I place the box down on the other side of me and open another box. Inside is a quilt I must have started years ago, but never finished it. Squares of different fabrics are stitched together in a large rectangle. This must be the simplest looking quilt I have ever made, and maybe even the ugliest. None of the fabrics coordinate or match. Red plaid flannel squares stitched next to light blue daisy cotton. *What a strange combination.*

I lay it out across my lap to see all the different fabrics. All that is left is to stitch the border around the quilt and then do the embroidery stitching to hold all the layers of fabric and batting together. "Maybe this is something Alice was making when I was teaching her to sew?" I mutter to myself.

The next few boxes I open contain old magazines, mismatched mugs, and forgotten tax returns from decades prior. I stack them back into separate piles. "I really should spend a week and clear out all these things," I continue to talk out loud to myself. "Maybe even turn it into a sewing room?"

My brain is far more motivated than my body and a yawn gives me away. The weight of the quilt on my lap feels quite comforting and begs me to lie down under it. I stretch my body out on the bed and cover myself with the quilt. In slow circles, I let my fingers trace over the different fabric textures. *I'll just close my eyes for a second and then I'll find that rooster.*

Margo

 **Growing Up and Moving On** - Margo in the Past

THE FIRST TIME I REMEMBER my dad ever getting angry with me, I was seven years old. The weather was finally warming up, and it had been a month since all the snow had melted. I was playing outside near the cornfields when I was supposed to be feeding the chickens. Feeding and cleaning up after the chickens was just one of my many chores. I had already helped my mom sweep the house, feed the dog, and gather the dirty laundry. Chores were an ingrained part of farm life, and they weren't like household chores that could be put off. If you don't sweep the floor for a day or two, it gets more crumbs. But, if you don't feed or milk the animals, then they suffer.

I felt like I could put off feeding the chickens for another thirty minutes, or one hour tops. I just wanted to sit in the spring sun for a bit and play with my doll. The best place to hide was behind the chicken coop by the tall cornfields. That way, I could either quickly duck inside and act like I was doing my chores all along, or I could hide away in the rows of corn.

"You better be done feeding the chickens by the time I let the horses out of the barn," Henry chastised me while leaning against the fence around the chicken coop with his arms folded. He had found me quickly after searching for me inside the house. What I always failed to count on was a big brother who could always sniff out my plans.

I probably stuck my tongue out at him, as I often did. Brothers are so annoying. "You don't get to tell me what to do. You're not the boss of me," I taunted.

"No, but Dad is. And I'm not mucking out all the stalls by myself." He turned and walked off towards the barn.

All my other friends got to play and have fun on weekends. But, because my parents decided to live on a farm, that meant I had to do farm things. I often felt like I got the short end of the stick with farm life.

I trudged off to the chicken coop to give them their food and swap out their water. My mom had already come to collect the eggs this morning for breakfast, but feeding them was my job. It was the perfect beginner-friendly farm chore. I could see the first two horses leaving the barn and knew Henry would be out yelling for me in a couple of minutes. Hastily finishing, I ran off to the barn before he could yell at me again. I figured if I mucked out my stalls fast, I could hide back in the cornfield until lunch.

Well, I ended up back in the cornfield, but not to play.

"Margoooooo!" My dad's voice had boomed and echoed off the barn walls. Henry and I both jumped at the sound. My dad wasn't a scary man, but he was a loud man. When he was angry, you would rather have it directed at someone else. Someone far, far away. "You didn't close the door on the chicken coop! Both of you come and help. Now!"

I could see the words *But, Dad!* forming in Henry's mind. But we both knew better than to talk back. It was better to just do as asked until the anger deflated enough that we could slink into the shadows.

We spent a couple of hours hunting down the roaming chickens. Most of them wandered through the rows of corn, happily pecking at the ground. In the end, only two of the chickens remained on the run. The payment for them came out of my money.

Henry was mad at me for the rest of the week because he had to spend so much time hunting down the chickens. He lost out on his time to play with the neighbor boy because of my mistake. I mucked out the stalls by myself the next weekend in my attempt to make it up to him. He enjoyed his extra time to play baseball with his friends, but he never said thank you.

I could brush off Henry's anger, but my dad's disappointment always hung heavy. The *I love yous* were not a spoken currency around the farm. He showed his love by providing and teaching. We showed our love by obeying and respecting him. Unfortunately, each of my errors was an offence to him. And I bore the cost by longing for any scrap of praise or approval he could throw my way.

Henry was no different. He scraped together more of it than I did because he could work harder. He could be better. But, ultimately, it cost him so much more in the end. I learned I could get through life without whatever bits of affection were thrown my way.

I always knew my parents loved each other. They worked hard to provide for us kids and to tend their farm. Farm life wasn't easy, and farm kids were raised to be tough. I had more chores and responsibilities than most of my classmates. Of course, many of them loved to come to the farm on field trips to visit the animals. But, once they went back home, the fun was over and it was just work for Henry and I. Everywhere you turned, a mouth always needed to be fed, or a stall that needed to be cleaned.

Mom was your typical stay-at-home farmer's wife. She rolled up her sleeves when needed to assist my dad with any work outside. And kept them rolled up for the cooking and cleaning inside. The farm came first and her husband came second. Although the farm and her husband were the same thing. Whatever energy she had left to give, she split between Henry and me. I didn't realize or appreciate it back then, but they raised us to be self-sufficient and that life wasn't handed to us to be easy.

She never had an empty lap to crawl into for a snuggle, to listen to a story, or to play a game. It didn't mean we weren't loved. It was simply shown differently — a patched knee on our pants, a home-cooked meal, and a kiss goodnight.

Dad was even more hands-off with his parenting. Go to school, do your chores, and don't get underfoot. Henry spent more time with him than I did. They would work the farm fields and Dad worked to train him up to be a farmer, just like him. I think Henry knew early on he didn't want that life for himself, but you don't disagree with Dad.

I was fine with Henry being under Dad's wing because I was more prone to messing things up. I wasn't stupid, but

I didn't always live with both my feet planted firmly on the ground. There were other worlds out there and things that I could be. I loved my dad, but I hated disappointing him. I was afraid that it would eventually become too many times and he would retract his love from my life altogether.

I figured the best way I could make him proud was to stay separate. Eventually, I would find someone to marry, and I would become one less mouth to provide for. My plan had always been to turn the farm into a bouncing-off point. I would visit with their grandkids and they would love to ride the horses and feed the chickens. Then we would say our goodbyes and leave. The perfect kids for Dad were capable ones. Henry had proven himself, although be-grudgingly around the farm, and I would make a life for myself elsewhere.

Henry moved away to go to college while I still lived at home. Dad didn't see the point and thought it was a waste of money. I knew deep down he missed having Henry around, and not only for an extra set of hands to do the hard labour.

I think Henry felt this was his last moment to spread his wings and see what was out in the world before locking himself down on the farm. He was a people pleaser, unlike me. He would stay at the farm and work until the day Mom and Dad died, if that's what Dad wanted. I could see it now, a second house built on the edge of the property for Henry with his future doting farm wife and kids. And, by the time my parents would pass on, he would stick it out because it's all that he would have known.

When Henry left, that was the first time I saw a crack into something wishful beneath my mom's *I'm so blessed* exterior. Henry was spreading his wings and experiencing life outside all this. I think her wings were curious about what it would be like to know what else might be out there for her.

She loved my dad. He was her whole life, aside from us kids. But, as we grew, we needed her less and less. After all those decades, she never resented her hard life. She always put in the same effort to make a meal my dad would love and a clean house for him. Tending and caring for a place for him to hang his hat proudly at the end of the day. But her heart and soul beat and breathed so in tune with him. I think she forgot how to think and feel about herself. I don't know who she would have been without the farm, but I would have been interested in meeting her.

I wasn't married yet, so I thought maybe that's what marriage was. And I wasn't sure if that was a good thing or not.

I moved away before I got married. It wasn't something my parents wanted for me, and it was something they were vocal about more than once. Henry agreed with them, as per usual.

"I want to live as just me before I get married," I had told Henry when we helped me move into the basement suite a couple of towns away. *Helped me* was maybe an overstatement. He drove my items in the back of his truck, but left them all sitting on the front lawn before driving back to the farm. I had to haul them in one by one on my own. Well, until the neighbor took pity on me and helped with the last few heaviest boxes.

"That's the dumbest thing you've ever said. Mom could use your help while you wait to get hitched," he had grumbled. He pulled out a cigarette from his front pocket and took a long inhale as he lit it. A habit he had picked up back as a teenager thanks to long hours working with our dad. Blowing out a stream of smoke, he gave me a long look. "I took you for a lot of things, but never selfish."

I didn't have the best relationship with my brother, but words can still have a sting, no matter who's the one slinging them. I watched as he drove away and wondered where our relationship would go from there. It was scary, though. I had left the nest, but were my wings ready to catch me so I wouldn't hit the ground? What I did know was that this was my life. And my decisions wouldn't be hinged on anyone making them for me.

A few years into my marriage with Jake, I got the call my dad had suffered a heart attack while out working. He had been working in the fields by himself and no one noticed anything was wrong until he didn't come back to the house for lunch. They had hoped he was just caught up with his tasks and lost track of time, but when Henry found him lying on the ground, it was far too late to save him. I wouldn't have expected it to happen any differently. He lived on that farm and died on that farm. But the news still shook my world. Henry had made the call, and I hadn't talked to him in years. It was surreal, like a whole different lifetime ago.

"If you can pry yourself away from your new life, there's gonna be a small service next week." Henry was still jaded, and the bitterness had completely eroded our relationship into a giant chasm. Now, the farm was squarely on his shoulders. He hadn't walked away by then, and he never would.

I had stayed at the farm instead of a hotel to spend time with my mom while she grieved. That was my last time staying at the farm. I went there only a handful of times after that. But I never returned for the joy of a visit, only for the few times when my time and service were needed. My dreams of a car full of their grandbabies bumping along in the backseat and going down the dirt road for a day of chickens, horses, and cows were only a mirage.

Nothing had changed since any of my other visits there, even since I was a kid. Not even me. Sure, I had grown up and moved on. But had I managed to become my own person? Or had I just found a new shadow to live within?

My mom died within a year of lung cancer. Her smoking habit of *just stepping out for a breather* had taken her last breath from her. I also think it was a broken heart. Even if it wasn't the love and relationship I wanted for myself, I could always see how strong their bond was. My dad may have been a tough nut to crack, but my mom was the only one able to do it. After Mom died and I pulled away from the farm, I guess deep down I knew it was going to be my last time seeing my childhood home. But I'm not even sure if I bothered to look back in the rearview mirror.

And, Henry? Well, he let his anger push everyone away. He took up the yoke of that farm and strived for Dad's approval from the grave. Incrementally, he drove himself into that ground. He never spoke to me again.

I LAY OUT THE BLUE SNOWFLAKE wrapping paper on the living room floor and reach for the scissors to cut off a piece. Sadie's at school, so it's the perfect time to get a head start on wrapping Christmas presents. Sure, it's only the start of December, but most of my shopping was already wrapped up shortly after Halloween. I'd rather miss out on a potential sale and be prepared than wait and rush to be ready.

It is also one of my favorite traditions every year. As I buy things, I wrap them secretly while Sadie is at school or at a friend's house. I stash the hidden presents throughout the house and pull them out after the Christmas tree is up and decorated. Traditionally, Travis takes Sadie out for a treat or shopping of their own, and they come home to see the pile of shiny presents with their crisp ribbons and bows. Each year, some of my hiding spots shift and change as Sadie gets older, taller, and more curious.

Placing Sadie's new doll in the middle of the wrapping paper, I fold over the edges and take care to make neat creases along the folds. I know full well Sadie will have this ripped open in two seconds flat, but I will look at it wrapped under the tree for the next three weeks. So, I might as well make it look as nice as I can.

For the past months, I have found myself unsure how I will feel as the Christmas season approaches this year. I know it will differ from the Christmases in years past, but I'm surprising myself with how much I'm still looking forward to it. I feel optimistic we can still capture some of the same joy from years prior. Hopefully, Mom will have a good day and maybe we can pretend everything is normal for just a day. *Who knows what next Christmas will bring?*

Even though I have been thinking about Christmas a lot recently, some things have slipped from my radar. Important things, like the little traditions and moments connecting Sadie and my mom. I was not expecting Sadie's reaction to Mom's already decorated Christmas tree, and it broke my heart.

"I can't believe I forgot about their tradition!" I had cried to Travis that night after tucking Sadie into bed. Sadie had been in a better mood by the time Travis came home from work. Partly thanks to my quick thinking with the star on top of the tree that distracted her from not decorating it. But, I couldn't relish in that victory since I was ultimately the cause of the whole situation to begin with. *I should've remembered.*

Travis had rubbed my back and muted the television. "You can't remember everything. There are too many moving parts. Even I forget things at work, and I have Amanda helping me."

"But, as wife, mom, daughter, and caregiver, they're all *my* moving parts," I had moaned. Moms should get an extra couple of hours added to each day. I could draft a thoroughly convincing letter, but there would be no one to mail it to.

"Maybe Sadie and your mom could make some ornaments for her tree?" Travis had glanced at our Christmas tree box sitting in the corner waiting to get put up. "Or could we drive her over here one weekend to decorate it with Sadie?"

Almost every year, Sadie and I decorate the tree after school on a Friday as a surprise for Travis. I'm not so sure it's a surprise anymore after seven years of doing it, but he always plays the part and acts surprised.

"I suppose we can blend the two traditions. I'm sure Sadie would love it." I had thoughtfully played out in my mind what I could pull together to create some Christmas magic.

I can still feel the kiss Travis had placed on the top of my head before unmuting the television. "That's my girl."

Thinking back on that conversation reminds me I should talk to Jennifer about it the next time I see her. I'm sure she would appreciate a day off to get her own Christmas preparations in order. It has been a while since Mom came to our house, too. I'm not sure how it will affect her, but I hope it will make it feel a bit more normal again.

My phone rings, and I lift the wrapping paper and ribbons to look for it. My living room looks like Santa's workshop has exploded, a much different look from its usual neat and tidy order.

I follow the sound coming from behind me and lean down to look under the couch. Tucked off to the side, I can see that my phone has been pushed under. I grab the scissors beside me to give me the extra inches necessary to pull my phone towards me. When I pull it out, I see I missed a call from Jennifer and she has left me a voicemail.

I unlock my phone and type in my code to listen. "Hey Alice, it's Jennifer. When you get this, can you give me a call? Or if you're available, maybe stop by your mom's. Everything is fine, there was just a bit of an incident-"

"You're going to worry her. I'm fine, Alice!" My mom's voice cuts into the message in the background.

Jennifer interjects, "Yes, yes. Everything is fine. Ok, I'll talk to you shortly."

My anxiety spikes with all the potential scenarios that swirl through my head. *Mom was talking. Mom said it was fine.* I keep repeating these lines to myself like a mantra as I grab two of the unwrapped gifts and stick them back in the hall closet. Then I push all the wrapping supplies to the side of the living room to be dealt with when I get home. I will head over to Mom's and see what's going on. Maybe I'll call Jennifer on the way, too. Let her know I'm on my way and see what's going on.

I had called Travis on the drive over to my mom's asking if he could get Sadie from school. Amanda, his receptionist, had told me he was in court. Thankfully, a quick call to Rachel's mom, Helen, sorted out Sadie's pickup. She was gracious enough to invite Sadie to stay for dinner, too. Helen, true to her helpful nature, was quick to say yes. I shouldn't have been so resistant to reaching out to her. Funny how I spend so much time being a village to everyone else, but I resist it so much for myself. *You can't be a burden, remember?*

I wasn't sure what I was going to be walking into when I arrived at Mom's house, but Jennifer stepped outside the front door as soon as my car pulled into the driveway. I had sent her a quick text saying I was on my way and she must have been watching out the window, waiting for me.

"Hey, what's going on?" I ask as I open my door and climb out, the thin layer of snow crunching under my boots.

Jennifer zips up her black puffy coat that she threw on as she came outside. "Let's talk for a couple of minutes out here before we go in," she says as she walks towards me, sidestepping a patch of ice that I should sprinkle some salt on.

I close the door to my SUV and nod for Jennifer to continue. My nervous hands find the warmth of my pockets and my right hand fiddles with my keys.

"I settled your mom in for a nap, as usual, and headed out for some errands. I guess she didn't end up going to sleep and made her way into the kitchen to eat something. When I got back to the house, a pot of something was burning on the stove and your mom was sleeping in the bedroom across from your old room," Jennifer explains.

"Is she okay? Oh my goodness, there could have been..." My voice trails off, the shock setting in. There are so many scenarios my mind wants to jump to, but it's rapid firing too fast to land on any one disaster.

Jennifer squeezes my arm. "Your mom is okay. When she woke up, she was mainly confused about why she was sleeping in that bedroom. She doesn't remember making any food in the kitchen, though, which is concerning."

"Are the two of you coming inside, or what?" Mom's face pops out from the front door. "It's freezing out there!" *She's okay.*

Mom holds the door open for us as we walk inside and remove our coats and boots.

"Hello, Mom. How are you?" I lean in and hug her. She holds onto my arm as we walk into the living room and settle into our usual spots.

She smiles at me. "Much better, now. Did Jennifer tell you about my room mixup? I should go into that room more often, though. There are so many things to sort through," Mom chatters away completely unphased. Then, reaching down beside her, she pulls up a quilt I have never seen before. "I found this in the room upstairs."

I'm still surprised to hear Jennifer found her sleeping in that room. For as long as I remember, that room has been banished to collect boxes and dust. A couple of times, when I was young, I would sneak inside to see what treasures might be lurking. I never found anything that excited me as a young girl, but maybe now as an adult, there would be something worthwhile to find. I make a mental note to look through the boxes with my mom. Maybe there would be more of her photo albums hiding in a forgotten box.

"Was that a quilt you were making?" I ask and reach out to grab the quilt from her.

"I guess so. It's pretty ugly, though, isn't it?" Mom chuckles and reaches behind her to grab one of the last quilts she made that rests on the back of her chair to compare them. The one Mom holds is full of pinwheel designs and is a blend of corals, whites, and mint greens. She had finished that quilt shortly before her memory started slipping. Mom had always been an avid crafter, and quilts were often cut and assembled on our kitchen table. When it was time to eat, the fabric squares and rotary cutter would be shifted off to the side temporarily to make room for dinner.

Knowing that the quilt on her chair was the last one she had ever made, makes it feel like the ending of a chapter. A door closing on one of the many rooms that make up Mom's life and who she is. So many of those doors have closed, some faster and more abruptly than others. *How many doors can close before a person is no longer the person they are at all?*

I trace my fingers along the different clashing fabrics of this forgotten quilt. "I think I remember you cutting out some of these squares, Mom."

If I close my eyes and focus, I remember one night that I had a bad dream when I was much younger than Sadie is now. Mom and Dad weren't in their bed, so I had walked down the stairs to see if I could find them. I had found Mom at the kitchen table with a stack of shirts and was cutting them into squares.

"Here, come sit with me," Mom had said with open arms for me to crawl into. Her lap and arms were always wide open for those she loved.

I fiddled with the buttons on one of the red plaid flannel shirts while she cut a square out of a light blue blouse with small daisies scattered on it.

"What are you making, Mommy?" I had asked, curious why she was cutting up perfectly good clothes into squares.

"Just weaving together some memories," she had hummed into my hair until I must have fallen asleep.

I point to the flannel shirt and look up at Mom, who is watching me study the quilt. "You were cutting these out from a stack of clothes, Mom. I don't know whose clothes they were though, do you remember?"

Mom shakes her head. "Not a clue. But I figure I will sew on the binding and finish it, though. It will give me something to do. I wonder why I started it." She reaches to grab it back from me while studying it more. "And I wonder why I stopped it. Maybe because it was so ugly," she chuckles lightly.

I know as well as she does, it's a memory that will probably stay lost forever.

I snuck into the house while Travis was putting Sadie to bed and went straight to the pantry closet. I should go in and hug Sadie and kiss her goodnight, but I'm confident that Travis has it under control. What I need is a mini vacation in the pantry. Tonight is a two chocolate bar kind of closet break. Two chocolate bar breaks are the top tier of needed breaks. Saved for the days when Sadie had skipped a nap, when Travis had a late-night meeting and the day was three hours too long, or when someone was up during the night with the latest stomach bug in circulation. Now, days like today could be added to that qualification. Days where I was struggling to captain both of my ships.

I am ripping open my second chocolate bar when Travis opens the door, so it's a narrow crack.

"Hey you," he says as his face pops in and offers a sympathetic smile.

I take a bite and give a small smile back. "Should I peek in on Sadie?"

Travis shakes his head and steps into the closet with me. I appreciate him climbing in with me instead of pulling me out to him.

"She's out like a light. How's your mom?" Travis asks.

I sink to the floor of the pantry and bring him up to speed. What happened, what could have happened, and the spinout of my brain since then.

We sit in silence for a few minutes and pass the chocolate bar back and forth between us. I take large bites, and Travis takes small nibbles.

"We should move your mom in with us," Travis says, breaking the silence.

I rest my head on his shoulder and let out a sigh. "I know."

Travis passes the chocolate bar back to me for the last bite. "Sadie will love it. An extended sleepover with Granny."

"I think Mom will hate it," I confess. She's spent most of her life in that house. A short time with my dad, a longer stint with me, but the longest on her own. It's not that she would hate living with her family, but that house is deep in her bones and another door to be closed in her life.

"Maybe." Travis knows how independent my mom is and how determined she is to stay independent and not be a burden. "We're not moving her into a care facility, though. We can also have Jennifer help out still, too."

I nod. "Mom will like that. They've really connected."

"And the house will stay right where it is, unchanged," he says. This man is good at reading my mind.

I poke the pantry door with my toe. "Can we stay here for a bit more?"

"As long as you need."

chapter 21

Margo

JENNIFER RUMMAGES THROUGH my closet while I sit on my bed. "How about we only pack your winter clothes and leave the rest in your closet?"

"Is that okay?" I ask. I am folding a couple of my fleece jumpsuits and placing them in the box beside me on the bed. "We can just leave them here?"

"It's your house. You can take and leave whatever you want." Jennifer turns back to look at me and smiles.

"The house stays?" I hadn't thought to ask Alice about what the plans for the house would be after I moved in with her, Travis, and Sadie. It occurred to me in the middle of the night after getting up to use the bathroom, but I wasn't about to pick up the phone and call her. *Will we sell the house? Would they sell their townhouse and move us all back to this house?* I know Alice, and I know she has a master plan. She also will have a corresponding task list, milestone markers, and even a backup plan for how this transition will work. I had hoped the house would stay inside of that plan but was too scared to ask.

"Of course, the house stays," Jennifer says and crosses off *clothes* from the list on the dresser. I recognize that printing anywhere, it's a page right out of Alice's plan.

"Did Alice send over a list?" I don't need to ask, because I already know the answer. "So, what's next?"

"This closet looks to be mostly cleared out. Well, except for a couple of boxes in the back." Jennifer reaches in and slides them out across the carpet. She opens the first one up to look inside. "Looks like this one is full of shoes."

I lean over from my perch on the bed to catch a peek as Jennifer tilts the box towards me to get a better angle. "Oh, those can be left or passed on," I say and turn back to folding the last of my sweaters sitting beside me on the bed. "Is the other box full of shoes, too?"

"No, this box is full of some papers and documents, it looks like. Did you want to look through it?" Jennifer shuffles through some papers on top.

I wave my hand dismissively and shake my hand no. "We can pack that up for Travis. It's probably just stuff to be shredded anyway."

Jennifer grabs some tape off the dresser to seal the box of clothes I have finished packing and adds it to the stack on the floor of the bedroom. She pushes the list off to the side and places her hands on her hips. "What would *you* like to bring with you, Margo?"

I still don't understand why it's necessary to move into Alice's townhouse so soon. Yes, I remember the stove incident. Well, the aftermath of it, anyway. I didn't let on to Alice or Jennifer, but it scared me when they asked me about it. It still concerns me that I can do things, and then they immediately vanish from my brain without any rhyme or reason. I don't remember heating any food, and I know they're both concerned about how much worse it could have been. But, this is my home. Mistakes and memories were made and sealed within these four walls, and I'm not sure I'm ready to walk away while I still have parts of my brain intact.

I've spent more years in this house than anywhere else. Almost twice as many years were spent here compared to my childhood home. Leaving my parent's home was like rebuilding a part of my life. Leaving this house feels like it's tearing my heart out of my chest.

"My quilt from downstairs," I say, starting my own list of items. "Oh, and the one I have been working on." I have finished stitching on the binding and now need to embroider the quilting stitches. I figure I will slowly work at stitching it by hand to pass the hours in the days. So many of them merge to be the same as the one before.

"I will grab those when I bring this box downstairs. Do you know what you will do with that quilt when it's done?" Jennifer grabs the box and heads for the door.

After Alice told me about cutting out the clothes when she was young, I think I remember it. Or maybe I just remember it through her memory's eyes. The red flannel triggers memories of a shirt Jake would wear when outside doing yard work in the fall weather. Those shirts were a dime in a dozen, though. Why would I have cut up one of his shirts to make a quilt? And I don't remember ever wearing that daisy fabric.

"I'm not sure, yet. But, I don't want to leave it behind unfinished. That entire room is full of unfinished memories and parts of my life," I say. "Before I went into the room for a nap, I'm certain I haven't set foot in there for many, many years."

"Is it a room you would like to open up and go through? We can always come back once a week, or I can bring a box or two to Alice's each week."

I appreciate Jennifer's helpfulness and her desire to make this adjustment easy on me. "I don't know if it's worth digging up."

"Granny!" Sadie calls out the moment the front door swings open. She runs into the house and crawls up beside me in my chair in the living room. "You're going to come live with us!"

I give her a tight squeeze as she curls into my lap. Soon she will be too big to fit, which is hard to believe. It feels like just yesterday Alice was small enough to fit into my lap. "Are you sure you're ready for an old woman like me to move in?" I tease.

"Mommy says it will be like a big sleepover. And I heard her and Daddy talking that it might help you remember some things better because you will be around us all the time. So, now you'll always know I'm Sadie! Isn't that great?" She's beaming up at me and talking a mile a minute.

"Of course you're Sadie. Who else would you be?" I watch as Sadie's smile falls away. *What was it that I said?*

Sadie slides off my lap and looks down at her feet. The toes on her left foot are burrowing circles into the carpet. "Sorry Granny, I don't think I was supposed to say that."

I grab her hand, and she lifts her head sheepishly to look at me. "Never apologize for speaking your mind." I squeeze her small hand in mine to drive the point home. "And definitely don't worry about your 'ole granny's feelings, okay?"

Sadie nods her head but still looks unsure.

"Hey, Mom." Alice pokes her head into the living room, allowing Sadie to slip away and scamper upstairs to her beloved dolls. "Travis is almost done loading up your boxes. Are you sure you don't want to bring more things with you?"

"Your house isn't big enough to hold both of our lives," I say. It's true, but I also couldn't bear to watch everything in this house be emptied, one item at a time. "I would like this chair, though, please. We can tuck it into my room if that's okay?"

I stand, moving over to the couch to take a seat. Taking in the view of my living room from a different angle, I notice how different everything looks when you're accustomed to seeing things the same way for the last multiple decades. I immediately spot the Christmas presents under the tree that Jennifer has helped me buy and wrap. "We should take those with us, too. Unless we come back here for Christmas?" I ask, unsure of what any plans are day-to-day.

"Oh, umm," Alice hesitates. "Did you want to come back here for Christmas? We can…"

"I suppose that's foolish." I wave her off. "No, no. I used to sleep over for some Christmas Eves, so let's do that."

Alice comes and sits beside me and grabs my hand in both of hers. "We can come back here whenever you want, though, okay?"

I nod. I like that idea. This will always be home.

Alice's townhouse is smaller than my house but still is a decent size. I'm settled into the bedroom beside Sadie. A queen-sized bed with my bedspread from home is tucked into the corner of the room. Along the opposite wall is my red armchair with my favorite quilt draped over the back.

As soon as we arrived home, Alice started calling out tasks to Travis and Sadie. I was ordered to sit in the chair to watch as they all buzzed around me. Now and then, I had answered a question of where I preferred something to go as they unpacked everything. I wasn't useless. I could roll up my sleeves and unpack my clothes at the very least.

"You don't need to do this all now," I had said. It was a weekend, and I didn't want them to change all of their routines more than they already had.

"The sooner we get everything unpacked, the sooner you can settle in." Alice had reassured me. I knew this was more for her than for me, so I let her buzz away. Sadie ran in and out of my new room, watching all the activity and the novelty of me being right next door.

Sadie would tap on the wall from her room and then come running into mine. "Did you hear that knock, Granny?" she had asked before running back in to try a different series of knocks and taps. "We can have our own secret code!"

It had taken me a while to settle down for a nap once they finished. These were all my things, but not my place. My brain was on high alert for what was missing, out of place, or strange. Life at my house was quiet. I was used to it, but I didn't love it. Even with Jennifer hanging around during the days, there were many moments just me, my thoughts, and stillness. Here, even when they were trying to be quiet so I could rest, there was a buzz in the house. Soft footsteps climbing the stairs, a faucet being turned on to fill a glass of water, the flipping of pages from Sadie reading a book next door. It was a house, alive.

"Do you think she's settling in okay? Should I have insisted she bring more things from home?" I can hear Alice's hushed voice as she talks to Travis down the hall in the kitchen. Without carpet in the house, all noise and conversations bounce off the floor and walls.

"We don't need to bring everything right away. We can always go back and get more." Travis' deep voice carries down the hall much more easily.

Alice notices it as well. "Shh, I don't want her to hear us talking about her," she chastises him.

"Alice, you don't need to walk on eggshells around your mom. You know what? I'm more worried about *you* adjusting to this than Margo." I agree with Travis. Alice has always been so high-strung, and me moving in might be too much of a weight to keep her world spinning on its axis. But you can't tell a helper not to help, and hopefully, with me moving in, she won't have to help as much.

"I was thinking I could go over to Mom's house sometimes while Jennifer is here. I could sort through some of her things and boxes in storage. Maybe I'll find some more photo albums in that room."

"Your mom might want to join you for that," Travis suggests. "You digging through her things might upset her more than looking through old, forgotten memories."

I wouldn't be offended if Alice wanted to sort through the room. I was more concerned she would find something that I wouldn't be able to answer her questions about. Alice always has questions.

"Mommy! Can I stop my quiet time now?" Sadie's voice bellows out from the room beside me, and I laugh.

Alice's brisk footsteps rush down the hall to Sadie's room. "Sadie, shh! Granny's napping, remember?"

Oops, that's my queue to intervene. I get up from the bed and open the door to my bedroom to stand in the doorway. "I'm awake," I announce.

"I'm so sorry, Mom. Did we wake you?" Alice studies my face, and Sadie pops her head out into the hall looking guilty.

I shake my head. "No, I don't think I was tired enough for a nap today. But I have a favor to ask of all of you."

"Of course, Mom, what is it?" Alice, the ever-dutiful daughter, is already ready to sign on the dotted line before even hearing my request.

"I moved in here because I can't be on my own, I get that." I reach out and squeeze Alice's arm. "But I need you to understand something, too. I'm moving into your life. You guys first, me second, okay?"

Alice covers my hand on her arm with her own and squeezes it.

There will come a time when I will surely be a greater burden to them than I am now. But I refuse to start now.

chapter 22
sadie

IT FEELS STRANGE to be at Granny's house without Granny here. It's like we are breaking a rule, or maybe we are secret spies. The house is so quiet, dark, and lonely. Last week, Granny moved into the room beside mine. And she's going to stay living with us forever now.

"Granny needs to spend more time around her family," Mommy had told me while we ate dinner the night before Granny moved in. "This will also mean I won't have to go back and forth between our houses so much."

I slurped up a long spaghetti noodle, my favorite, and nodded. "Like a big sleepover?"

Daddy had smiled at me while he twirled noodles around his fork like how boring adults eat their noodles. Granny likes to slurp hers, though, when Mommy and

Daddy aren't looking. "Exactly. She'll sleep in the room next to yours," Daddy had explained.

"Where will Jennifer sleep?" The room next to mine only has one bed that is used for guests.

"Jennifer will sleep at her house like she always has. But she'll still come by each day to keep Granny company," Mommy had answered.

Granny has been living with us for almost a week. It is different having Granny around all the time. She is better at remembering that I am Sadie, though, and I like that a lot. But having to be quiet during her afternoon naps is really hard. Usually, she wakes up as I come home from school, so that isn't too bad. Since it is a Saturday, I came with Mommy to get some things from Granny's house while she naps. Being quiet on a weekend so Granny can nap is really, really hard.

"Why don't you go play with the dolls in my old room while I put together some boxes?" Mommy suggests as we climb the stairs and she flips on a couple of light switches.

"Can I bring the dolls home with us?" I ask, since I won't be coming over for tea time anymore. I don't want them to be left here all alone.

Mommy heads into the room across from her old room. "Sounds good, Ladybug."

I peek a look into the mysterious room before heading to the dolls. Granny always keeps the room closed, but I sometimes wonder what is in there. Mommy is a lonely child like me. *Or is it called an only child?* I snuck into the room a couple of years ago, but it was only full of boxes. Most of the boxes were taped closed. The boxes that I could look into only had old pictures and clothing. Just boring stuff.

I don't know how long Mommy and I will stay here, so I hurry across to Mommy's old bedroom. I start by pulling out all the dolls and their clothes and placing them into a pile on the bed. Daddy said we are going to leave most of Granny's things in the house because she won't need all of them at ours. That's good because I can't imagine this house not having things inside of it. But it also feels weird to just leave it sitting here holding everything. Something must have happened to make Granny move in with us and never come back here. But don't ask me what happened. *No one ever tells me anything.*

I remember the picture I found of Granny and her bike inside the closet. I go into the closet and check to see if it is still where I left it. I carefully pull it back out and look at the picture again. *Granny and Mommy will be so excited to see this.*

I lay the picture on the bed and go check for a box in the hall. Mommy hasn't come out of the room and I don't want to interrupt her and ask for one. Mommy doesn't love interruptions like Granny does.

Granny especially loved it when I interrupted her when she was cleaning. "Thank heavens you found me Sadie-bum. I was trapped here scrubbing the floor and I couldn't stop." She would drag a soapy hand across her forehead and make her face look like she was really scared.

I would giggle and promise to save her from the cleaning curse. "We have to do something fun to break the curse, Granny!"

Granny would hold her soap-covered hands out like a zombie trying to touch me with the bubbles. "Quick, before you get trapped, too! And then we will have to clean the house from top to bottom."

I would giggle and run around the kitchen to get away. "Hide-and-seek, Granny! Quick, do it!"

"Okay, go hide and I'll count to ten." And that was my sign to take off to find the best hiding spot I could find.

Mommy can be pretty fun, too. But she needs to finish her list first before the fun part of her brain clicks on.

I find a box near the door that's small and empty. Perfect! I carry it back inside the room and lay the picture at the bottom to hide it. Then, I take my time to pile the dolls and clothes on top of it.

Once I finish packing the box, I'm not sure what else to do or if I should unpack one of them to play with while I wait. I decide to head across to see what Mommy is doing, but I won't interrupt her.

Mommy is stacking boxes into piles and looks up at me right as I poke my head in. *Mommy's have the best spy senses.* "Hey Ladybug, did you get all the dolls and their clothes?"

"I found a box in the hall-" I am cut off as one of the boxes falls from the tower beside Mommy and crashes to the ground.

"Gah! Please don't be breakable," Mommy cries out.

She grabs the box and some baby girl clothes slide out of it onto the floor around Mommy's feet.

"More doll clothes!" I excitedly reach for them to add to my pile in the other room.

Mommy grabs them first. "No, I think these were maybe mine when I was a baby." Mommy starts holding them up, one by one, to look at them.

I dig through the clothes still in the box before Mommy can stop me to see if there is anything else inside. At the bottom of the box, I spot a small cloth with pink and gold stitches.

"No, Mommy. I think these are from Jennifer," I say and lift the square cloth out of the box. I trace the little X stitches with my fingers.

Mommy laughs and reaches for the cloth. "Why would you think Jennifer has her baby clothes here?"

"Because it says Jennifer," I say matter-of-factly, turning the cloth towards her so she can see I'm right. *Duh*.

Mommy shifts on the bed and reaches out to grab the cloth from me. She looks back and forth between the cloth and the clothes. Mommy rubs her forehead like she's thinking too hard. "Huh. So there is a Jennifer, after all?" she mumbles.

"A different Jennifer, Mommy?" I hold up one of the baby blankets that Mommy hadn't scooped up with the other clothes when the box fell.

"That's a very good question, Ladybug."

An hour later, the room Mommy was working in looks as full of stuff as when we first arrived. She managed to fill a couple of boxes with some photo albums she found, some old quilts Granny had made, and some extra bedding.

"Alright, I think we're ready to start carrying these boxes out and head home," Mommy says as she stands up from the bed and stretches her back. I carry my box of dolls downstairs and place it by the door for Mommy to carry outside.

"Why don't you wait for me in the living room while I load these up? It's warmer than being outside." Mommy is balancing three boxes as she climbs down the stairs, angling her body slightly so she can see where the last step is.

I run into the living room to get out of her way. Most of Granny's furniture is still here and the Christmas tree is still sitting by the front window. The lights aren't turned on, though, and her favorite chair is back at our house in her new bedroom. Pictures still sit in frames on the ledges and bookshelf by the couch. I stand on my tiptoes to see the picture of me on Granny's lap from when I was a baby. I am a pretty cute baby.

"Wait! We can't leave Granny's memories here, Mommy!" I notice the bowl of Granny's memory stones sitting beside some pictures higher on the bookshelf.

Mommy is bending over to grab the last box to bring outside. "Granny doesn't need those anymore. She used them to remember things, but she hasn't used them in quite a while."

I climb up on the arm of the couch to reach the bowl on the shelf. *Who put them up so high, anyway?* "But, Mommy! She will forget everything without them," I whine.

Mommy has no choice but to put down the box she was holding so she can grab the bowl before I knock it off the shelf. "Okay, you can bring them home. I know they mean a lot to you, but you need to remember they're not actually magical." She walks over beside me, grabs the bowl, and hands it to me after I climb back down. "You know that, right? Granny's still going to lose her memory, okay?" Mommy asks.

"Maybe. But I can still keep them for her." I hug the bowl to my chest and know I will guard them forever. Even if no one else will.

"Put them in the box with the dolls so they don't go flying while I drive," Mommy says.

I run for the front door and quickly shove my feet into my boots. Then I fly out the front door, cradling the bowl of rocks under my arm.

"Your coat, Sadie!" Mommy calls behind me, but it's too late. I'm on a mission.

I had Daddy carry my box of stuff from Granny's into my room once we got home. I didn't tell Mommy about the picture in the box. My plan is to wait until Christmas to show Mommy and Granny.

Now that I'm in my room, the first thing I unpack is the bowl of memory stones. *Maybe I should put them in Granny's room so she can use them.* But, if Mommy is right and she will still lose her memories, maybe she will forget the rocks are special. I can't risk that. I add the painted rocks from under my bed into the bowl. Then I slide the bowl under my bed to keep them all safe. Maybe being in the room next to Granny is just as good as being in the same room.

One by one, I pull out the dolls and set them up by the dollhouse on my floor. Only my tiny dolls can fit into the dollhouse, but these dolls can lie beside it and keep them company. Once everything is set up, I look at the picture again. It's still strange to be riding a bike in the snow, but maybe Granny's farm had snow for a long time. I remember in school learning about some places that never get snow, and other places that have snow for a ton of months! I can't imagine living in either of those places. If things don't change, I get bored. Well, there are a couple of things I would like to stay the same.

"Sadie, do you want a snack?" Granny's voice calls down the hall.

"Yes, please!" I call back.

I push the picture under my bed beside Granny's rocks. I'll ask Mommy about it later when I show her. Probably soon, because I don't know if I can wait until Christmas. The space under my bed is getting a bit too full of secrets.

I run down the hall and see Granny sitting at the kitchen table with a plate of sliced apples and a basket of things in her lap. "What's that Granny?" I ask as I climb onto the chair beside her and grab an apple slice off the plate to bite into.

"How would you like to learn to sew, Sadie?" Granny asks me and places her basket on the table in front of me.

I dig through the basket of threads in every color of the rainbow. "What are we going to sew? I don't see any fabric in here."

Granny smiles and grabs a wooden circle with fabric over the top. It looks like a small drum. "This is called a hoop. We are going to stitch pretty designs onto this fabric. When you practice more, you could sew a picture of something and then hang it on your wall." ·

"You can also stitch up the holes in your jeans for me," Mommy calls over from the kitchen counter. She's chopping up ingredients for dinner tonight.

Granny scrunches up her face and says, "That's boring sewing. But you could stitch flowers and designs into your jeans."

"That sounds cool! Can I do that, Mommy?" I ask, bouncing on my chair.

Mommy tilts her cutting board and uses her knife to drag the chopped onions into a bowl. "Learn to sew first and then we will talk."

"Alright Granny, what do I do first?" I ask ready to get started.

"First you choose a color and then we will thread the needle." Granny tilts the basket for me to pick a color.

"That's easy! Let's start with orange." I grab the bright orange thread from the basket and hold it out to Granny.

Granny shakes her head. "You're going to thread the needle. If you're going to learn to sew, you need to do the steps yourself."

Granny helps cut the thread and after a few attempts with my tongue sticking out, I get the needle threaded. "I did it!" I exclaim excitedly.

"Now we will practice some straight stitches. Like this." Granny passes the needle up and down through the fabric and then passes it to me to try.

"How did you learn to sew, Granny?" I ask while doing my best not to stab my finger with the needle.

"My mom taught me when I was little. I mostly helped her patch clothing, but when I got older, I realized sewing can also be fun."

"Is sewing quilts fun?" I ask while digging through the basket to find some purple thread to use next.

"Sewing quilts is a lot of fun. But teaching your mom and you to sew is the best."

chapter 23

Margo

☕ **The Highs & Lows of Love** - Margo in the Past

THE JAKE I SAW THE MOST was the Jake that was never around. Just the shell of his presence in our marriage and in our house. But I would be crazy if that's all that Jake was, and I still stayed in the marriage. I may have regrets, and I may have made some poor choices, but I was not crazy.

Scattered among the cracks of heartache were these pockets of moments that pieced together the image in my head of who Jake is. Each part making a mosaic and I, the observer, fighting to hold all the pieces together. Justifying that it was enough to stay, to make it work.

One time, Jake was working overtime for days on end. Each night, he would barely lay his head down to sleep before his alarm was yelling at him to get out of bed. After almost a week of this, he came home with barely the forethought to put his uneaten dinner into the fridge so it wouldn't spoil before quietly creeping to bed, thinking I was either asleep or rocking Alice to back to sleep for the second time. Instead, he found the bathroom light on as I lay on the bathroom floor feverish and covering my face with my arm.

"Mar, what's going on?" He brushed his cool hand across my forehead and helped me to sit up against the bathtub.

Alice answered for me as she cried out in the background, wanting me to come back and soothe her. It had been a long time since I had been so sick. "I'll just go rub her back while I sit by her crib," I had said to him. I wasn't getting any sleep right now anyway, and Alice had never settled for Jake during the night.

But before I could force myself to stand, Jake scooped me up and tucked me into bed. I was too weak to protest, and could only sink into the mattress hanging on to a thread of hope that Alice would settle for him. Well, she did settle for him, but it took an hour. I faded in and out of restless, feverish sleep, intermixed with thoughts nagging me to get out of bed and shoo Jake out to get some sleep of his own. But the thoughts wouldn't connect to my body to get out of bed and do anything about it.

I ended up waking the next morning to the light pouring in and feeling much better. Jake wasn't beside me in bed and I couldn't hear Alice crying like she should be in the morning. I had puttered cautiously out of the bedroom, only to find our neighbor holding Alice while she made some tea in the kitchen.

"Jake came and grabbed me before he headed to work. How are you feeling?" she had asked me with Alice snuggled in close on her hip.

I couldn't believe he had gotten up to go to work still after being up with Alice and me the night before, but I don't know if I could have done it without him. And I think he knew that, too.

Then there was the memory of Jake after Henry and I had gotten into another disagreement. Mom had injured her back lifting some posts while working in the fields with my dad. They were trying to get the fencing fixed before the heat of the summer set in, so Mom had pitched in to help as she always did. I vaguely remember my dad asking if Jake could come out for a couple of weekends and lend a hand. But Jake wasn't in the right state of mind and I made up some kind of excuse.

"Work is really busy right now for Jake. Could you wait until next month to do the fencing?" I knew they couldn't wait, so I was banking on that when I implied another month would be better. I hoped another month would be better, but I never knew if it would be.

I should have had the courage to tell them Jake and I were struggling. But their marriage was nothing like ours, and I wondered how they had managed it. It would sometimes wake me in the night, thoughts of if they knew. Did they know Jake was battling demons that threatened to rip us apart? Did they know I was trying to fix it all, but I couldn't be the same wife that my mom was? But, in the end, they never asked me. And I never said anything.

Henry called the second weekend into the fencing project to say Mom pulled a muscle in her back and could use some help around the house. I should have dropped everything to go help, but I had Alice to take care of. If I was around, maybe they would read it on my face about what a failure my marriage was. They would notice that I wasn't rushing to get home to make my own dinner, because Jake wouldn't be back home until too late.

I stopped by a couple of times, my arms full of meals and groceries for their fridge. I cleaned the dishes, swept the floor, and fed the chickens.

"Okay Mom, I need to get Alice back home," I would say as I hung her apron back up on the hook tucked beside the pantry. "Make sure you rest and I will try to come back in a few days."

She would nod at me and stroke Alice's cheek as she stacked a block tower on the floor beside the couch. "Don't worry about me. I'll be back on my feet in no time."

And then I would scoop up Alice and head out the door.

Each time I left, Henry would express his frustrations to me out on the driveway. He was a dutiful son for staying and helping take care of the farm. I was a disappointing daughter for leaving. *And I didn't even have a happy family to show for it.*

"I should sit Henry down for a chat. He can't treat you like that." Jake had been angry when I came home in tears that third time. He had been home from work early and brought some pizza for us as a treat.

I felt bad complaining about my family drama to him, especially when I was being accused of not helping my parents out more. I knew Jake would give anything to have another day to help his parents out with anything.

"I know what you're thinking over there, Mar, and stop it." Jake could always read me so well. "Being your brother does not give him a free pass to belittle you. You are a strong, independent woman. You are kind. You make everyone around you a better person."

A few days later, when I went back to check on Mom, she was moving around more. When I left to go home, Henry followed me outside again as I loaded Alice into her car seat.

"Thanks for coming out and checking on her," he said as I clipped the buckle to secure Alice's squirming body. Then he gave a firm knock on the hood of my car before turning back into the house.

I always wondered when Jake sat him down. There was no doubt in my mind that he must have. I just wish I had been a fly on the wall for that conversation. Henry and I never formed a new relationship after that. He still threw barbs my way and grumbled about this and that. But, whatever was said, some boundary lines were drawn, and the fights stayed fair.

For all my favorite glimpses of Jake, there was also the moment that broke everything.

Once we decided we were going to start a family, we snapped right to it. Stolen moments before Jake left for work, a trip home on a slow day between cars to pick up lunch was his excuse, and date nights by candlelight. Jake was here with me, and I almost secretly hoped it would take a while to get that positive test result. But, we were quickly blessed with a growing baby burrowed deep inside me, and I prayed that as this wee one burrowed, Jake would delve into our family instead of retreating from it.

As Alice went from rolling, to crawling, to walking, we debated when was the right time to grow our family again. I watched and studied how Jake was coping. I weighed what would happen if I timed it wrong, or if I waited too long trying to time it right.

It was an ordinary weeknight and Jake was building a tower of blocks for Alice to kick down for the hundredth time.

"Yay! Daddy do 'gain!" her little voice cheered as the colorful blocks crashed into a pile again.

"Let's do it again, Mar." Jake grinned up at me as he stacked a red block on the yellow one.

I looked up from patching the hole in his pants, needle in hand. "Do what again?" I had asked, confused.

"Alice. Well, not Alice, but a child. Let's have another one."

I grinned, mirroring the joy and hope in his eyes. "Okay," I agreed. It never took much for Jake to say something that would make me jump right in.

What I never weighed in my considerations for timing was the fact babies come when they're ready. Months went by and we were no closer than we were before deciding to take this next step. We let time go by when I lost my hope, and we pulled the plug when Jake no longer had that joy to cling to.

Alice's next birthday came and went. And, somewhere in the chaos of it all, my cycle had come and gone as well.

"Just one more thing and then we will go home," I said to Alice. I had added a bag of oranges into the grocery cart and headed toward the pharmacy at the back of the store. I diligently scanned the shelves while Alice chattered away. Grabbing the box that would soon tell my future, I placed it into the cart and headed to the checkout.

Why now? I had thought to myself later that day while I sat on the edge of the bathtub staring at the positive test. I should be excited that we finally had success, but I feared the timing. I wondered if growing our dysfunctional family was wise, and whether nine months from now we would be bonded together or ripped apart.

I didn't tell Jake for quite a while, and he wasn't around long enough to notice me bent over the toilet fighting for every last calorie I forced myself to eat. Once the nausea had passed and the waistline of my clothes grew snug, I knew this baby would out my secret sooner than later.

"Jake, we're having another baby," I had blurted out, almost nonchalantly over dinner one night at the beginning of my second trimester. "Can you pass the carrots?"

Jake's eyebrows had shot up and Alice broke the silence by throwing some potatoes on the floor with a squeal. "Pregnant? But, Mar, we umm… We haven't…" Jake stammered over his words like a newborn fawn finding its footing.

I nodded and reached across the table to grab the carrots myself. "I'm about 15 weeks along. I got pregnant around Alice's birthday party," I informed him.

He jumped out of his chair so fast and whisked me up in his arms. He laughed, he kissed my neck, and we twirled around the kitchen. Alice smacked her hands on her highchair, loving the show.

I swatted playfully at him. "Put me down, Jake."

He was exuding so much joy that I couldn't help but wonder if I shouldn't have told him months ago when I first found out myself. Maybe it would have pulled him out of his hole sooner.

The one thing that I should have learned early on, but never did, was I could not control how to pull Jake out of his darkness any more than I could stop the world from spinning. Nothing was truly within my control, no matter how much I felt the responsibility to hold it together. Eventually, I could let the control go and let things be as they wanted to be. But that wasn't until much later. Much too late.

A few weeks later, when the aches turned into pains, the blood-splattered stains on the bed turned into my future ripped from my life as our baby was ripped away, too.

"We can try again, whenever you're ready," Jake had said as he held me weeks later when the tears would keep flowing.

"I don't think I can. Jennifer was our last," I responded and held on to him as my life raft.

Jake shifted to look at my face. "Jennifer?"

My hand went to the flatness of my stomach where she once was safe until my body failed to hold on to her anymore. "She felt like a girl, right from the start. I would have liked to name her Jennifer. It means *blessed*, and we tried so hard for her."

Jake shifted again, uneasy about the idea of putting a name to this child who did not exist anymore. It made her short life more real, more tangible. A name was attached to hopes and dreams, a personality, and something for the grief to latch on to. He wanted the grief to pass by us, like a dark winter wind. But its hooks were deep in me and I needed to heal. For most of the pregnancy, it was just Jennifer and me, our little secret together. I felt guilty for worrying about the timing. I felt ashamed that she may not have felt wanted enough.

What I didn't know was that Jennifer also meant a *white wave*, and it was ultimately the last wave to wipe Jake out.

Our family could never go back to the three of us. We were forever a family of three, plus the ghost of Jennifer lurking in the shadows. The taste of what we wanted, what we held for the briefest of moments, and then gone.

We tried again six months later. We tried for a year. We tried until Jake wasn't around to try anymore. There was only so much loss that Jake could take. His family, his child, and that life he was aspiring to live.

When I think of Jake, I think of him as a person first, my husband second, and a father third. I imagine most people think of their spouse as being their spouse first, and to be honest, I sometimes even forget to think of him as being a father. Even when we were married, I think I often viewed myself and Alice on one island in my brain, and Jake and I on a separate island. Jake may have been battling his demons and adrift from us many times, but he was also a present father when he could be. The separation in my mind, I believe, was my own problem. For whatever reason, I just couldn't blend those worlds together, and maybe that's why I stopped trying.

If you asked me when I knew Jake wasn't coming back, I could tell you the exact day. Alice was 12, and her school was having a father-daughter dance.

"Why does the school have these stupid dances anyway?" Alice had complained after bringing home the poster handout from school. She wadded it up into a tight ball and threw it across the room. It had bounced off the kitchen counter and landed in the corner.

"You know, some of the other moms are going to be going instead of the dads. Some dads work and some of the other kids don't have a dad around, either. Would you like me to go with you?" I had offered.

"No. I'd rather just stay home and have pizza with you."

I had wrapped my arms around her in a hug while she tried to hide her stray tears. The topic of Jake came up less and less as she got older. I always wanted to keep the good memories alive for her, but she had made it clear she didn't want them around. I could have pushed more. *I should have pushed more.* I had promised Jake that I wouldn't let his name be a foul taste. Maybe I was afraid of him breaking her heart again, or maybe I was selfishly protecting mine.

We had a bond, Alice and I. She was on the cusp of being a teenager, and so far, she still loved confiding in me and spending time with me. If I let Jake back around now, what sort of ripples would that new adjustment set off in her world? How many questions would she have for why he returned now, and why he left at all? Right now, in her world, Jake was the enemy. And as much as it pained me for her to see him that way, the thought of her changing her sights to be set on me for the part that I played; well, it took all the breath from my lungs.

If you asked me when I knew Jake wasn't coming back, I could tell you the exact day because it was the day I subconsciously, or maybe consciously, decided he wouldn't.

ROLLING OUT OF BED, I head down the hall to the kitchen to put some waffles in the toaster for Sadie's breakfast. With Mom at the house now, our regular schedule has shifted and changed, but with only mild growing pains. Since Jennifer doesn't come by until mid-morning now, Travis has shifted his hours at work so he could take Sadie to school on his way to the office. Mom rarely wakes until after they are gone for the day, and I prefer not to leave her on her own before seeing how she is feeling for the day.

Travis is already seated in the corner of the kitchen with the newspaper and a cup of coffee. I have always been the first to rise in the house, but not necessarily the first to leave the bedroom. My natural clock always wakes me before Travis' alarm clock sets his day into motion. But that hour or so in bed while the rest of the world seems to be at a standstill is one of my few moments to breathe. Once my feet hit the floor, I can't help but feel forced to propel myself into motion. And so long as my family is sleeping, and I am tucked into my bed, the world around me can wait.

This morning in bed I had ticked through my mental list of things to do and made a couple of notes on my phone to add to my master list in the kitchen. Tomorrow is Sadie's last day of school before Christmas break. She has been very excited all month for this day to come. Just one step closer to Christmas. Travis is also going to be off from work for a couple of weeks, and I am looking forward to that time as a family to hibernate.

"Hopefully, this case wraps up for us today." Travis lowers his newspaper on the table and acknowledges my presence in the kitchen.

I grab the waffles that have popped up from the toaster and place them on a plate. Their sweet, warm smell wafts down the hall to Sadie's bedroom. Food is the only surefire way to wake that child from the deepest of dreams. "Wouldn't that be nice to have one less thing on your mind during your holidays?"

Travis stands up to head down the hall to make sure Sadie doesn't come barrelling down and wake up my mom. "I might be home late tonight, though. I want to get as much handled as I can before handing over things to the others on the team," he says.

"Just a girls' night tonight, then. Maybe we should watch a Christmas movie." I fill the kettle and place it on the stove so it's ready for when Mom wakes up.

Shortly after Travis and Sadie left for their day, there was a quiet knock on the door. Mom still hasn't come out yet, but I can hear her turning under the covers. I head down the stairs before they decide to ring the doorbell and wake her up for sure.

I open the door and smile. "Suzanne! What a surprise!" I exclaim, reaching out to hug my mom's neighbor.

She's holding a plate of cookies and other sweet treats that she extends out to me after our hug. "These are for you guys. Merry Christmas."

I take the plate in my hand and see the pile of assorted delicious goodies that will not last long in our house. "This is so sweet of you. Thank you, we will enjoy these. Did you want to come in?" I ask as I open the door wider.

"I'll step inside so you're not letting the cold in, but I can't stay," Suzanne answers. She steps into the house and out of the way for me to close the door.

"How have you in and Peter been?" I ask, placing the plate of cookies on the stairs to grab when I go up.

"We've been good. Just getting ready for Christmas. Peter was going to call you, but I told him I was going to swing by with some treats," Suzanne pauses for a second before taking a tentative step out into whatever conversation is stewing inside her. "Your dad came by our house a couple of days ago. I guess he hadn't heard from Margo in a while and was concerned something had happened."

My legs feel weak and I want to sit down on the stairs, but I grab onto the railing with my hand instead. "Why would he go to your house, though?"

"Poor guy seemed upset and didn't know what to do. He was rambling on about not being sure if he should call you since he figured he was the last person you would want to hear from," Suzanne explains and places her hand on mine. "I guess he calls her every week. If she's having a good day, they chat. But, no one was around to answer the phones for the last couple of weeks, so he made the drive to check on her himself."

"Did he want anything else?" I ask, suspicious about his intentions.

Suzanne shakes her head no. "I told him she had moved in with you, but everything was okay. I hope that was okay. You can call him if you want." She offers me a slip of paper with his contact information written on it, in case I need it.

I smile a tight smile and grab the paper from her hand. "Thanks for letting me know, Suzanne. I appreciate it."

Mom is settled into the sectional in the living room, working on the last of the embroidery stitches for the quilt. She had woken up shortly after Suzanne had left, giving me just enough time to gather my wits about me and head upstairs to make our morning teas.

"Alice!" Mom calls to me from the couch. "Get me some new thread from my room." Mom's voice is tense and irritated.

I come back from her room with a new spool of white thread and hand it to her. "Is this the color you wanted?"

Mom grabs it and measures out a length of thread to cut. "The other thread isn't working," Mom says without looking up at me. Her left hand is shaking slightly as she holds the needle. The thread in her right hand misses the eye of the needle once, twice, then three times.

"Damn it, this thread isn't working either," she grumbles. Then drops the needle and thread in her lap on top of the quilt.

I kneel beside her and grab the needle from her lap before it gets knocked down to the floor. "Here, let me try. The lighting in here isn't the best," I offer.

Mom snatches it back from my hands. "I didn't ask for help! I have been quilting since before you were born."

It's going to be a day. I stand and retreat to the water boiling on the stove. "I'll get us some tea, Mom," I call over my shoulder.

I pour out the tea and think back on the conversation I had with Suzanne. At first, I had a strong reaction to the idea of Jake coming to check on my mom. But I'm surprised how that reaction hasn't festered inside to a larger response. No, not a tantrum, but a movement of the knife that's been deep in my gut all these years. The knife that twisted and enmeshed itself deeper inside me when I found out Jake and my mom are still married. I would have expected that knowing, one hundred percent without a doubt, they had an ongoing relationship would have sliced me right open and left all my hurts and anguish spilled out for everyone to see.

Instead, I managed to say goodbye to Suzanne and walk upstairs to start my day. I didn't like what I had heard, but it was like this small moment of clarity that Mom and I are connected but also separate. Maybe if I had been born more easygoing like my mom, I could have broached the topic of my dad leaving years ago. I could have asked her what had gone so wrong between the three of us as a family and told her how much it still hurt. I should have asked if it still hurt her, too. *Could've, would've, should've.*

There were no answers for her to give now, though. She was here with me, but she lived partially in a different reality.

Given how agitated she is this morning, maybe I should try to join her in her world to help calm her down.

I walk into the living room, holding two steaming cups of chamomile tea. "Oh, Mom. Jake," I pause to correct myself. "I mean Dad, called wondering how you're doing." It feels foreign to my tongue and my bitterness inside screams *imposter* at me. It's still a tender bruise inside me and I feel it as I push on it, albeit gently.

Mom reaches over to grab the mug from my hands and bobs her tea bag up and down. "Did you tell him that I have moved in with you?" she asks, and the ordeal with the needle is temporarily forgotten.

I don't even know if I'm doing the right thing by telling her or encouraging her. *What doors am I opening or closing in the process?* I'm realizing there's so much of her life I don't know or understand. I most likely never will, as I'm sure is the case for all kids as they grow up and realize their parents are more than the image they have created in their heads. They're fully functioning adults with their own lives that started before yours did and ebb out both alongside and away from yours.

I blow on my tea, and Mom carefully places the quilt beside her. "Yes, he knows. Next time he calls, would you like to speak to him?"

She's chosen some kind of relationship, if you can call it that, or connection with the man for this many years. The three of us have a shared history, but we each have a different outlook on the situation, I guess. If Mom wants to hold on to this part of her life, maybe I can learn to accept that this is her reality. And it doesn't take away from my experience.

"Of course I would," she responds. Then lifts her tea, still steaming, and takes a long sip.

Later that afternoon, while Mom went for a nap, Jennifer stayed to help me sort through some of the other photo albums we brought over from the house. Most days, Jennifer heads out and runs errands when my mom lays down, but the snow decided to come down and not stop.

"There's no point in you going out in that weather, only to turn around and come back in a couple of hours," I had told her as she finished sorting out Mom's pills for the week. It felt odd having her around doing things I could do myself, but she was a part of Mom's world now and it was a blessing to have an extra set of helping hands. I also wasn't sure if Mom was going to wake up agitated again after her nap, and wanted some moral support.

"Well, if it's not an interruption for you, I didn't have anything I needed to do," she had responded, relieved to not have to brush off her car for at least a few more hours. "You can carry on as you normally would, and I'll just flip through some magazines and keep busy out of your way."

I didn't have anything I needed to do either, so on a whim, I had decided to sort through some boxes. Maybe it felt safe to look through old photos because she was only mildly attached to the family. Looking through them with Mom felt like there could be unexpected landmines of finding things she had forgotten.

So, Jennifer and I settled onto the couch, side by side, balancing a photo album between the two of us, gently turning each of the yellowed pages.

"I had no idea she had more photo albums in her house. I thought we had moved most of them here already," I say, thinking of the boxes in the basement still waiting to be scanned into the computer. "But, I still remember some photos so clearly in my head, but never found them in those books. So, I am hoping we will find some more."

The first two pages are full of baby pictures. "Look at all the rolls your mom had," Jennifer says as she points to the top right photo of a baby lying on a crocheted blanket. The baby is wearing a shirt, a folded cloth diaper secured with a large pin, and the roundest cheeks grinning up at whoever was taking the picture.

There's another picture of a young boy holding the baby across his lap. "That must be my Uncle Henry. I never did meet him. Mom and him had a falling out a long time ago," I explain.

Jennifer flips the page, and we have jumped ahead to what looks like photos from a first, second, and third birthday all collaged together across the two pages. "Funny how different film pictures are from digital ones. I have probably a thousand pictures on my phone of this past year alone. I can't imagine compiling three years of Sadie's life into a dozen pictures spread across two pages in a scrapbook." The idea of having to decide when to take a picture, and which ones to keep, almost makes me break out in hives.

The picture on the top left catches my eye. "That must be my grandparents." I point to a photo of a mom and dad smiling proudly, sitting on either side of a young child celebrating what looks like a first birthday. The colors from the photo have mostly faded over the decades, but what stands out to me is the shirts they are wearing. "Doesn't that blouse look like the blue flower fabric on the quilt my mom found?" I ask Jennifer as I look around for where I had placed the quilt before we ate lunch.

Jennifer spots the quilt sitting on the bench by the window and gets up to grab it. "It's hard to tell for sure, but it does seem to match." She squints at the photo and looks back at the quilt in her hands to compare. "And you know what? It looks like her dad is wearing a plaid flannel shirt, which could be the same as this," she says as she points to the matching fabric on the quilt.

"I guess she was making a quilt of items from her parents, then?" I wonder aloud, flipping to the next page to study more of the clothing for potential matches to the quilt.

"Wait, maybe this is a photo album for your uncle? The pictures on this page are clearly of a young boy and not your mom." Jennifer points at a boy around eight years old grinning a big toothless grin that reminds me of Sadie. She then points to a photo at the bottom right that is a family portrait. The mom and dad are on opposite ends of the photo, with five children spread out between them. "I didn't know your mom had so many siblings."

I look at the photo Jennifer is pointing at. "Mom only has a brother," I say, studying the picture some more. I flip further ahead into the album and watch as page by page the young boy becomes taller, older, and resembles a face that is faded and just out of reach at the back of my memories. "I think this album might be my dad's."

chapter 25

Margo

"AND THAT'S THE LAST STITCH," I say to no one but myself as I knot off the embroidery thread and pull the ends of the thread through to the back of the quilt to hide them. I place my needle back into the small tin case beside me on the couch and snip the stray threads with my scissors. The quilt is officially complete. It was an enjoyable project to pass the time at home, and as satisfying as it is to have finished it, I'm disappointed that now I have nothing to do.

On a typical day, Alice would be at home with me puttering around the house while I offer to do something, but she always declines. A couple of hours after Travis dropped Sadie off at school, the teacher called to say Sadie had hit her head during recess and wasn't feeling well. As soon as she hung up with the teacher, she went into fix-it mode and started calling Travis at work and then Jennifer. Travis was in court, wrapping up a case before his Christmas holidays. Jennifer was, Jennifer was… *Hmm, Jennifer was doing something.*

"Are you sure you will be okay at home by yourself?" Alice had asked while buttoning up her coat and gripping her gloves tightly in her hand.

I had looked up from my stitching, mildly amused at her unique version of chaos, not so different from Sadie's chaos and spunk. "I've been home by myself ever since you moved out," I reminded her.

"I called Jennifer, and she's going to head over as soon as she can, but maybe I should just wait until she gets here before picking up Sadie…" Alice had trailed off, trying to decide.

"Shoo, shoo." I had motioned her away with my hands and nearly dropped my needle in the process. "The sooner you pick up that sweet granddaughter of mine, the quicker you can get in line at the doctor."

Alice had still hovered, uncertain. If she had figured out a way to clone herself by now, she would have.

"I'll be fine," I had reassured her. To drive my point home, I placed down my needle and folded my hands in my lap while looking at her. "I promise."

And that was all the push she had needed before she grabbed her keys and rushed out the door with that magnetic pull of a mama hen to her baby chick.

Being called for an emergency for your child is one part of motherhood that is never enjoyable. Thankfully, a bump to the head would be an easy fix. As a single mom of Alice, I was the only parent on call if something went wrong. It was a haunting concern in those times when I would make the long drive to Jake's therapy appointments.

I was not prone to worrying, though, so I always pushed off the *what-ifs* and focused on the task at hand. I suppose the fears never fully vanished, because there was no denying the immediate relief as I was back within the borders of our town.

Alice has never been a wild child or a risk-taker growing up. You could always find her on the swing set or with her nose buried in a book. Only once in Alice's life did I find myself sitting in an emergency room with her. When she was ten, she felt brave enough to attempt the monkey bars. She spent recess swinging from bar to bar, making it almost halfway across before dropping to the ground with tired hands. Her friends showed her how to climb up and sit on the top of the bars with their legs dangling down. They would then hook their legs over a bar and hang upside down. Everything was fine until she fell and landed on her arm.

I had been getting groceries when I got the call. I left my cart, half full, abandoned in the dairy aisle while I rushed to the school. We had waited for two hours in the emergency room for a doctor to check out her swollen arm. After countless word searches, magazines, and a lollipop, we were called behind the curtains for an X-ray. It was just a slight fracture, a sticker for waiting so nicely, and orders to rest it and take it easy. Alice's takeaway from the entire ordeal was to never climb the monkey bars ever again. There was no dusting herself off to try again.

I fold the finished quilt and place it beside me, resting my sewing tin on top, and reach for the magazine on the coffee table when there's a knock at the front door. I stand up and look out the front window to see who might be knocking, but from that angle, I can't see anyone. The visitor rings the doorbell as I head for the stairs.

"I'm coming, I'm coming!" I holler out, taking one stair at a time and gripping the railing as I go. Before I reach the last step, they knock a second time. "What's the rush?" I mutter to myself.

I open the front door and am greeted by a delivery man holding a couple of boxes and a clipboard with a pen attached.

"Delivery for Alice?" The man asks and holds out the clipboard for me to sign for the packages.

I grab it and write my signature across the bottom. "You are an impatient man, aren't you?" I chastise him for his urgency for someone to open the door.

"Sorry, Ma'am, but I've got a van full of last-minute Christmas shopping to get delivered," he explains and grabs the clipboard back from me. "We don't all have Santa's magic." He winks at me, and my frustration with him fades away.

I grab the parcels from his arms and turn to head back up the stairs. The packages aren't heavy but as I turn my body, my feet lag just slightly. I crash to the ground before I can steady my feet to stop it from happening.

"Oooof!" The wind rushes out of me as my hip collides first with the bottom step, followed by the rest of my left side and head on the steps further up. The packages hit the stairs and wall with a series of chaotic thumps. Then they tumble back to the bottom.

The pounding in my head nearly drowns out the delivery man, who is now rushing to my side. "Ma'am, Ma'am. Are you okay?" he asks while hovering above me, no longer holding onto his clipboard.

"Mmm," I mumble through my clenched jaw. I try to push off the stairs to sit up, but can't move my body. The throbbing is paralyzing, and every attempt to move weighs me down through a dark haze.

The delivery driver grabs my arm and rolls me to my back. I can't feel him, but an explosion of pins and needles courses through my lower body at the change of position. I groan and am vaguely aware of tears trailing down my cheeks.

I think I hear him say something about an ambulance as I close my eyes and hope the darkness wraps around me in some relief.

"She took quite the fall-" A female's voice is coming from somewhere in the room and I urge my eyes to open, but they are too heavy to obey.

"-no concussion, but we will need to operate." I move my hands and their phantom weight is almost like they're not a part of my body. I fumble to clasp them together and notice the wires coming from my left hand.

"Lucky the delivery driver was there-" The mystery woman is talking again. I try to roll to my side, but my body feels empty and rubbery.

"Oh, oh, careful there Mom," Alice says. My eyes slowly pry open and I focus on Alice's face hovering over mine.

"Good to see you awake, Margo." I move my head toward the woman's voice, my eyes lagging, and land on a doctor standing on the other side of my bed. She reaches over to push some buttons on the machine sitting beside my bed. "Do you remember falling?" she asks me.

"Yes," I mumble in a whisper and cough. "Yes, on the stairs," I say more clearly this time while she lifts my eyelids and flashes a light back and forth.

"You fractured your hip, Mom. You're going to have surgery to fix it, okay?" Alice squeezes my arm and I focus my attention on trying to mentally locate my hip.

"My hip doesn't hurt," I say out loud when I realize I can't feel my hip or much of anything.

The doctor chuckles. "We put you on some good meds, Margo. I doubt you feel much of anything," she explains, then turns to look at Alice. "Should we wait for anyone else to arrive before we get her prepped for surgery? Any siblings or husband?"

Alice shakes her head no.

"I'm so sorry Alice. I'm so sorry…" I say, turning my head back to Alice.

Alice reaches over and wipes the tears on my cheek. "You didn't mean to fall. You're going to be just fine, Mom."

My stomach is churning, and the room feels like it's starting to wobble. "Jake should be here. Your dad should have been here. I am so sorry. I ruined it all." I close my eyes in hopes of resetting the spinning and making the world back to normal.

"Mom, I just need you to relax, okay?" Alice's voice hovers by my ear.

"Let's get her to the back and prepped," the doctor interjects.

"The more time we wait-" The voices are floating around me again.

"-more agitated and confused."

chapter 26
sadie

"GOOD THING WE GET TO take you home today, Granny!" I beam at Granny as she sits on the hospital bed eating orange Jell-O with a spoon.

The Jell-O tumbles off the spoon and Granny looks down to scoop it off her chest. "And why's that Sadie-bum?"

I giggle because surely Granny must know. "Because it's two days until Christmas!"

Almost a week ago Granny fell while at home by herself. That was the same day Scotty was spinning me around in the tire swing during recess. I like it when he winds the chains tight and then when he lets go, you whip around really fast. My other friends hate it and never go on. So, instead, Scotty and I take turns making each other dizzy. When I climbed off, everything was still moving around and

I crashed into one of the wood beams holding the swing up. I got a bump on my head and it really hurt. So, Mrs. Anderson called Mommy to pick me up early.

Mommy said Jennifer got to the house at the same time as the ambulance. I wish I had got to see the ambulance. Maybe I could have ridden in it with Granny, so she didn't have to be by herself. And then I could tell all my friends that I got to ride in one! After we had finished at the doctor, Mommy rushed us over to the hospital to see Granny. On the way, Mommy called Daddy, and he was waiting at the front entrance when we got there. Mommy went inside to see Granny while Daddy and I sat in the waiting room. I didn't want to go back home, so Daddy and I read books and ate fries at the cafeteria while we waited for Granny to come out of surgery.

I only saw Granny for a couple of minutes after her surgery. She was still sleeping and everything was so white in her room - her sheets, her bed, and her face. I like Granny when she's wearing all of her colors. But I was so glad that she was going to be okay. I wanted Granny to come home with us, but she had to stay at the hospital for a few days before the doctors would let her leave.

"Granny will have to do a lot of resting when we bring her home, remember?" Mommy ruffles my hair and grabs Granny's food tray to move it out of the way. "How are you feeling about coming home, Mom?"

"I'll be excited to sleep in peace. And I guess I will have Sadie to keep me company during the next couple of weeks." Granny winks at me. "What should we do first? Go sledding or skating?"

I giggle. "Granny! You can't do those things."

Mommy shakes her head at both of us. "I fear you both will keep me on my toes."

"We can read books and maybe we can sew some more," I say.

"Those sound like approved activities to me," a voice behind me says. I turn around and see a doctor standing at the end of the bed. "Well, Margo, looks like we're going to be kicking you out of here today," the doctor continues.

"I'm just too much trouble for you," Granny teases.

The doctor laughs. "Never too much trouble, but I do hope not to see you in here again." She turns to look at me. "I need you to keep an eye on your granny for me, okay?"

I nod and give her a thumbs-up. "I will make sure she follows all the rules."

Mommy laughs. "I'll believe it when I see it."

When we got home, Mommy and Daddy helped carry Granny up the stairs and settled her into the bed in her room. Mommy had said she was going to make lunch and told me I should find something in my room that I could quietly do with Granny to keep her company.

I am still here, looking around my room for something to do. I've never really played with my toys with Granny before, so I'm not sure what she would like to play with. Normally, at her house, I play with the dolls by myself, and then we talk. *That's it!*

I bend down by my bed and pull out the memory stones. Granny can just lay and relax while we tell stories. I grab the painted rocks on the top of the bowl and wonder if I should hide them. I still haven't told anyone that I painted them, but I think Granny might like them. But, just in case, I put them into my sweater pocket and carry the bowl with both my hands into Granny's room.

"What did you find, Sadie?" Granny peers to look at me as I walk into the room and carefully sit at the end of her bed. Mommy keeps reminding me I have to be careful and not bump Granny because she will be in pain for a while.

"They're your memory rocks, Granny," I answer and push the bowl a bit closer to her. She picks up a couple from the top of the pile to hold in her hands.

"Well, would you look at that? What would you like to do with them?" Granny runs her thumb over the top of the white rock in her hand and flips it over to look at the bottom.

I shrug. "I guess you could tell me a story from one of them."

Granny reaches out to pass the rock back to me. "How about you tell me a story with them?" she suggests.

I grab the rock from her and frown at it. "But I don't know the stories of each rock. Only you do."

Granny urges me on. "That's the magic of memory stones, Sadie. They can be whatever memory you want them to be."

I place the rock back on the pile in the bowl. Slowly, I reach my hand into my sweater pocket and pull out the painted stones. Too scared to look up at Granny yet, I lay them out in the empty space on the quilt between us.

"Did you paint these?" Granny asks as she picks up the rock closest to her with the purple butterfly on it. "This butterfly is beautiful. It's purple, your mom's favorite color."

I brave a glance at Granny. "Yes, I stole these from your house because I wanted to help you not forget,"

I mumble and look back down at my hands, feeling the tears pooling in my eyes. "I'm sorry. I shouldn't have taken them from you. Maybe if I-"

"Sadie, look at me," Granny says gently, and she reaches out her hand for me to hold. "That was very sweet of you to be concerned. But you can't steal a memory."

"I know, Granny. I'm so sorry. I won't do it again," I promise her.

Granny squeezes my hand. "No, you shouldn't have taken something without asking. But, I mean it's not possible to steal a memory. I am going to forget things with or without the rocks, or anything that anyone does."

"Oh," I breathe out and the tears drip off my chin. Mommy had told me the stones weren't magical, but I just knew she *had* to be wrong.

"I love these paintings you did, Sadie. Memories can't be stolen, but they *can* be shared. How about you keep these rocks safe for me and help remember them for me?" Granny holds out the purple butterfly rock to me. "Why don't you tell me what this memory is?"

"That was the time your mommy made you a butterfly cake for your birthday. You thought she made you a plain white cake, and she surprised you with a cake covered in purple butterflies." I smile proudly at remembering the story she had told me before. *I can be the best memory keeper ever!*

Granny smiles and nods. "Too bad I can't bake like my mom. I would love to have made beautiful cakes for you or your mom."

"You *can* bake, Granny!" I reach excitedly for the rock with the chocolate chip cookie painted on it. "You and I baked cookies when Mommy and Daddy went on a date.

You let me eat them before dinner, but it was our secret." I hold one finger to my lips in a *shh* motion.

Granny mirrors me and whispers, "I guess you better hide that rock to keep it a secret. Were they yummy?"

I beam at her and lick my lips. "The best!"

"Can I keep this rock with me?" Granny asks and points to the red heart painted with *L-U-V-E* on it. "This looks like a great memory to keep with me."

"That one was so you would always remember we love you," I explain and place the rock on the table beside her bed.

"Thank you, Sadie." Granny smiles a big smile at me, the skin around her eyes crinkling. "I will always love you, too."

Mommy wanted to make sure Granny had a long nap after lunch, so I am watching a show quietly in the living room. Mommy and Daddy are in the kitchen sorting through some boxes that still haven't been unpacked from Granny's house. I was curious at first to see what was inside them, but so far it was only clothes and boxes of old papers.

"This one looks like a lot of old documents and receipts that can be shredded now." Daddy's voice drifts into the living room and I move closer to the television to hear my cartoon better.

"Well, we should still go through it to make sure there's nothing important in it," Mommy answers.

They're quiet for a few minutes while shuffling through papers and I'm focused on the blue dog running around on the screen, trying to solve the mystery of the missing shoes.

Mommy carries in a glass of juice for me to drink. "Careful you don't spill this, okay?"

I nod excitedly and take a sip of the cold apple juice.

"Hey, Alice. There are some letters in here for you," Daddy calls over to Mommy.

Mommy walks back into the kitchen. "Letters?"

"They're addressed from Jake," Daddy says.

I set my juice down on the coffee table and creep closer to the kitchen. *Who's Jake?* I peer around the corner of the kitchen cabinet and see Mommy pull out the envelopes to look at them.

"It's already opened," she says, looking into the box and digging through what's still in there. "There's a couple dozen in here, at least. They're all open."

Daddy grabs them out and stacks them on the counter. "Did you know your dad had sent you these letters?" Mommy shakes her head and places her letter on top of the stack.

Dad? So, Jake is my Grandpa? Mommy always said I only have one grandpa, Daddy's dad.

"Why don't you have a daddy, too?" I had asked Mommy when I was working on a family tree project in kindergarten. Mommy's side of the tree seemed small and empty.

Mommy had placed a flower sticker to cover some of the blank space. "I only needed Granny," she had explained to me.

"But you had to start with a daddy," I insisted. I had always been a stubborn kid, I guess.

Mommy had shut down the conversation, though. "I stopped having a daddy when I was younger than you. But you're lucky to have one special grandpa and an even more special daddy. And he's not going anywhere." She had kissed the top of my head, and that was that.

"Aren't you curious to read what they say?" Daddy asks, nudging the pile closer to Mommy.

Mommy places them back in the box. "Not now, Trav. They've sat in this box for all these years. They can wait." Then, I watch as Mommy places the box in the cupboard above the fridge and moves on to another box.

I go back to watch my show. I wonder what my grandpa is like. Mommy likes to say Daddy and his dad are twins, which is silly. Mommy and Granny are so different from each other, though. So, maybe Mommy is more like her dad. And I love Mommy, so I guess I would like him too.

chapter

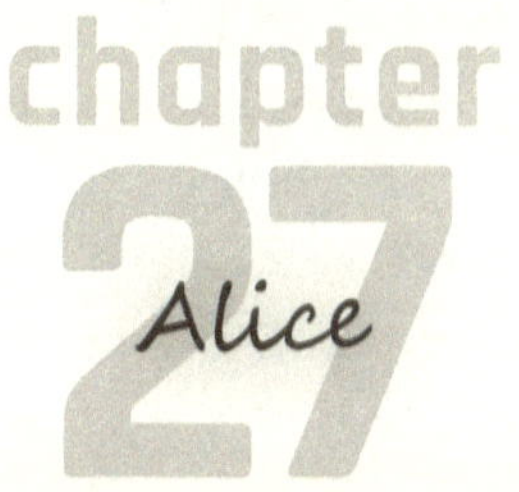

27

Alice

"How could Mom never tell me about this?" I ask out loud to myself as I stare at the box of letters spread out on my bed. Travis and Sadie are outside playing while Mom is resting in her room. Her surgery sucked out her energy, but the rest will be good for her. The doctor gave her strict orders to rest when tired, but also to move when awake to help with her healing. Jennifer has been so helpful in keeping her company. Mom has been teaching her embroidery stitches at the same time as Sadie. They've been puttering away for hours in her room each day since she's been home.

I chose to retreat into my room to process the discovery of these letters. I keep picking up and putting down the letters without reading them. The printing on the envelopes is foreign to me. I could hardly sleep last night because the knowledge of this box's existence haunted me as I tossed and turned. I have no memories of ever seeing these letters before, so my mom must have been the one who opened and read them.

If she read them and stored them away without ever telling me, then that should tell me I don't need to read them myself. She knew me best and chose to shield me from whatever they contained. *But she also withheld the secret that they never did divorce.*

I take a shaky breath and grab one from the pile at random. Mostly because I don't want to see the first words he chose to write, and I don't want to see the last.

The note is short and dated around my 8th birthday.

> Happy birthday Alice! I hear you made the team for soccer at school. I'm so proud of you! Last month, I bought a house only an hour away from you. There's a playground a few houses down from me and a large field that would be perfect for kicking the ball. Maybe one day you can come with your mom and play some soccer. Remember that I always love you and I'm working to be together as a family again soon.
>
> Love Daddy

I wish I could ask Mom why he left in the first place, and why he was still trying to come back so many years later. *Clearly, he failed.* These are the questions I should have asked years before, back when she remembered. But would she even have told me? There's so little that I know, but the feelings surrounding it all are drowning me.

The next few letters are similar to the first one I read. A few lines about something that had happened in my life-missing a tooth, straight A's in school, and a handful of missed birthdays. Some years multiple letters were sent, other times long gaps of time had passed. After reading each letter, I place it on the bed, forming a patchwork timeline of my life. The missed father-daughter dances, empty family tree projects, and take your kid to work days staring up at me, missing from his notes. *Was he aware of those moments, or was this only what he saw of my childhood?*

The last letter feels heavy in my hands, and not just because it is the last one he sent me before stopping. Inside the envelope, a coin falls out on my bedspread. I know what it is when I see it, even though I've never actually seen one in person before. *One Day at a Time* is emblazoned on the surface. I hold it in my hand, feeling its weighted meaning, while unfolding the letter.

Alice, to be honest, I don't know if you read these anymore or if you throw them away. I respect your decision either way. I added my chip, hoping it would at least make you curious enough to open the letter. You're about to turn 16 years old, and it's my fault that you don't even know who I am anymore.

I wanted to give you a milestone of my own for your birthday. And a promise, if that even holds worth anymore.

Your mom did everything she could to protect you from the heartbreak I caused her. I agreed to not come back into your life unless I was gonna stay in it. She couldn't bear to watch you fall apart again and have to rebuild yourself.

I want you to know I have been sober for a year. I'm still a mess inside, and I may just always be that way. I promise that one day if you ever come

knocking, I'll have more chips to match this one that
I'm giving you. I promise if you ever want to know me,
I will be here working to be someone worth knowing.

Love you always, Your dad, Jake

I add the letter at the end of the grid on my bed and look up to see Travis hovering in the doorway. I hadn't even heard them come inside.

"How long have you been there?" I ask, embarrassed, like I am caught doing something I shouldn't be.

Travis walks over to the bed but looks at me and not at the letters. "Not long. So, answers or more questions?" he asks, now eyeing up how I've spread them all out in order on the bed.

"Both," I answer, tossing the chip on top of the last letter and then looking up at Travis. "I wish I could see this from the full picture like you do. Subpoena the evidence, interview the witnesses, and make a ruling about how I'm supposed to feel. What am I supposed to do?"

Travis crouches down in front of me and grabs my hands. "Lawyers don't ever get the full picture. We are staked on a side and tell a story from that perspective. You can't be on the side of Jake is guilty and also look at the big picture at the same time."

"So you don't think he's guilty of leaving me and Mom?" I ask accusingly.

Travis shakes his head. "I didn't say that. But you can't be a judge and jury while you believe guilty is the only thing he is."

I chuckle lightly. "Okay, maybe this analogy went a little far. Do I need to do anything with this, though? Is it supposed to change anything?"

Travis stands up and rubs my back. "You can do whatever you want. But there's only one person left in this history that can offer you any answers," he says.

He heads out of the room and I stack the letters back together in the box. The idea of asking Jake the questions swirling in my head makes me nauseous. Some questions have been bouncing around in my head since I was a little girl. But, I also live in a very real world where I never knew I would have questions I wanted answered by someone who can't. *And maybe he can.*

But, surely, this can all wait for now. Tomorrow is Christmas.

Two hours ago, I felt I could simply box everything away again and wait until I was ready to unearth it. But, turns out thoughts and emotions can't be beaten into submission so easily.

"I need to get a couple of things for dinner tomorrow night," I had told Travis while he made Sadie a snack in the kitchen. "Are you okay if I just run out quickly?"

Travis raised an eyebrow at me. "It's not like you to run out at the last minute for something. Don't you have lists and backup lists to prevent that?" he asked teasingly.

"Life happens." I had shrugged, as if this was all normal. "Are you all good here?"

"Of course." He had eyed up the folded paper and the bag I was holding, but didn't ask me about it. "Are you good?"

I nodded and then left.

Now I'm sitting in my idling vehicle while I am parked across the street from a mechanic shop. I glance down at the address on the paper on the passenger side, but I don't need to confirm it because the sign has Jake's name written on it. *So this is where he works.*

All the other businesses I had driven past were already closed up. Everyone headed home to their families for the Christmas season. Jake was still open, likely because he had no one to go home to. There was a time when that would have given me a sliver of satisfaction.

"*That's what you get for abandoning your family,*" I would have said to myself. "*A lonely Christmas by yourself.*"

But, instead, I was feeling a mix of sadness for him, and also I couldn't deny being curious. What was Jake's day-to-day life like, and has it been the same for all these years? *Who is my dad?*

This impulsive trip out here is not who I am. The entire 40-minute drive I looped through the same question in my head. *Why are you going?* The best answer I could come up with was, *I don't know.* Now that I am parked here, I still don't have an answer to what to do next.

I grab the bag from the passenger seat and touch the quilt inside. I should have asked Mom before taking the quilt, but I wondered if asking about it would have been more upsetting. Maybe it would bring light to missing links in her memories. After seeing the photos of Jake and his parents, I knew this quilt was a connection to them. I was already being plagued with secrets from my dad. I didn't need to be haunted by his parents, too.

His relationship with his family was before I even existed. And his relationship with my mom seemed to be separate from mine as well. So withholding the quilt was only me interfering in something that had no connection to me. But my real reason for not asking for permission about the quilt is that if I had said my intent about the quilt out loud,

I would have been committed to doing it. As of right now, I can stay idling and drive away if I choose. No harm, no foul.

I watch the minutes tick by, one by one. If I want to be home in time for dinner, and before it gets dark, I need to decide. Like a flip of a coin, I count down. *Three, two, one.* And my hand fell to the door handle instead of the gear-shift. With my other hand, I turn the key to shut off the engine, and then grab the bag with the quilt. Before leaving home, I had scribbled a quick note that I tucked into the bag.

Margo fell and broke her hip, but her surgery went well. She finished this quilt, and I thought you should have it for Christmas.

Alice.

P.S. You should call her tomorrow for Christmas. She would like that.

Pulling my coat tightly around me, I look both ways across the abandoned street and cross to the mechanic shop. The bell over the door jingles loudly as I open the door.

A young girl jumps at the sound. "Oh, hello! We were just gonna be closing up, but how can we help?"

She has blonde hair, cut to her chin, and straight across bangs. Her piercing blue eyes look at me through the lenses of her thick, bold yellow glasses. She looks to be around 15 years old and it startles me. *Would that have been me as a teenager?* Hanging out at the shop after school and answering phones for my dad?

I find myself frozen in place and only come unglued when a tool clatters to the ground behind the shop walls. I shake my head and walk to the counter to place the bag on it.

"No, I just was dropping this off for Jake," I explain to the girl.

She stands up and turns to the door that leads to the back of the shop. "Oh, he is only cleaning up. I can go get him if you don't mind waiting a minute."

I feel the blood drain from my face at the thought of actually seeing him and talking to him in person. Driving by and dropping something off was as much as I had prepared myself for. "No, no. That's not necessary. Merry Christmas." And then swiftly turning, I head out the door.

chapter 28
Margo

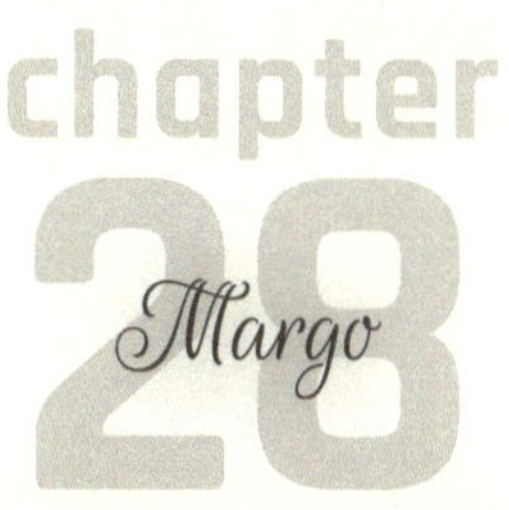

☕ **Ghosts of Christmas Past** - Margo in the Past

SOMETHING ABOUT THAT FIRST Christmas together as a married couple made me feel like we were an actual family, doing real family things. We went out and got our own Christmas tree; we went shopping for each other, and we made our decorations because it was expensive to outfit an entire house for our first Christmas together.

"Do we really need to have decorations?" Jake had asked me as I rolled out some clay on the counter.

I smacked his hand away as the soft dough was too tempting for him to not push into it, leaving a fingerprint behind. "It won't feel like Christmas without all the decorations. Besides, I'm only making a handful of ornaments for our tree. We can add more each year."

Jake held up a cookie cutter, inspecting it. "I suppose. But at least if we made cookies, we could eat them."

"You mean, if *I* made cookies, then *you* could eat them."

I gave him a knowing look because the poor man could barely make himself toast. Before marrying me, he survived on pre-made meals from the grocery store and anything that came in a tin can.

"You, me- it's the same thing." He winked and headed into the living room to see what was on the television.

When he was happy like this, my world was complete. And as much as he could be a pest with his teasing, I couldn't help myself from doing everything I could to pull more of it out of him. It was my addiction, and I always needed another hit of it.

The temptation was too great, so I called out to him, "Give me an hour to finish here and then we can go caroling."

I grinned to myself and waited no more than a second before hearing him snort and chuckle to himself, "Not a chance, Mar." *Yeah, I made that happen.*

I so badly wanted to make that first Christmas magical for us, but mostly Jake. I knew holidays were hard for him and I wanted to start our lives together by opening a new chapter on what Christmas could be for him. Christmas was always my favorite holiday, and I desperately wanted someone to share it with me. Or, at the very least, let me pour out my love for it on them.

"Doesn't that seem kind of pathetic?" Jake pointed to the small pile of presents under our Christmas tree.

This was our third Christmas in the house, and the ornaments on the tree grew each year. Even our first clay ornaments were still hanging. Jake had joined me in the process and painted delicate snowflakes, farm scenery, and snowmen on them with some watercolor paints. Every year, I wrapped them carefully when packing away the decorations. Other years I had made our initials out of slices from a log and hung them with red ribbons. This year, I had dehydrated orange slices to give the tree a pop of color. The orange slices were also easier to make with a little one underfoot.

This would be Alice's second Christmas- not that she understood what it meant or why a large tree was sitting in the corner of our living room. She especially didn't understand why she couldn't pull at the needles on the branches.

I looked at the pile of silver and red-wrapped Christmas presents. "What do you mean? It's only three of us who live here," I had reminded him.

Jake shook his head and headed for the front door. "Just seems like we must not have a lot, if that's all we managed to give each other for Christmas."

I knew he didn't mean what I was getting for him. He never cared about that. That Christmas I was planning to give him a beautiful set of high-end watercolor paints. I had tucked away some money of my own by secretly watching a couple of the kids on our street while Jake was at work. The other moms loved having a couple of hours to themselves to get ready for Christmas, or nap and pretend that Christmas wasn't looming over them. They also always dropped off and picked up in the middle of the day while Jake was at work. And they always paid in cash.

I knew that the family bank account was for both of us, even though he was the only one working. But he would never be okay with me spending that much on a gift for him. Even if he loved painting and wanted to do more to improve his skills.

With Alice still being so young, I hadn't seen the point of spoiling her with gifts she couldn't even play with yet, anyway. I had thought Jake would be happy with my logical reasoning for once and how I avoided my impulsive urges to buy every cute thing I saw at the store.

But seeing the small amount of spending for our small family, it made Jake feel like he wasn't doing enough. Like he wasn't enough. And whenever he didn't feel like he was enough, he would remove himself from the equation entirely.

That first Christmas without Jake, we were really without him. He had been moved out of the house for multiple months already. I wasn't expecting him to show up on the doorstep right after I had asked him to leave. But, deep down, I had hoped he would have found his way back to us by then. By putting my foot down, it was equally impulsive and bravado as it was finally setting a boundary in my life. A big reason I dared to do it was believing it would finally snap him out of his stupor and come back to us with open arms.

"I can't believe what a mistake I was making all these years, Mar," he would have said to me and I would've been so happy that I finally took that step to force that change in him.

But you can't decide for someone else to change, and you certainly can't be the one who does the changing for them. I get that now, many years later, but not then. And not when I sat outside the front door asking him to leave. I had finally taken control of my life, but I couldn't let go. I still felt like I could make the best decisions for him and our family, and I was still trying to pull those strings.

Right after leaving, Jake regularly deposited money into the family bank account. He never withdrew money from it, so it essentially became my account with a drip feed of money to pay for our living expenses. A larger deposit came that first December that he was gone, and a phone call telling me to buy something nice for me and Alice.

"What will you do for Christmas this year, Jake?" I had hesitantly asked him, knowing he had no one.

"All that matters is that you and Alice have a good Christmas. Don't worry about me." I'm not a worrier but, of course, I worried. My brain spun in circles, seeking an answer about how to maintain the boundary I firmly set when sending him away. I continually ran into every dead end of that maze, slamming into the guilt of knowing I was the one who forced his world to shatter. And he had no one left anymore to help him put it back together.

By the time Christmas came around the next year, Alice and I had found a rhythm. We were out of the *firsts* now. It was no longer the first Easter, first Christmas, or first birthday without Jake- without her daddy.

Jake had settled in a town a driving distance away. He had started up his own mechanic's shop and did handiwork on the side. He was seeing a therapist somewhat regularly and sometimes dipped his toes into the AA meetings. Committing to going to the meetings and maintaining sobriety were two different decisions to make, and he flip-flopped between them both. But he seemed to have found a rhythm of treading water, barely enough to keep his head afloat.

Sometimes we spoke on the phone, and sometimes I attended a therapy session with him. It hurt less each time to hear from him. We would talk a lot about Alice, and I would give him pictures every few months when I saw him. In exchange, he would give me a letter for Alice. I would stay up at night and read each of the letters, usually through teary eyes. Not once did I give the letter to Alice, and Jake never asked if I did. Deep down I'm sure he knew because he only got pictures from me and no replies.

You can't keep Alice from her dad. The guilt would eat a raw wound inside of me after each conversation with Jake. But after some days would pass and our routine would flow, that guilt would subside to a dull throbbing ache I could learn to live with.

I'm not keeping her from him. I am only protecting her until he comes back. This script ran through my head often enough to create a deep trench in my brain, as I would rationalize my decisions to myself. It would all be worth it in the end when he would come back and we would be a family again. It was harder to buy into it as each year passed, but with each year, the stack of letters grew and the hole I dug myself into was deeper than I could climb out of.

But, that third Christmas without Jake, he did show up at the door. He knocked, but he left before Alice or I saw him. Resting against the railing by the front door was a shiny red bike with glittering streamers hanging from the handlebars. The bike was new and must have cost Jake many extra side projects to afford it on top of paying for our two households.

The card simply said *Merry Christmas* and Alice assumed it was a late delivery from Santa that he had forgotten in his sleigh from the night before. I hadn't even realized my heart was racing with panic until I saw it wasn't signed by Jake. There would be no domino effect to unfold that Daddy had been back home. That Daddy had been there and then he left. *Again.*

But, years later, I would find myself continually wondering what would've happened if Alice had opened the door to see her dad standing on the front porch with a bike. Or if he had signed his name, and we called to say thank you. What exactly could've happened if I wasn't holding onto controlling everything so tight?

Christmas as a mother is such a joy, but Christmas as a granny is the greatest gift for the heart. Watching as things you chose to do as a mom become part of a family tradition as they are then passed down. No longer was Christmas only the two of us. We were now a family of four nestled around the tree.

Travis was such a welcomed addition to the family. His relationship with Alice was a pleasure to watch as it unfolded. I could see so much of my parent's marriage in their love- the steady devotion and commitment. They were able to sand away any of the roughness Jake and I experienced, or maybe they were blessed to never have it in their marriage in the first place. Travis worked hard to provide for his family, and he dutifully showed up repeatedly.

Their marriage was surrounded by myself and Travis' parents supporting them, and cheering them on.

Alice, my precious daughter. Oh, how much she reminds me of Jake. Her strive for perfection, her thoughtful eyes, and the love she shares with others. I had spent Alice's childhood so fully wrapped up in her; we were inseparable. I loved her so much that my heart ached. I wondered if my mom felt that way about me, even if she rarely expressed it outwardly. My tap remained open, on full blast, pouring it generously upon Alice every chance I could. If my mom had more of a silent, trickling stream of her love, I had likely been in danger of drowning Alice in mine.

If only Jake could have seen that the goodness in him had grown into this beautiful young woman. She had thrived, despite both of us.

Sometimes I wondered what it would have been like if Jennifer had lived to be Jennifer. If she had been part of our family, would Jake be sitting here with us, too? The ghosts of the life that could have been, the memories and kids we were supposed to have here. If those moments ever surfaced, all I had to do was stare down at pudgy Sadie with her wide eyes of wonder.

"Up Granny!" she would squeal at me, oozing joy, and I would lift that little bundle into my lap and kiss her neck until her giggles filled the room.

The more I chose to live in the moments in front of me, and how they blossomed and grew, the more I could let my regrets and guilt retreat away. As the years continued to march on, the less and less space there was for the *what-ifs*. Even if they festered in the darkness, I gave them very little of my time.

"Merry Christmas, Jake," I had said when he picked up the phone. Now that Alice was an adult, we didn't have the same need to stay in touch as we did when she was young.

If my call surprised him, he didn't let me know. "Merry Christmas, Mar."

The call was brief, but it felt right. I had just finished celebrating Christmas with Alice, Travis, and Sadie. Sadie was quickly approaching four years old. The full circle of Alice being that age when I set off the domino effect of the last couple of decades wasn't lost on me.

We didn't chat long, but I felt like it wasn't Christmas without calling to wish him well.

"Hope it's okay that I'm calling you, but I found this painting of a stained glass window and thought of you," Jake had said when he called me a few months later out of the blue.

"Did you buy it?" I had asked while unloading some groceries in the kitchen.

"I always buy them."

I remembered the empty space above the mantle in the living room. "You should start painting them instead of buying them," I had suggested.

"It's easier to collect something than to make it."

There was a familiarity to visiting with him again. Alice wasn't a weight on the conversation. I was just Margo, and he was just Jake. We could pretend that's all we were.

"I don't work on Fridays," he had said one day. "Can I call you again, then?"

"I'd like that, Jake."

"Talk soon, Mar."

chapter 29

Margo

"GRANNY, IT'S CHRISTMAS! It's Christmas!" I open my eyes in time to see Sadie flying into my bedroom, still wearing the candy cane-striped pajamas she got for Christmas Eve. Her hair is still separated into two braids, but just barely. The frizz of her curls is poking out like a halo around her head and her cheeks are the perfect rosy pink. She climbs up onto the end of my bed and pats my foot that is buried under the bedspread to make sure I know she's there.

Before I can even open my mouth in response, Alice comes in hot on her heels. "Sadie Margaret!" Alice is whisper-yelling, as if I had slept through Sadie's Christmas greeting to begin with. "We told you to wait until Granny woke up!"

Alice is already dressed for the day in a fuzzy purple sweater and a pair of black leggings. Her hair is pulled back in a ponytail, likely because she's already been busy in the kitchen getting the day started.

"Merry Christmas Sadie. Merry Christmas Alice." I grin at them both. "It seems like Santa's elves didn't sprinkle the same magical energy on me that you got." I wink at Sadie, who I am sure has been anxiously waiting to tear into her presents for the past hour already. I'm surprised I have managed to sleep past her first waking up.

In years past, when I would sleep over on Christmas Eve, I was woken up around 6am by Miss Sadie. She would skip her parent's room and come straight to me. "Can we open presents while Mommy and Daddy sleep?" she would ask me.

I would pull her onto the bed with me and snuggle into her body, which was buzzing with excitement. "We better not. If we break the rules on Christmas, the magic will disappear."

Eventually, I would feel her body relax into mine. Once or twice we both drifted back to sleep, but usually, we would lie there and wait for Alice's slippers to shuffle down the hall.

"Mommy says we can open presents as soon as you are awake." Sadie hops off the bed and is ready to run back to the living room. "And now you're awake!"

"Sadie, you don't touch any of those presents until everyone is sitting by that Christmas tree!" Alice calls after her as she takes off back to the living room. She lets out a breath and then follows Sadie down the hall. "Let me know when you're ready to get up and I'll come help you, Mom," she calls back down the hall towards my room.

I tentatively stretch out my legs, stiff from laying in the same position all night with my tender hip. I probably could have done with another hour or two of sleep, but there are only so many Christmas mornings like this. *I've got the rest of my life to sleep.*

Travis helped me out to the living room and got me settled comfortably on one of the couches. I opted to stay in my pajamas like Sadie. It's too bad we don't match. Although, given my hip, my light blue plaid nightgown is much easier to get on and off. My favorite quilt is wrapped around me and Alice is boiling some water for tea. Travis returns from the kitchen carrying a tray of banana and chocolate chip muffins for us to eat for breakfast. *So this is what Alice was busy with this morning.* He passes me a plate with a banana muffin and then settles on the ground near Sadie. Sadie is looking less and less patient by the minute.

"Sadie, did you know some people don't open their presents until after dinner on Christmas? Do you think we should try that tradition?" I tease and bite my tongue as I watch Sadie's jaw fall open on loose hinges.

"That's crazy, Granny! No way!" She shakes her head and her frazzled braids go flying.

Alice enters the living room with two mugs of hot tea and sits beside me on the couch, passing me a mug.

"Alright Sadie, you can pick *one* present with your name on it and open it," Alice says, and that's all the encouragement Sadie needs before wrapping paper goes flying.

"It's a doll! Look, Granny! A friend for your dolls!" Sadie wraps her arms around it with a big hug, the plastic head tucked into the crook of her neck.

I smile at her. "Your other dolls will be so happy to have another friend."

We take turns going around opening presents until all the adults run out and Sadie is the only one left with a few more tucked under the tree. I am spoiled with a new robe and slippers, some quilting cotton, and a new mug that says *Granny's Have Extra Spice*. Sadie has a pile of new toys, books, nail polishes, and her doll surrounding her.

"Well, Ladybug. I think that was the last present," Alice says as she checks to make sure nothing got pushed to the back of the tree.

"Granny, could I paint your nails?" Sadie is eyeing up the nail polishes Jennifer picked up for me. "I could paint each nail a different color! Or I could try to do polka dots."

I laugh. "That sounds very colorful, Sadie. Exactly what I love, but how about you practice on yourself first?" Mischievously I glance at Alice. "And maybe your mom, too."

Alice gives me a look. "We can *all* get our nails done, Sadie. How about later, though?"

I yawn and shift slightly on the couch. "I think later is a good idea. Granny might lie down for a bit of a rest now that the presents are over."

Alice turns to face me. "Everything okay, Mom?"

"Oh yes, just an early start to the day." I smile to ease her worries that are never far away. "And the more rest I get, the quicker this 'ole hip will heal." I tentatively pat my hip.

"Wait!" Sadie shouts as she leaps up from her kingdom of presents. "I have a gift for Granny and Mommy!" She runs down the hall into her room.

Alice looks at Travis. "Are you behind this?" Alice asks.

Travis looks as curious as the rest of us and raises his hands in defence. "I don't have a clue."

Sadie walks back in with both hands behind her back. She has a giant smile on her face and I could squeeze her onto my lap if it wouldn't hurt me so much. "What's behind your back?" I ask her.

"I found it!" Sadie exclaims as she thrusts a photo towards me.

Alice comes back over to sit beside me on the couch and looks at the photograph. "I knew that photo was somewhere. Mom, this is you and that red bike you told me about."

I gently brush my fingers over the two faces in the photo, smiling at the camera. "Where did you find this, Sadie?" My voice comes out as a whisper.

"In the closet in Mommy's old bedroom. Why were you riding your bike in the snow, Granny?" Sadie giggles at the idea of biking in the winter.

"That's not me, Sadie," I breathe out.

"Sure it is, Mom." Alice reaches to grab the photo to look closer. "Oh wait, that's not at the farm. That fence in the background, wait…"

"That's you," I finish the sentence for her.

Sadie is scrambling to see the photo again. "It's Mommy?"

"Careful, Sadie!" Travis jumps up to help guide Sadie to move around me instead of across me.

"Why did you get me a bike for Christmas, Mom?" Alice asks. "I don't even remember this."

Some of the memory comes back to me. I remember our neighbor, Peter, shoveling outside on the driveway when Alice saw her bike on the porch. He was nice enough to take a picture of Alice and me with her new bike. I think I remember her begging me to let her ride it down the driveway only once. But, I don't think it was me that bought it for her.

"I don't think I did, Alice." I rub my head, the dull ache of my headache coming back again. "Travis, would you mind helping me back to my room?"

"Of course." Travis comes over to help me to my feet. I lean into him for balance and use the cane from the hospital in my other hand for extra support.

Alice and Sadie are still looking at the picture. "Then who did buy it for me?" Alice asks.

I yawn and shrug my shoulders as I shuffle slowly towards my room. "I don't know. Maybe your dad? He was really trying."

I doze in and out of sleep, shifting my weight, and trying to find a comfortable position. Instead, I focus on relaxing and enjoying the sounds of Sadie chattering to herself while playing with her new toys in her bedroom. The phone rings in the kitchen and I consider getting up to join the rest of the family, the clock shows it's almost time for lunch, but I'm not feeling too hungry. The problem with sitting and lying around most of the day is you don't work up a big appetite.

"Oh, hi Jake." Alice's soft voice carries down the hall and I perk up at the mention of his name. "Actually, she's lying down for a rest right now. Can I have her call you back once she's awake?"

I feel myself getting up and walking down the hall to hear his voice, but it's all in my head. I can't urge my muscles to actually do anything but lie here and listen. My mind floats to the red bike, and I try to unearth the memory. *Was it Jake?* Was he there for that Christmas? Did I tell Alice?

Let them be.

"Merry Christmas, Jake," the words flow out like a whisper and I settle back into my dreams. "We will chat again soon."

"DO YOU THINK SHE had a good Christmas?" I roll over and snuggle into Travis.

It's Boxing Day, and it's only a matter of minutes until Sadie is awake and looking for food. Christmas is all the hustle for Travis and me, but pure magic for Sadie. Boxing Day is a holiday for us. The fridge is full of leftovers and Sadie will be occupied with her new toys.

Travis brushes my hair out of my face. "She seemed very happy. Did *you* have a good Christmas?"

I nod. It was not our usual Christmas, but at the same time, it was. We were all together and happy. "That photo Sadie found- it got me thinking again about journaling Mom's memories. Honestly, I've been putting it off because I don't even know where to start," I confess.

I had bounced around the ideas of a joint journal project, or a scrapbook, and even went so far as to consider bringing in someone to help us put something together. When I sink my teeth into an idea, it can very easily snowball. But this idea had become stuck, wedged into my brain, nagging at me. I didn't know which direction to run with it so it just sat there and festered. And then it kept feeling like a bigger and bigger *thing* that I needed to deal with.

"I think you're making it into a bigger project than it needs to be. You don't need to overcomplicate it," Travis says.

I roll my eyes. I know I'm a perfectionist, but of all the times to get something right, it's now. These are my mom's memories and I want to, no, I *need* to remember them. I prop myself up on one elbow to look at Travis. "And what do you suggest I do to simplify it?"

Travis stares up at the ceiling, thinking for a bit, before turning his head to face me. "Did you ever see those rocks Sadie was painting for your mom?" he asks.

When I saw the heart painted on the rock by Mom's bed, I asked her where she got it from. She told me Sadie had been working on a special project to protect her memories. I hadn't seen the other rocks Sadie had painted besides that red heart, though.

"I saw the red heart by Mom's bed." Her spelling of *L-U-V-E* still tugged a smile at my lips.

Travis drums his fingers along my back. "Sadie found a way to keep the memories alive by painting the rocks. It's as simple as that."

It is a simple idea, and I'm sure it will help keep Mom's memories alive for Sadie. "Do you think she'll remember Mom? Like the real version of Granny?" I ask, my brain hopping down another rabbit trail. Sadie is still so young. I only have a handful of memories of myself from that age. The further that Mom's memory deteriorates, the more memories Sadie will have that will be fractured and disjointed from the Granny that she was. My chest aches at the thought of Sadie not remembering Mom. My mom is the best granny to Sadie, and she was supposed to continue being that awesome granny for a long, long time.

Travis interrupts the runaway train of my thoughts. "I think Sadie will remember your mom however you want her to be remembered. You can tell Sadie stories and pass on traditions to keep those moments alive," he reassures me.

I lay back down on his chest and wrap my arm around him.

"Why don't you paint some memory rocks of your own? Your mom already has a whole bowl of them," Travis offers.

I suppose Sadie's idea could work for me too, and it would be easy to do. "But what memories do I paint? And how do I know if they're true?"

"You paint the ones that feel like they matter." He kisses my head and then wiggles out from under me so he can climb out of bed. "Focus on the feelings, facts make it complicated."

"Says the lawyer," I smirk at the irony and roll to my back so I can stretch out in the bed. "Besides, I like facts."

Travis walks to the chair by the window, pulls a white shirt over his head, and then tugs on a pair of grey joggers. "And that's why you need Sadie and your mom to help you. You can all paint the rocks together, all of your favorite memories combined."

I watch as he heads down the hall to make breakfast. I guess I know how to spend our Christmas holidays while Mom recovers.

"Are you sure you're fine to paint at the table, Mom? We can move you to the couch or do this another day," I offer. I want to get this project started, but I also don't want to set back my mom's recovery. I've already waited this long; I can wait a few more weeks.

"Nonsense. Let's paint!" Mom holds up a paintbrush in the air, like she's going to lead a revolution. Sadie shoots hers up in the air too, beaming at all of us.

"Sadie," I gently chastise. "Paintbrush down. We're painting the rocks, not the kitchen."

Both Sadie and my mom obey, lowering their brushes in defeat. "Guess we better listen to the captain, Sadie-bum." Mom turns to me, smiling. "We could paint the kitchen, though, too," she offers mischievously.

I turn to Jennifer, who is sitting beside me, and shake my head. "I should remember to hide the paints for when her hip heals. Otherwise, I might come home to striped cabinets."

"Ah! That's what I'm going to paint. A daisy, like the cabinets in my kitchen," Mom says, smiling. I remember painting them with her when I was quite young. She had been on a mission that month with project after project, desperate to keep us both busy. They always made me smile when I entered the kitchen. None of my friends had cabinets in their house that they were allowed to paint. Looking back, I'm surprised we never had a mural going down the hallway to match.

The rocks are spread out in front of us to choose from. Mom has already selected one to start painting her daisy.

Jennifer is also joining us in our crafting mission. She had Christmas Eve and Christmas off work, but the change in routine was upsetting Mom. So, Jennifer decided to come back to the house, but only on a part-time basis over the Christmas holidays. Even though this feels like an intimate family moment, I'm glad to have Jennifer here. It takes off the pressure and keeps me from overcomplicating it.

Sadie is trying to decide between the dark round rock and the grey oval one.

"What are you going to paint, Sadie?" I ask as I squeeze out some paints on the tray in front of me.

"A Christmas tree!" she exclaims as she picks up the grey oval rock. "Because this year I got to put the star on top."

I smile at her. I wonder if 20 years from now that's all she'll remember from that moment, or if she'll still remember the disappointment of not decorating the tree with Granny too.

Travis startles me when he puts his hands on my shoulders and leans down to whisper in my ear, "Feelings, babe. Feelings, not facts."

He pulls away and nods to Mom, Sadie, and Jennifer. "You ladies have fun and don't cause too much trouble. I'm going to shovel the driveway."

"Out Daddy! No boys allowed!" Sadie points to the door with her paintbrush in hand, green paint dripping to the floor. "Oops!"

Jennifer grabs a wipe and cleans up the mess while Travis heads outside. She settles back into her chair and

I watch Sadie and Mom happily painting away. Jennifer is eyeing up her rock and starts looking through the paint options. The blank rocks taunt me and my indecisiveness.

"I'm going to paint a needle and thread," Jennifer announces while studying the paintbrushes. "Well, maybe a quilt instead. These brushes aren't very tiny."

Mom smiles. "Ah yes, I do love to sew." She glances up at Jennifer. "And I have loved teaching you."

"And teaching me too!" Sadie pipes up from the end of the table. She's learned a few different stitches and has almost filled her embroidery hoop with different colors. Soon she will be begging to stitch some flowers into her jeans, and I can't wait to see the results.

"Yes, I've loved teaching you too, Sadie," Mom says. She puts her paintbrush down and pats my hand. "I love having all my girls together. Even if only one of my daughters inherited my sewing genes."

Jennifer gives me a knowing nod and I grab the closest rock to me, a round white one. It's getting easier each time to let one of Mom's confused comments roll off my back. Jennifer has reminded me it will be all-consuming to spend my time correcting every little thing. I never did ask Mom about the box of baby clothes and the cloth marked Jennifer. Either she won't remember, or I'll question the story she tells. Either way, I'm trying to let the questions gradually slide away.

"What are you painting, Mommy?" Sadie asks from her end of the table. She has somehow managed to get a streak of yellow paint across her left cheek already.

"I think I will paint a sunflower. We used to grow them in the front yard every year." I squirt out some yellow paint and start painting the leaves.

"We should plant sunflowers again this year. Maybe I can get Jake to water them for us," Mom chatters away while grabbing another rock to paint.

"Grandpa?" Sadie pipes up and then clamps her mouth tight, looking back at her rock.

Jennifer and I stare wide-eyed at each other and then at Sadie. *How would she know that?*

Mom doesn't even miss a beat. "Yes, your Grandpa."

"He will probably do a good job remembering," Sadie replies, not scared anymore that she let a secret slip. She's staring down at her rock, adding dots of different colors to decorate her Christmas tree.

"Why do you say that, Ladybug?" I manage to clear my throat and ask.

"Well, you're not much like Granny. So I guess you must be like your daddy. And you love lists and are good at checking things off." She sets down her paintbrush and holds up her rock. "Done!"

Mom looks over at Sadie. "Your grandpa and your mom both love to get everything done and always try to do it the right way. But sometimes the lists just get too heavy."

"Mommy's lists aren't heavy, they're just really long," Sadie responds.

We laugh and fall into silence as we finish the rocks we are painting. I wonder what is going through everyone else's heads. Sadie is concentrating on painting her third rock, this one is a slice of pizza. Jennifer is rinsing her brushes in a cup and watching my mom. I have finished my sunflower rock and am now painting a cat's face.

I had spent an entire year begging my mom to get a cat when I was nine years old. You would think Mom was a cat person given how much she loved to sit and sew or read.

But, no, she wasn't interested in having a cat around the house. That entire year, I drew cats, dreamed of cats, and wore clothes with cat paw prints on them.

Our neighbors, Peter and Suzanne, had a cat who ended up having kittens. Mom woke me up a couple hours after I went to bed and we walked over to their house to see them right after they were born. She never said it out loud to me, but I think she was considering letting us bring home one kitten once they got bigger. Turns out, though, I was allergic to cats. But I loved the fact that Mom was willing to do that for me.

"I can't believe I almost brought that cat home with us," Mom says and laughs to herself. "I should've guessed you would be allergic since I am, too."

"You are allergic to cats, too? How did I not know that?" I ask.

Mom shrugs. "It's not something that ever affected us."

"But you were going to let me bring one of Peter and Suzanne's kittens home with us while you were allergic to cats?" I had always loved that my mom was willing to get me a cat, even when she wasn't a cat person herself. But being allergic to them and still willing to do it? That's next level.

"I figured if I kept my room off limits, then maybe we could find a way to make it work." She dips her paintbrush into the water to rinse it off. "I was mostly just going to wing it."

Jennifer laughs. "I could never imagine my mom doing that."

I finish painting the whiskers and look over at Mom, since she's not painting anymore. She is rubbing the side of her head with her hand.

"You still have that headache, Mom?" I ask her, concerned.

She drops her hand to her lap. "It comes, and it goes. I just need to lie down again. I usually am better after a rest."

I glance at Jennifer and I know she is mentally making a note of how often these headaches have been occurring the last week since her surgery.

"We should call the doctor tomorrow if it doesn't go away," I say. I'm going to call the doctor regardless, but Mom hates when I hover and worry. "Sadie, you can keep painting, but Jennifer and I are going to help Granny settle for a nap."

Jennifer and I help steady Mom between us as we walk her back toward her room. "Don't you worry about me. I'll only have a quick rest and then you can show me all the rocks you painted."

chapter 31
sadie

I'M SITTING ON THE FLOOR in my room, hiding from Mommy and Daddy. I'm supposed to be getting dressed, but I don't want to leave the house. Especially not in the dress Mommy wants me to wear. She laid it out on the bed before going to take a shower. Instead of putting it on, I keep playing with my dolls. I don't want to make Mommy upset with me, but I don't understand. I keep asking her why I have to wear it, why I have to go, and why no one will answer any of my questions with real answers.

At school, Mrs. Anderson always talks to us like we're teenagers. She says we are all mini adults in training and she won't baby us anymore. I like that. She lets us use oil pastels and acrylic paints too. Some kids have wrecked some of their clothes, so she's not supposed to use those with us anymore unless she gets permission from our parents. I only messed up one of my shirts, but Mommy and Daddy always say that my clothes never last me, anyway.

At the start of the year, we all had to say our favorite color and create a painting using only that color. Robbie chose black.

"Black isn't a color," Mrs. Anderson had told him. "Black is what you get when you take everything away. It means it is absent of any color."

I don't understand what *absent* has to do with it. But I agree that black is definitely not a color. Black is empty, but it's also full. It's *too* full. It's overflowing with being sad and alone.

Mommy went out to the mall a few days ago and got me a special black dress to wear this weekend.

"I hate it! Why do I have to wear it?" I had asked when Mommy brought it home to show me. She wanted me to try it on, and I did because Mommy looked too tired to fight me.

"Because that's what happens," Mommy had said. She cut off the tag with her scissors and gave me a big hug. *But that's not a real answer.* I wish Mommy and Daddy would talk to me like Mrs. Anderson does. Maybe then I could finally start to understand things.

I have been hearing *not real* answers a lot lately. Well, I didn't want it to happen, but I still want to know why.

The only answer I know is that I hate that dress. I don't want to wear it, and I won't wear it.

Even Daddy is on Mommy's side. He wants me to wear the dress, too. "People wear black to show they're sad while they say their goodbyes, Ladybug."

I want to ask how we can say goodbye when Granny is already gone? But they probably won't give me a real answer.

And besides, Granny likes pink.

Our house has been very busy since *it* happened. Lots of people have come to bring us food, some delivery trucks brought us flowers, and there has been lots of crying. Mommy and Daddy take turns coming into my room to talk to me. I don't like leaving my room because then I have to walk past Granny's room.

The front door is closing again, and I stand on my bed to see out my bedroom window. A silver truck is backing out of the driveway slowly. It looks like the truck that Peter drives. Peter was Granny's old neighbor. Their truck has already come to the house three times this week. Each time they drop off something for dinner, and usually a plate of cookies, too. I hope they brought some chocolate chip ones this time.

"How's it going, Ladybug?" Daddy pokes his head in. Mommy's crying in the bedroom, so I guess it's Daddy's turn to check on me.

I shrug my shoulders and climb down from the bed. Daddy knows I'm not supposed to stand on my bed, but his face says he's not going to get mad at me. Sitting on the bed, I reach for my doll from Christmas and fidget with the hair. I have been trying to put it into braids like Mommy does with my hair, but I can't figure out how to do it. I doubt she's going to show me for a while.

"Did you want to come watch a show with me? I think someone dropped off some yummy cookies too," Daddy offers. *I knew it.*

"No thanks. But can I have a cookie later?" Daddy glances down the hall to their bedroom since Mommy's crying has stopped. "I just want to play some more," I say.

"If you want to do something though, you'll tell me, right? I'm going to check on Mommy quickly."

I nod and push my doll off my lap.

"And you will need to get your dress on too, okay? But if you're going to eat, do that first." He starts to close the door to my room but leaves it cracked open instead.

What I want is to go back to last week. I want to get rid of that black dress and everyone knocking on our door with more food. I don't want to hear Mommy crying anymore. And I don't want to feel a big lump of sad inside.

I don't understand why we have all these things we need to do, places we need to be, and clothes we need to wear. Granny is dead. She's gone, and she isn't coming back. I just want to stay in my room and not have to do anything.

When Granny left, it was very loud. I had woken up to sirens and Mommy talking loudly in Granny's bedroom. There were lots of other voices too, but I couldn't hear Granny's. Daddy had come into my room to see if I was awake.

"What's going on?" I had asked while rubbing the sleep out of my eyes.

"Can I lay in bed with you for a bit?" he asked, climbing into bed with me and wrapping his arms around me. We lay quietly for a few minutes until I started to squirm because I wanted to go out into the hall.

"Sadie," my dad whispered to me. "Something happened last night while Granny was sleeping, and it made her stop breathing."

"Will the doctor make her breathe again?" They had already fixed her hip, so maybe she would only need to be in the hospital for a few days again. Maybe this time I could ride in the ambulance with her. "That's what doctors do. They fix us."

Daddy took a big breath, and I wondered where Mommy was. *Did she go with Granny in the ambulance?* "No, Ladybug. The doctors won't be able to fix Granny this time. She died, I'm sorry."

The world was so loud outside my bedroom, thumping and talking. But everything was so silent and still in my room. "No Daddy. Granny wouldn't have left without saying good-bye," I had said. *Granny always said goodbye.*

I tried to fight the dress, but Mommy's face looked so tired. I still have my nail polish on my nails that I got from Granny for Christmas. Mommy had already removed hers because she said she couldn't wear colorful polka-dot nails for a funeral. I think Granny would have liked it though, Granny loves color. I decided to leave mine on my nails and Mommy said that was okay.

"Is *everyone* going to be wearing black?" I don't think I have ever been in a room where everyone is wearing the same color before.

"Yes, everyone will be wearing black." Mommy carefully guides the brush through my curly hair.

"Will Granny be sad that everyone is wearing black? She doesn't like black," I mumble.

"No, Sadie. Granny won't be sad," Mommy replies. That makes me happy because everyone else is already sad. I'm glad Granny won't be one of them.

I am wearing my pink socks with my black dress, though. Mommy didn't feel like fighting me on that. "I think my socks will make her smile," I say, wiggling my toes.

"Maybe, Ladybug," Mommy whispers. She uses a comb to separate my hair so she can put it into a long braid down the back of my dress. "I think Granny would like that very much."

Sitting for a long time makes me squirm, so I watch in the mirror's reflection for when Mommy will be done braiding. I don't even look like Sadie right now in this black dress with my wild curls in a braid. I wonder what Granny looks like now.

Mommy and Daddy went to something called a viewing last night. Mommy said it was a chance for them to say a last goodbye to Granny.

"But I want to say goodbye, too!" I had cried at the top of the stairs as they were getting their shoes on. Mommy had asked Jennifer if she would be able to stay with me while they went. The viewing was only for family, and Jennifer had said she would love to hang out with me. Jennifer sat beside me at the top of the stairs and held my hand while I cried.

Mommy had knelt in front of me. "Granny's not really in her body anymore, Ladybug."

"Then how can you say goodbye to her?" I had asked. *Adults make no sense.* Jennifer stayed sitting with me and rubbed my back.

"It's something that adults do to help them feel better. Granny loved you very much and she wouldn't want you to see her like this. She doesn't look like the Granny you remember," Mommy tried to explain.

But that didn't answer my question at all.

I had tried to argue with Mommy this morning that maybe I shouldn't go to the funeral today either. But Mommy said there would be lots of people who loved Granny there, and we were going to go as a family. I'm definitely one of those people and I bet the place will be full. Granny was the best.

"You're all done, Sadie." Mommy places the brush down my desk and smiles at my reflection in the mirror. "It's okay if you cry today, Sadie. Everyone there is sad and misses Granny. Even Mommy might cry."

That doesn't surprise me. Mommy has been crying a lot this last week, even if she tries to hide away in her bedroom. I have cried too and I really miss Granny. Sometimes, though, I play with one of my toys and for a little bit I forget Granny is gone. Then I feel extra sad, because I'm scared that means I forgot to miss Granny.

"Can I bring Granny's heart rock?" I ask as we head out of my room.

"I think Granny would have wanted you to have it, Ladybug."

I stand outside Granny's door, too scared to go in. "Can you get it for me, Mommy?" I ask.

"Of course."

I wait by the stairs while Mommy brings the rock out, quietly closing Granny's door behind her. It reminds me of Granny going down for a nap and we would all be quiet. I wonder if Granny has to take naps anymore.

Mommy places the rock into my hand and squeezes my fingers around it. "Alright, Daddy is outside waiting for us."

I rub the rock in my hands. Now I won't forget that Granny always loves me.

chapter 32

Alice

TRAVIS, SADIE, AND I are tucked together in a pew at the front of the church. The pastor offered for us to wait in the back and walk into the room at the beginning of the service, but I didn't want to see everyone's sad faces as we found our seats. Sadie is holding the red heart rock she painted for Mom in her lap. I reach over and squeeze her hand. She's been such a trooper through everything, but I worry about her being so young and going through all of this grief.

"How are you doing, Ladybug?" I ask, knowing she's heartbroken like the rest of us. No one had seen it coming. She had been recovering slowly from the surgery, but she was at home and getting better. The doctor figured it was a stroke during the night. He said she would have left peacefully and without pain. I wondered if maybe I had gone to bed later, or woken up earlier, if I would have noticed. *Could I have helped?*

Sadie nods her head and squeezes the rock. "What happens after this, Mommy?"

I kiss her head. "After today, we go back home. And we snuggle, talk, and cry as much as you want, okay?"

"Okay." She leans into me and I wrap my arm around her.

Travis leans over to whisper in my ear, "Your dad just came in and is sitting at the back. Just so you know."

I instinctively turn to look at the back of the room. I instantly regret my decision because there are so many faces looking towards me and at the front. They're all a mixture of sad, crying, and giving me soft smiles with heavy eyes. Some faces I recognize and others I don't. Sadie is right, though. It is strange to see everyone all dressed in black. Funerals equal black, and grief equals black. I had never thought of anything else before, except that's the way it is done. Mom would have loved that Sadie wore her pink socks and her bright nails. I hope she will always have Mom's spunk and spice.

As I finish taking in all the faces, I spot a man tucked into the back pew. His eyes instantly remind me of Sadie's. The way his hands are nervously folding and unfolding in his lap makes me certain that must be him. Everyone else in the room looks like they belong here, but don't want to be here. He looks like he doesn't know if he belongs here at all.

I turn back to the front and reply to Travis, "He shouldn't be sitting back there."

"Alice, I'm by your side all day today," he says and reaches over and takes my hand in his. "If he comes over,

I'll let him know you don't want to talk. But I think he just wants to slink in and out without causing a scene."

I shake my head because he misunderstands me. "No, he was her family. She would have wanted him up here." Our pew is empty except for us, but I also notice there are a couple of pews behind us with some empty seating. "Just not sitting beside us, though, okay?"

Travis squeezes my hand and releases it. Instantly, I miss his warmth. "Okay, babe." He stands and exits the pew to go back to talk to Jake.

I wrap both my arms around Sadie so she can snuggle more into my side.

After a few minutes, Travis settles back beside me and places his arm behind me across the top of the pew. "He's sitting a couple of rows behind us. He wanted to give you space," he whispers.

I nod. "How did you know it was him?" I ask Travis. It crosses my mind that neither of us has met my dad before.

"He looks like you, and I heard someone say they never thought they'd see the day Jake would be here."

Sadie looks up at me. "Is Grandpa here?"

Ever since we painted rocks, she has been curious to ask more about her mysterious grandpa. I have mostly been sidestepping the conversations and questions. I give her a small smile. "Yes, he is."

That sparkle in her eye lights up and it feels so comforting, it feels so normal. "Will I get to meet him?" she asks, looking around for who he might be.

Travis interjects on my behalf. "Probably not today, Ladybug."

Sadie pouts a little but accepts his answer, snuggling back into me.

I stroke her hair and ask, "Would you like to?"

"Was he Granny's best friend like you are Daddy's best friend?" she asks.

How else would you describe two people who fell in love, and had a family, but even when separate couldn't cut that last cord? "Yes, I think so."

Sadie smiles and passes her rock between her hands. "Then yes, I want to meet him."

I smile softly at Travis, and he holds my hand again. "Ok, Ladybug. One day you can probably meet him."

Somewhere between Suzanne playing the piano and the Pastor shuffling his papers, I am called to the front. I wasn't sure if I was going to get up in front of everyone and talk about my mom. I wasn't even sure where to start with what to write to say. But, here I am, walking to the front with a tight grip on some notes I wrote late last night, and a crumpled tissue in my other hand.

"Growing up, my mom was my everything. That never stopped, even as an adult," I begin shakily and take a deep breath in before continuing. "Where my mom saw her failures, all I saw was her love. She wasn't perfect, but none of us are. All this time, I thought she was this carefree, confident woman. I aspired to be like her, but felt stuck in my need for control. Turns out we weren't all that different after all. My mom spent her life believing she was the shadow and not the sun. But she was neither. To me, she was the whole world."

My voice catches and I look to Travis, who is nodding at me, encouraging me to keep going.

"I'd like to take a moment and share a story that she told me and Sadie a couple of months ago. She told us her version, but these past couple of weeks I've had too many hours to think back and recount our time together. Her version of the story wasn't entirely correct, so I figured I should give her the credit she deserves."

Sadie has perked up now, listening to what story of Granny's I am going to share. "I always thought my earliest memories were forever just my mom and I. But, I remember what was probably my third birthday only vaguely. I'm not even entirely sure I can piece together how it happened. Regardless, my mom worked hard to decorate a special birthday cake for me. All I saw was a plain, iced cake when I snuck into the kitchen and was so disappointed. But, to my surprise, my mom and my dad…"

I look up again and search the sea of faces for my dad's and see a knowing look on his face. "They revealed to me this beautiful cake covered in purple butterflies. And honestly, I'm probably rambling, but I'm just chasing the memories at this point. I'm clinging on to what connected me to her and searching for anything else cast my way."

I pause again and then continue, "In the last year, I have learned that we only see our lives through our own lens, and that's such a narrow view. My mom's life was full, vibrant, and overflowing when you look through it from each person's perspective who knew her and had the blessing of her touch on their life. I'll never know the whole woman that she was, but I'll always know who she was to me. I love you, Mom."

I expected her memories to be gone. I expected to grieve for her before she left us. In some ways, it's a bitter and twisted mercy that we still had most of her until her last day. And she still had the comfort and knowledge of us. But we weren't ready yet for her to leave. There was still so much left to share.

I am shaking outside by her grave, and not only because it's the start of January and the wind is ripping through my black dress and coat. I lean against Travis while holding Sadie's hand. I'm sure the pastor is saying perfectly pleasant words that are meant to comfort everyone here, but I only hear the rise and fall of his voice.

Slowly, people drift away to their vehicles to give space for the family to have their final moments. Travis had extended the invite to Jake to come to the cemetery as well. We also included Jennifer because she became such an important part at the end of my mom's journey. *The end*, it sounds so final.

"Travis, maybe you should take Sadie home. It's so cold out here and I just need a moment." I motion to Jennifer, who is making her way to the parking lot to give me some space. "Jennifer already offered to stay and give me a ride home."

Travis pulls me in for a hug and kisses me on the head. "Take all the time you need."

Travis scoops up Sadie to carry her back through the snow and I spot Jake lingering to the side before turning toward the parking lot.

"Jake, you called Mom on Fridays, right?" My voice startles both of us.

He nods and scratches his beard. "Like clockwork." His voice is more gruff than when I have heard it on the phone.

"Maybe one Friday you could call me and we could talk about her," I suggest tentatively before chickening out.

"I'd like that," he agrees.

I turn back to the grave and stare at the coffin that's still waiting to be covered by the pile of dirt on top of the snow.

"Oh, and Alice." I turn around to see that he has stopped to call back to me. "One of your birthdays hadn't turned out so good. Well, I had messed up, to be perfectly honest." He digs the toe of his boot into the snow. "Your mom had the idea of a do-over. That's why she worked so hard on that cake. It's why she worked so hard on all of us. She really wanted that do-over."

The tears stream down my cheeks, and the chilly wind makes them sting. I don't know what to say, so I just nod and watch him turn back and walk away.

I'm not ready to forgive him, but I would also like to talk about my mom and learn more about her story before me. My relationship with my dad, or lack thereof, isn't a weight that my mom bears alone. I could have asked questions, as an adult I could have gone looking for him. It feels a bit late in my life to add a dad. But maybe in time, I could find some room for Jake.

I think my parents were both dysfunctional in their own ways, both fighting their own demons. I love her, but I am also angry with her. She's not even here anymore, but I have to just sit with my anger and my grief. I don't know if talking with my dad will help heal those wounds or open them more. But I don't want to stay in one place stuck anymore. I won't know what a do-over will look like unless I take a chance and turn over that rock.

I kneel by Mom's grave, and the wet snow seeps through my dress around my knees. Everyone has left and Jennifer still stands off in the parking lot, waiting to drive me away. I dig my hands into the snow until I reach the frozen earth that Mom has been lowered into. My fingers probe at a rock that's embedded in the frozen grass and soil. I pull it up and brush it off. I remove my glove and rub my thumb over its surface. It's soothing. I can see why my mom did it.

Stroke stroke stroke. *Always my Mom.* Stroke stroke stroke. *I love you.*

epilogue

Alice

KNOCK, KNOCK.

"I'm coming!" I call to the person at the front door. I finish tying the yellow balloon in my hand and bounce it across the room to Travis, who is in the middle of blowing up a red balloon.

"Is someone here, Mommy?" Sadie calls from her room down the hall.

I head down the steps to the door and call back to her, "Yes, I'm getting the door now."

I open the door and step aside for him to enter the house. "You're early," I say, double-checking the time on my watch.

"Only by ten minutes," Jake responds and steps into the house, juggling a large cake box and a gift bag hanging from his wrist.

"Well, let's put you to work, then. We need to finish hanging up the balloons and streamers." I close the door and start climbing the steps before turning back to my dad. "Here, let me grab the cake from you."

"Hey Jake, good to see ya." Travis waves from behind his pile of balloons as we reach the top of the steps.

"Thanks for having me," Jake replies. "Where's the birthday girl?"

Sadie takes that as her queue to make a grand entrance. Her door flies open, bouncing off the wall, and she runs down the hall with her hair and dress flying behind her as she crashes into Jake. "Grandpa!!"

Without missing a beat, Jake scoops her up and spins her around in a circle as she squeals. "So, how old are you now, four?"

Sadie shakes her head, giggling. "No, silly. I'm ten!"

"What? No way, I don't believe you. If you're ten, you're probably too old to be getting spun around and having birthday parties," Jake teases.

"Never! Granny always said you're never too old for anything."

I pat her head and smile before heading into the kitchen to set the cake down. *Mom would have loved this party.* You would never guess that Sadie and my dad's relationship is only a couple of years in the making. They immediately formed a bond that, at times, has made me jealous of what I missed with him as my dad. But it's usually overshadowed by how relieved I am that she may have lost my mom, but she gained my dad.

Jake's and my relationship has not clicked together as easily as his with Sadie's, but we're making progress. There was still so much hurt and grief to process after Mom passed away, and I was not in a good place to open the door to my dad. Almost six months after the funeral, I called Jake and asked if he would meet me for coffee. We met in town, somewhere neutral. I wasn't ready to have him step into my house, and I wasn't ready to step into his world.

"Thanks for calling," he had said after we found a quiet spot in the corner with our drinks. Tea for me, coffee for him.

"I'm not sure how this is supposed to work." I fidgeted with my mug, blowing at the steam.

He mirrored my fidgeting and stirred his coffee aimlessly. "Me neither, but a start is a start."

That coffee visit was more silent and sipping than talking and bonding. But a start was a start, and our monthly chats slowly became weekly visits. Then the long silent pauses turned into hard questions and conversations.

A year ago was the first time I invited my dad over to the house. Travis thought it would be a good idea to have him over for dinner. It felt too personal to have him enter into the very heart of my life, but I can't try to form a relationship with the guy if I don't fully open the door and invite him in. It wasn't as awkward as the first coffee chat we had, and Sadie and Travis were a helpful buffer to keep the conversation flowing.

I open the box on the counter and see a beautiful cake. Sadie had requested a colorful birthday and Jake wanted to be the one in charge of the cake. "You really nailed the theme, Jake," I call out from the kitchen. The cake is covered in butterflies in every color and a rainbow-swirled border is piped around the edges.

"I had my niece make it for me. So I guess that makes her your cousin," Jake says. "You should have seen the explosion of icing in her kitchen when I picked it up."

Cousin? Logically I knew I had cousins, aunts, and uncles that I had never met. My dad had talked about his family during our visits, but he had always referred to them as my sister, my brother, my niece, or my nephew. I had never thought of them concerning me, though, as my aunt, uncle, or cousin. Turns out I have an entire family out there that would fill my side of the family tree, and I don't even know their faces or their names.

"Well, she did an excellent job," I say and wonder if or when I'll ever meet any of them.

"Alright, Sadie, make a wish and blow out your candles," I say, and hold my phone up to get a few more pictures of her behind the birthday cake.

The lights are dimmed down, and the light of the candles is giving her face an orange glow. Everyone around me cheers as she takes a big breath and blows out all ten candles in one pass.

"Let's eat cake!" Sadie announces and pumps her arms in the air, hoping the room will break out in a chant of *cake, cake, cake!*

A hand squeezes my shoulder and a woman leans into my ear to say, "Thanks for having us over."

I turn and hug her. "Thanks for coming, Suzanne. How are you guys?"

Suzanne, my mom's old neighbor, smiles at me. "We have been great. Peter is trying to cut back his hours at work and we are hoping to travel somewhere this winter. Be more adventurous and winter away and come back for the sunny weather."

"That sounds lovely! Will you rent out your house?" I ask.

I'm curious because Travis and I have talked a lot about what to do with Mom's house. Jake is still listed as the owner of the house until we decide what to do with it. So far, we have landed on the idea that we might rent it out and hold on to it as a future investment for Sadie. The idea of strangers living in it makes me very uncomfortable, but we can't leave it sitting empty anymore and I can't sell it.

Peter comes to join the conversation and passes Suzanne a paper plate with a slice of cake on it. "We actually listed our house for sale last week. Our realtor thinks it will sell fast, so the pressure is on."

I'm shocked. First, my mom is no longer living there, now Peter and Suzanne. "That road just won't feel the same anymore," I frown. "What will you do when you're not traveling, though?"

"We will find a short-term rental somewhere and purge our belongings so we won't need to have anything more than a storage unit for our sentimental items," Peter explains, and takes a big bite of his cake.

"Why don't you rent Mom's old house when you're not traveling?" The words are out of my mouth before I have even finished my thoughts. "We were thinking of looking for renters, and I would rather know the people moving in than strangers."

"Are you sure?" Suzanne asks and squeezes my arm. "We know how much that house means to you."

"I'm sure," I nod. "I'll talk to Travis tonight and we can put together the details."

"Talk to me about what?" Travis asks from behind me, holding a slice of cake.

I grab the fork from his plate and steal a bite. "I offered Peter and Suzanne to move into Mom's house. They listed their house and are going to be traveling."

"Sounds like a perfect fit to me," Travis says, swiping the fork back from me to eat a bite for himself.

"Well, I guess it's settled," Peter says and sticks out his hand to shake Travis'.

"Mommy! It's time for my wish," Sadie runs over to us and wipes her face with a napkin.

"And what was your wish?" I ask.

"I wanted a camera for my birthday and I got one! Now I want a picture of everyone together." Sadie turns to face into the room where everyone is finishing their cake. "Everyone squeeze together on the couch!"

I join in with everyone on the couch, squeezing together tightly to fit into Sadie's frame. She's directing people like she's a professional to make sure no one is getting cut off.

Jake walks over to Sadie and holds out his hand. "Here, let me take the picture and you go find a spot in the middle."

Sadie shakes her head and shoos him away. "No way! I want a picture of everyone I love. Go find a spot."

I squeeze in closer to Travis, so there's room at the end of the couch. "Here Jake, there's some room beside me." *Calling him dad still feels unnatural. Maybe one day.*

Jake sits beside me, half hanging over the edge. "There's no arguing with that one, is there?" he asks.

"Definitely not. She got a little bit of stubbornness from each of us, and that includes you," I smile.

"Cheese!" Sadie says.

Click.

want to know
more about Jake?

Turn the page for a sneak peek of the first chapter from the sequel, Memory Stains Left Behind, releasing October 2024!

follow for updates

Amelia
VENJOY

http://www.ameliavenjoy.com

@ameliavenjoy.writes on Instagram

did you enjoy the book?

Go to the link below or scan the QR code.
It takes just a minute to leave a star rating or a quick sentence about what you loved.

https://www.bklnk.com/review/1998100065

chapter 1

JAKE

WITH A FLICK OF MY WRIST, the camping chair in my hand unfolds so I can place it on the ground beside her grave.

"Last weekend was grad weekend," I say as I relax in the chair and sip from the coffee in my thermos. Most people turn to iced coffee during the summer months, but I'm a creature of habit. "Man, it would have been different if you were here for it all. You deserved that experience."

The early summer heat hits the top of my head and makes me wish for my baseball hat to offer some relief. I may not be a gentleman, but I can't disrespect the dead. *Especially not her.*

Talking to a headstone still feels unnatural, but it always is therapeutic when I have these moments.

I don't know if she can hear what I'm saying, but I like to think she is listening. "Mar, you should have seen Sadie. She graduated with full honors and a person can just tell she's going places."

Sadie's graduating class was not large, by any means, but that's to be expected when living in only a small town. A few dozen kids sat along the front wall in matching gowns and the iconic wildcat banner strung up behind them. The school hadn't changed its mascot, colors, or principal in the last few decades.

If I had let my imagination wander, while sitting in that hard plastic chair in the front rows of the town's arena, I could have swapped out Sadie's red curly hair for Alice's long brown hair. In another life, I could have been sitting in the same spot watching Alice in her black cap and gown with the golden trim and tassel. I would have clasped Mar's hand in mine while I blinked away tears as we reminisced about how only yesterday she was running around the backyard, naked except for her diaper, chasing the butterflies. But no, at Sadie's ceremony I sat proudly beside Alice and Travis, while during Alice's ceremony, I had snuck in twenty minutes late and loitered in the back by the door.

Fiddling with the loose threads coming apart at the edge of the canvas seat, I tug on one and watch it come loose from the chair. "I guess I got my second chance after all. I get a chance to experience things again with Sadie." I pause when I hear the crunch of a car's tires over the gravel in the parking lot, catching my attention and making me self-conscious. "She's a wild cracker like you, Mar. But I don't know if I'm worthy of carrying on being the grandparent in your place."

While I may never feel like the right person for the job, I know not filling the role at all is far worse. My relationship with Alice has come a long way over the last decade. She probably should have left her 'ole dad in the dust without a second glance in the rearview mirror. I'm not sure if I hold the role of dad in her life, but she accepts me as Jake.

While I get a front-row seat to witness what a lovely woman Margo raised Alice to be, I have also been gifted the privilege of becoming a fixture in Sadie's life. That alone has been thrilling, but terrifying to stare down at the risk of history repeating itself.

"Jake, I'm just going to be blunt with you," Alice had told me in the beginning during our weekly chat at the coffeehouse around the corner from my mechanic's shop. It was still fresh into navigating our relationship with each other. "I want to work on a relationship with you, but I am not a woman on my own. I have a family, and I can't let you into Sadie's life if there's any chance you will break her like you broke me."

What I had done was unforgivable, leaving her and Margo behind because I couldn't be the dad and husband I thought I should be. I thought I was doing them a favor by not dragging them down with me, but there was always the other option to fight against the tide. There was the option to fight for them. I should have chosen that option, but I couldn't see it. I wasn't worthy of it. I wanted that relationship with Alice, desperately. But did I have it in me to come back and stay?

I had shaken a pack of sugar before tearing it open. "I know my word means nothing," I had said as I poured the sugar into my steaming mug of coffee.

"But this is a chance I never thought I would have. And I'm not about to trash it now. We can take it as slow as you need for Sadie's sake."

Alice had nodded and bent her head to blow into her herbal tea. Her voice was only a whisper, the hum of conversations in the rest of the coffee shop almost completely buried her words before I could catch them, "And for my sake."

Somehow I had made it here, a recurring part in all of their lives, and watching my only granddaughter walk across the stage to begin the rest of her life. A group of college kids unpack themselves out of the blue car that had pulled into the parking lot, a few holding flowers and another a sports jersey. They linger off to the edge watching me, the old man with a few days' scruff along his jaw, hanging out in a camping chair beside a grave.

"Well, I think our time is up for today. Looks like some others want a moment in here and my ugly mug might just be scaring them off." I stand and fold my chair, tucking it under my arm. "They look awfully young, Mar. Maybe if you have an extra minute or two, you could pour some motherly love on them. You were always good at that."

"Sadie! I can smell the lasagna burning!" Alice yells as she runs into the kitchen. I only catch a blurry flash of her as I close the front door behind me. I had knocked, but no one heard me over the dinner fiasco happening inside. Years ago, I wouldn't have dared open the front door without being welcomed in, but Sunday night dinners were such a fixture in our routine now that I felt comfortable letting myself in.

"Hello? Everything okay in here?" I call out as I remove my shoes and place them on the mat at the entry before climbing the stairs into Alice and Travis' townhouse. Just before I reach the top step, a blur of Sadie flies by me into the kitchen.

"The timer didn't go off yet, Mom," Sadie explains as she spies the blackened top of the lasagna.

Alice sighs and pulls off the burned layer of cheese noodles to discard into the garbage. "That's why I asked you to keep an eye on it. What were you doing anyway?"

"I was just texting with Rachel about her going away party tomorrow." Sadie spies me standing in the entry to the kitchen and comes over to hug me.

"Hi, Grandpa! Welcome to Sunday's circus."

"Not funny, Sadie," Alice chastises as she pulls the cheese from the fridge to grate on the top of the lasagna.

Finding my voice to enter into this mother-daughter dispute, I say, "I'm sure it's still delicious."

Travis enters from around the other side of the kitchen and nods in my direction. "Jake's right. Just the top is burnt, and it still smells good. Sadie, why don't you get the plates out and help your mom set the table?"

Sunday night dinners are part of my routine, but I still never quite know how I fit into the moving gears. I tend to awkwardly hover and wait for someone to give me a job because if I ever volunteer, it's always an Oh no, we've got it. What I don't say is I know that she's had it for her entire life and I wish I could do something now.

I grab the stack of cutlery on the island and follow Sadie over to the table. "How does it feel to be graduated now?"

Sadie grins ear-to-ear. "I'm so glad to never take a test or stare at a textbook ever again!"

"For now, you mean. There's still plenty of learning in college," Alice corrects her as she carries the lasagna to place in the middle of the table. She's added a layer of freshly grated cheese to the top, which is slowly melting from the heat.

"If I go to college," Sadie rolls her eyes and heads back to the kitchen to grab the bowl of salad.

Travis carries in some garlic bread and shoots me a cautionary look to not become involved. "There's still plenty of time to figure out if, where, and when you go to college. Let's shelve it for another time," he says as the mediator, pulling out a chair to sit down.

After Alice sits, she dishes out a serving of salad on her plate and passes the bowl to Travis beside her. "So, Jake, what's new with you?"

I scratch the stubble on my chin and respond with my usual answer, "Nothing new with me. Work, sleep, eat, repeat. You?" Alice and her family are always bustling with appointments, events, and activities. My life looks like a single dot of paint compared with the colorful tapestry of their lives.

"I guess our lives will drastically slow down if Sadie ever moves out," Travis muses and digs into the lasagna.

"Somehow, I highly doubt that. You'll find something to fill it." I take a bite from the lasagna and you can't even tell it was burnt. "This is delicious, Alice, as always."

Alice smiles appreciatively at the compliment, even if I know she's still kicking herself internally.

"Well, I suppose there is something new, actually. I am now a grandpa to a graduate who is 18 years old," I smile at Sadie and then turn to Travis. "Did you bring home that paperwork from the office?"

"Yes, it's in my files," Travis confirms, and glances cautiously at Alice and Sadie.

"What paperwork?" Sadie asks and rips off a chunk from her garlic bread, shoving it in her mouth.

Alice sets down her fork and turns to Travis. "We're doing this now?"

Travis shrugs. "Jake brought it up and I don't see why not."

I should let Alice and Travis take the lead on this, but I'm too excited. I turn to Sadie and explain, "I don't know if your parents ever told you, but it was in your Granny's will that when you turn 18 years old, the house would be transferred to you."

Sadie swallows her bread with a gulp, eyes wide. "Granny's house is mine? What am I supposed to do with it?"

"Whatever you want- keep renting it out, sell it, or live in it," I throw out some options for her to consider.

"I was thinking," Alice interjects. "You could keep renting it out and use that money to go towards college. Or, if you applied for some scholarships for the winter term, you could put it into savings for when you move out on your own."

I'm only the grandpa in this situation, not on the strongest foundation either, but I don't want to rock the boat. "Your mom's got a good idea if you want to go to college."

Sadie sees right through me trying to play Switzerland in this decision. "But I don't have to decide what to do with the house right now, right?"

"No, you can talk it over with your parents and decide whenever." I glance at Alice and Travis to confirm they agree.

I know a college education is important to Alice, and I imagine Travis, too. I never went to college and barely scraped through high school. In fact, I almost dropped out more than once, but my Aunt Alice was always there to give me a swift kick in the rear to get back in there and finish what I started.

"I know it's hard, Jake, but your dad would be so proud of you for how hard you're working," she had told me after the principal called me in for skipping too many classes. Aunt Alice had to come to the office because they couldn't reach my mom. The reality was probably because she didn't want to be reached.

I had kicked the rocks in the school parking lot with my backpack slung over one shoulder. "Yeah, sure, so proud that his son is failing chemistry and math."

Aunt Alice had placed her hand on my shoulder and moved her face, so I was forced to return her gaze. "He couldn't care less what grades you got. He would have been proud that you showed up and kept trying because you're not a quitter. So, when you're ready to show up for yourself, let me know and I'll meet you there."

She was one of the few people in my life who always kept her promises. I finished high school, far from honors, but a diploma is a diploma. Aunt Alice showed up for me again, and again. Until I stopped showing up for myself, and then she was no longer there to show up for me either.

I don't want to step on their toes with what Sadie should or shouldn't do with her life, but I want to make sure she gets a chance to make her life how she wants it to be.

Now that I have brought up the transfer of the house, the air in the room feels heavy as everyone loses themselves in their thoughts. For years, Margo's house has been mostly out of everyone's mind, unless something needed to be repaired for our long-term tenants. Given Alice's attachment to her childhood home, I wouldn't be surprised if, once I leave, she offers to buy it from Sadie if she wants to sell it. It would be sad to have the house in someone's hands outside of this family, but Margo wanted to gift it to Sadie for a reason, and it's her choice to make.

Alice clears her throat in an attempt to regain control over the conversation. "Let's finish dinner and we can discuss this as a family once Jake heads back home." She blushes and stammers, "I meant family as in Sadie, Travis, and I. Sorry, Jake."

It hurt, but I shrug my shoulders because the unintended arrow was justifiable. I grab another slice of garlic bread to mop up the mess of sauce on my plate from the lasagna. Tonight is not the celebratory graduation dinner I was thinking it would be.

acknowledgements

First, this book would not have been possible without the unwavering support of my family. They continue to show up to celebrate with me on every one of my dreams I choose to tackle.

To my husband, who works tirelessly to provide for our family.

To my children, who love to cheer me on.

Thanks to Laurel, Emily, Ria, and Candice for being my "Walking Crew Plus One". You all keep me sane every day through our texts, walks, and chats. I can't imagine doing motherhood without you in my corner and loving on me and my kids in the process.

A giant thank you to my near and dear friend, Jenn. You encourage me to live my life by collecting experiences. Your dedication and hard work as you tackle life's challenges with a smile on your face is nothing short of inspirational to those around you. Alice, in this story, is a fraction of the caretaker and mom that you are.

Mama, spending my childhood under the same roof as you shaped me in more ways than you ever got to experience during your time on this earth. Your commitment to everyone around you and your duties as a caretaker to Papa blessed everyone in your life. 15 years ago, I wrote my first book in high school with you by my side, reading and editing chapter by chapter. If you were still here, I hope this book would also make you proud.

A big thank you to everyone who took the time to read my versions of the book as I wrote it.

To Nikki, your initial excitement at reading each chapter hot off the press spurred me on to keep writing and developing this dream into a reality.

To Kim and Amber, thank you for passionately reading the book from cover to cover. Your feedback, brainstorming, and thoughts while reading chapter by chapter of my first drafts helped to shape this book into what it is today.

To Andrea, your professional opinion and thoughts on the first sneak peek were greatly appreciated. As one of my longest friends, thank you for always being along for the ride on my adventures.

Finally, thank you to everyone who took a chance on me as a debut author and picked up this book to read.

books by amelia venjoy

Before the Tea Gets Cold
Memory Stains Left Behind

follow for updates

Amelia
VENJOY

http://www.ameliavenjoy.com

@ameliavenjoy.writes on Instagram